ROCK STEADY

DAWN RYDER

 sourcebooks
casablanca

Published by Sourcebooks Casablanca, an imprint of Sourcebooks, Inc.
P.O. Box 4410, Naperville, Illinois 60567-4410
(630) 961-3900
Fax: (630) 961-2168
www.sourcebooks.com

Printed and bound in Canada.
MBP 10 9 8 7 6 5 4 3 2

Chapter 1

THE FOG HAD SETTLED IN OVER THE CITY OF SAN Francisco. The locals put on their coats and stayed on the streets, casting off the chains of the workweek with excess. The bars and clubs were in full swing even two full hours after midnight.

"Where in the hell did you go?" Kate Braden propped her hands on her hips and sent Ramsey a seething glare. "We've been shaking the trees for you."

Ramsey offered her a smile that was a shot of pure sin. He curled a hand around her hip and pulled her against his hard body while taking a moment to enjoy the display her corset top pushed her breasts into. "Would have surfaced sooner if I'd known you wanted me."

He purred out the word "wanted."

A faint scent of scotch surrounded him, but it was a fine grade and only added to his dark-as-midnight persona. He was wearing leather pants and vest as usual, but it fit in with the crowd on the sidewalks of San Francisco. At least the crowd that was out at two thirty in the morning.

He started to nuzzle her neck.

"Hands off my wife there, Rams."

Syon Braden appeared, neatly lifting Ramsey's hand off Kate's hip. Syon slid in and took possession of her as Ramsey grinned.

"What happened to Tia?" Syon asked his bandmate.

Ramsey frowned. For a moment, his rocker image cracked, showing the very sharp mind of the man who lurked inside the Toxsin band member. It was only a momentary glimpse before Ramsey shrugged and offered them a bored expression, retreating into his bad-boy persona.

"Guess she's gone." He kept his tone nonchalant. If Kate didn't know him, she never would have guessed he cared at all about the girl in question. He shrugged again, his leather vest opening to display a peek at his six-pack abs.

But it also showed her a flash of something else.

Kate reached forward for the waistband of the leather pants he wore.

"She might be your wife, but she can't keep her hands off me," Ramsey taunted Syon.

Her husband shifted, trying to decide what she was doing. Kate nudged the leather down just an inch and gasped.

Syon cursed.

The other two members of Toxsin had found them and joined Syon.

"They're"—Kate pushed the waistband a little farther to get a better look at the new tattoo on Ramsey's lower abdomen—"cherry blossoms." Her voice was a horrified whisper.

Ramsey frowned and looked down. He was sobering up quickly, his expression turning deadly. "That bitch."

"Damn it, Ramsey," Syon snapped. "You can't slip the leash like that." He peered at the delicate, blush-pink blossoms.

"I wasn't drunk when I went off with Tia," Ramsey said.

"Damn straight you weren't," Taz said. "I would have stayed on your butt if you were."

Ramsey was struggling to remember how he'd ended up with a tattoo. "I didn't have that much." His forehead furrowed as he tried to concentrate. He popped open the button on his waistband and looked down.

"Oh, shit," Drake said, his British accent emerging.

"That's bad," Taz agreed.

"We've got to do something," Syon confirmed.

Clearly tattooed on the singer's body were two sprigs of pink cherry blossoms. They conflicted so badly with Ramsey's dark image, his bandmates stared at him for long moments as shock held them silent. It was a serious crash-and-burn moment.

Kate pulled him closer to a streetlamp, hoping the light might show it to be a temporary tattoo.

No such luck.

"You're screwed." Kate detected the faint red marks from the needle. There was a slight gloss from Vaseline too.

"We're screwed," Syon added. "We've got a show in forty-eight hours."

The members of Toxsin stuck together. Ramsey and Syon were tighter than most married couples. Kate had learned that firsthand when she'd met Syon and spent a season on tour with them as their costumer.

"It's Toxsin!" someone yelled from across the street. There was the blare of a horn as the fangirls stepped right into traffic in their quest to connect with their music idols.

Kate reached out and refashioned Ramsey's pants to hide the tattoo.

"I dreamed about this differently," Ramsey drawled. "You took my pants *off* in my dreams. I remember that detail perfectly."

"Right now, they need to stay on." She fastened up

his vest while she was at it, but the garment wasn't going to hide the top half of the second blossom.

"We've got to get this fixed. Now," Syon said. "That is going to show on stage, big time."

They might have been sporting long hair and leather, making them look like society's rejects, but all of them were dead serious when it came to their image. The potential for disaster the little feminine tattoo posed was off the scale.

As in…epic disaster.

The tabloids would have a field day if even one fuzzy picture surfaced. They'd just hit the Bay Area and had two days until show night. Ramsey was known for his guitar solos, and his lack of a shirt made sure his abs were on display.

"I don't think cover-up is going to do the job on that one," Drake offered.

"One little rub from the waistband of your pants, and it would be all over cyberspace," Kate added.

"We need tattoo rescue. Like, now," Taz said as he dug his phone out of his pocket and started searching the Internet. "The paparazzi get a shot of that, and we're never going to live it down."

"Well, gotta do what we gotta do for image…" Ramsey slid behind Kate, trapping her in front of him as a human shield as the fangirls made it to them.

Syon punched him in the shoulder, but all he did was smirk and rub his chin on top of her head.

"You're so hot!"

"Can I have a picture with you?"

The girls squealed as they tried to push their way closer to Ramsey. Kate ended up sandwiched between them.

"Got it," Taz said.

Drake went to work, settling his arms around the fangirls and steering them away as he charmed them with his British accent.

"Three blocks south. All-night tattoo parlor. Good references," Taz said once the fans were out of earshot.

"Let's check it out." Syon whistled. A young Korean man looked up from where he'd been leaning against a streetlamp enjoying the view of the bay. "Better get some sleep, Kate."

She let her bodyguard take her toward a black SUV with tinted windows. Syon and Taz surrounded Ramsey, guiding him away. They were three lean, hard bodies, and if she did say so herself, they were wearing really great leather pants. Kate took one last look at her work, as the leather showed off their prime butts, before she ducked into the SUV, Yoon holding the door for her.

Yoon claimed shotgun before the driver pulled the car away from the curb and took her back to the five-star hotel the band was staying at. The paparazzi were camped out as usual. They perked up as the car pulled up, raising their cameras as Yoon opened her door, ready to catch one of the members of the mega rock band Toxsin in a moment of inattention. There was a ripple of disappointment when they realized it was only her, but they were always ready to make the most of every opportunity to claim a headline.

"Hey, Kate, how is it being married to the Marquis?"

"Are you pregnant?"

"Is it true you've filed for divorce?"

"Are you allowing Syon to date?"

The paparazzi had no shame. They'd hound her with

the most ridiculous questions, and as far as personal boundaries went, they didn't have any. Taz had brought in his cousin Yoon to be her bodyguard and keep them at bay. The paparazzi stood behind velvet-covered ropes as Yoon swept them with a keen gaze to make sure they weren't breaching the barriers the hotel had set up.

Yoon escorted her inside. He'd finally stopped shooting glares at the more insensitive questions. Hotel security was waiting for her, making sure none of the camera jockeys followed her inside.

"The boys still out?" Brenton, the band's road manager, greeted her with a handshake and a room key card.

"Um…yes. And we have a problem, with Tia."

Brenton fell into step beside her, never losing his congenial grin. Managing a mega superstar band like Toxsin meant the walls had ears and telephoto lenses. He waited until the penthouse elevator door closed the curious spectators out before his expression went serious.

"How big of a problem?" Brenton asked.

"Cherry blossoms."

The road manager's eyebrows lowered as he listened to her.

"What do you think you're going to prove?"

Jewel tapped her fingers against the countertop and bit her lower lip. Her mom was just getting started.

"Don't you appreciate the education your father and I paid for?"

"I do, Mom." Jewel managed to keep her tone even and sweet. Really, it shouldn't have taken much effort. At this point, she should be well acquainted with her mother's disdain for her current employment choice.

But her skin wasn't as thick as she'd like to think. The tone of her mother's voice cut deep, slicing into the dream she was trying to live with the sharp blade of reality.

Don't hate the messenger…

"Well, you wouldn't know it by the way you're playing around in that tattoo shop like some sort of orphan who didn't have the benefit of a university education paid for by her parents," her mom said.

"I just love art."

"So love it." Her mother was completely exasperated now, her breathing rough on the other end of the line. "What I don't understand is why you aren't using that marketing degree. You need to get out and start your career. If it was your own shop, I might understand. I hate to think about you suffering. Living in a death trap apartment, wondering where your next meal is coming from, sleeping on a futon."

Guilt chewed on her. "Money isn't that tight."

Her mother made a low sound of disbelief. Jewel couldn't really form another argument because, well, it would be a flat-out lie. Her boss was a prick, who paid her only when she had a client, and he scooped up the best hours while the parlor was open, leaving her to mind the shop from three in the morning until lunchtime, when most of their clientele woke up.

And she did sleep on a futon. In an apartment building that had been built in the twenties. Plugging more than one kitchen appliance in at the same time was asking to break out her fire extinguisher.

It wasn't anywhere near the exciting adventure she'd

hoped for when she'd decided to try a year of being a struggling artist. So far, all she'd really experienced was the "struggling" part. Substandard wiring and plumbing were everyday challenges. So was scraping together enough funds to pay the landlord. She had a newfound understanding of the girls who resorted to stripping a couple of nights a week to supplement their income.

"Mom, I just wanted to venture a little off the beaten path. Just for a bit, while I'm not responsible for anyone else. I don't even have a houseplant, and I have the safety net of knowing I can come home. I do appreciate you. I just want to try walking on the wild side, to say I did it."

There was a soft sound as her mother sighed. "I was young once too," her mother confessed with a soft snicker. "Burned my bra at a concert once; bet you didn't know that."

"You didn't!" Jewel exclaimed.

Her mother smothered a giggle. "I did. Whipped that puppy off, tossed it into a trash can, and lit it up. It was the night I met your father. I wanted him to see me as a woman of the world: fearless, confident in my sexuality, a true wild child."

"Get out!"

"Your sign says twenty-four hours."

Jewel looked up and fumbled her phone. She was pretty sure her mouth hung open, but wasn't completely sure, because her brain decided to fry, leaving her staring at the decadent man prowling across the shop toward her.

"Tell your mom you'll call back. I need you right now."

Okay, *fried* wasn't nearly hot enough a word to

describe the sensation going through her. The guy in front of her was a god. Six and a quarter feet of raw muscle, with black eyes that looked like they'd been carved out of a moonless night sky at midnight. His shoulder-length hair was spiky and screamed nonconformity. But it was the flash of arrogance in his eyes that drove home just how raw he was.

This guy took what he wanted and never apologized for any of his desires.

It should have raised her hackles. Instead, it made her wet.

And she wasn't sure she liked it.

Scratch that. She was sure she didn't like it, because it felt like she was losing control.

"Mom, I've got someone in the shop."

Her voice had become raspy. She blinked, trying to scrape together some poise. It felt like mission impossible as the god grinned at her, his lips curving in a sensual way that sent a bolt of heat straight into her clit.

Shit.

The guy was sex on a stick. And his leather pants made it clear he had quite a stick.

"How can I help you?" she asked.

"So, you're open?" She hadn't realized the god had companions. One was an Asian man with short, spiky hair, black as a raven's wing, with a flash of blue fire that made it look amazing.

"Oh…sorry. I was talking to my mom." Her tongue felt like it had gone lame. "When you walked in, that is. We're always open."

And her day was suddenly looking up. "I'm Jewel. What are you gents looking for?"

"Do you do tattoo rescue?" The blond one was talking now. His hair fell just to his shoulders, and his eyebrows were slashes.

"You can only go darker. So if it's already black, your options are limited. But sure, I do rescues."

"Wait," the Asian guy insisted. "Do you have a portfolio?"

"Of course." Jewel pulled a large book from under the counter.

She was used to seeing leather and brawn in the shop, but there was a level of detail on all three of them that spoke of money. The pants were all custom-made, or she'd pack up and start sending out marketing résumés like her parents advised. She knew the difference between wannabes and genuine badasses.

These were the real McCoy.

"I mean, nothing personal, but we can't have this done by an amateur," the Asian continued as he started flipping through the pages of her work.

"Speak for yourself, Taz." The dark-eyed one was leaning farther across the counter, making the air between them sizzle. "I'd like to get very personal with you."

His voice was like black velvet. It would be super easy to just let it rub all over her. She got the feeling she'd end up purring. There was a flash of something in his eyes, sending a tingle of apprehension through her.

He knew exactly what sort of effect he was having on her.

God, that was sexy. It really redefined her concept of the word. He knew exactly what to do with every inch of her body.

She ended up rolling her lower lip in and setting her

teeth into it. His dark gaze dropped to the little nervous motion, his lips curving rakishly in response as he leaned on the counter, moving closer to her. He was too damned smooth, pushing in on her comfort zone with an ease that was annoying, but at the same time, forced her to admit she admired it. A ton of guys thought they were good at getting under a girl's skin.

This guy was amazing at it.

He was arrogant, but with a solid core of confidence that sent a shiver down her spine. Part of her really wanted to put him to the test.

Which wouldn't help her pay the rent. She dug deep, trying to get a grip on her professionalism.

"You might want to see these too." She lifted another album from beneath the counter and handed it over. "These are my awards, and the back half are rescues, before and after shots."

The blond took it in a flash, leaving her once again staring at the dark-eyed god. Her mouth actually went dry when he opened his mouth and bit the air between them. "Maybe you should let me in on the…problem?" she said.

His grin grew into a huge smile that showed off gleaming white teeth. "Thought you'd never ask me to open my pants."

He'd straightened up, giving her another glimpse of just how tall he was before he popped the button on his fly.

It was totally unprofessional for her to get a buzz out of his brazen attitude.

But frickin' awesome nonetheless.

She was actually holding her breath as he worked the buttons.

One…

Two…

Oh, hell, the guy was chiseled.

But the delicate pink blossoms hit her like a bucket of ice water. "Oh, that is just wrong."

She came around the counter, her attention fixed on his lower belly. Jewel sank to her knee to get eye level with the cherry blossoms. It *was* a sacrilege, like putting pink ribbons in the ears of a panther.

"Hmm…" The dark god made a soft sound under his breath and reached for her head. For a moment, she was caught in that second, waiting for his fingers to land on her.

"Don't be an idiot, Ramsey." Taz smacked the hand away. "These pictures are good. We don't need her getting pissed off because you get touchy."

"Looked to me like she wouldn't mind me…touching." There was a brazenness to him that should have pissed her off.

Really, it should.

Jewel straightened up, forcing herself to take a reality check. Ramsey was dark temptation, completely lickable, and he knew it. Yeah, she had that part of his persona pegged perfectly. The little cherry blossoms proved that she was far from the first girl to feel his magnetism. She'd better get a grip before she found herself driven to extremes, like the jilted ex-flame who had clearly lashed out at him through the tattoo.

"Pissed off your girlfriend?" she asked pointedly.

"She wasn't really a girlfriend."

Jewel clicked her tongue and looked back at the cherry blossoms. "By the look of that, she disagreed with you on the topic. She must have taken you to Spike Collar."

Taz was typing into his cell phone as she spoke. "Makes sense. You surfaced right around where that tattoo parlor is on the map."

"Just don't go back there," Jewel warned as she went behind the counter and pulled a blank sheet of paper in front of her.

"Why not?" the blond asked. "I've got half a mind to have my lawyer pay them a visit."

Jewel didn't look up from what she was drawing. "Won't do you any good. They never touch a client without a release of liability signed and sealed, with video footage to back it up. Whoever was gunning for you did her homework. The gals at Spike Collar don't like guys, and they really don't like any males who try to charm them." Jewel cast a look at Ramsey. "You are exactly the sort they hate. Bet they popped a bottle of champagne the second you cleared the doorway with that little gem."

Taz made a low sound under his breath.

But Ramsey was watching her. She felt his attention tightening, focusing on the motion of her pen as she inked a design on the paper. He'd sent a shiver down her spine before, but now he was warming her insides, melting her core slowly with the absolute devotion he was giving her. She looked up, locking gazes with him.

Her insides churned.

And her toes curled.

She'd never felt so connected to another soul. It was his doing, and she realized that his arrogance was something he'd earned.

That fact slapped her across the face and sent her into a full meltdown. He was the sort who could captivate.

Which was a damned dangerous place to go.

It wasn't like she had any personal experience with it. Still, she felt like she was on pins and needles. The sheer level of sensitivity the guy was able to elicit from her was off the scale. It was fascinating to say the least.

As well as a really bad place to go when he looked like he could afford to hire her.

She looked back at her work, forcing herself to focus on the art and get a grip on herself before he knocked her flat. Sweat popped out on her forehead, but her hands responded perfectly. Art was like a living force inside her. A place she could take refuge in as well as being a gift she might share. She let it consume her, the drawing coming to life beneath the strokes of her pen. It was a little like giving birth: first she had to let it grow and form before it was ready to breathe.

"That is smokin' hot," Taz said as he leaned on the counter to peer at her work.

"You're good," the blond said in a tone full of awe.

Ramsey reserved judgment until she'd shaded in the last few areas on her sketch. When she lifted her pen, he swept it up and studied the drawing. It was a metal dragon crawling down his abdomen toward his cock. Its front claws would be where the cherry blossoms were, and its tail would wrap around his lean hip and onto his lower back. It wasn't a reptilian dragon. It was a steel one, a merging of metal and mythical creature.

His eyes narrowed as he studied it, seeing more than just the black lines. He was seeing the attitude she'd tried to capture and portray. His expression gave her a hint of the man inside him. She got the impression he spent a lot of time covering up that man with his don't-give-a-rat's-ass attitude.

But she saw it.

His attention shifted to her, their gazes locking over the edge of the paper. For a moment, she caught a flicker of understanding in his eyes. Just a moment of awareness, a few seconds when he admitted to himself that she saw him.

Really saw him.

It didn't last long. In fact, she found herself questioning if it had really been there, when his gaze hardened and sealed her out of that place he was determined to keep private.

"You recognize me," he said.

It wasn't a question, but she felt inclined to answer anyway. "It isn't hard to peg you for a metalhead when you're wearing nothing but leather and have a stud bar through your nipple."

"I'm a metal god," he said.

"Right," she countered, feeling a rise of heat in her cheeks. "I'm good at what I do."

"You are," the blond interrupted. He was studying her portfolio. "So why are you working the graveyard shift?"

"I wanted to work at the best shop in town. That left me to choose between Spike Collar and here," Jewel said without hesitation.

"But you're not a lesbian," Ramsey finished for her. "Bet that was a bit of a problem with getting hired over at Spike Collar."

"Definite ripple in the pond," she confirmed. "Not on my side, mind you. They just don't like straight girls. Shame really, they know how to do tats."

"So do you." Ramsey was thumbing through the pictures of her work. He wore that businessman expression.

"Who are you?" she gave in and asked. All three men

looked up at her. "I mean, since it sounded like you were trying to impress me."

"Impressing you will involve more than my name," her client said. His lips curved, and his expression became sensual. He flattened his hand on the counter between them and leaned toward her. In one flat second, it felt like her breath caught in her lungs. She was hyper-aware of him, fighting not to take a step back. There was a flicker of approval in his dark eyes as she managed to stand her ground.

"Count on that fact." Her voice had turned raspy, but his arrogance was rubbing her pride raw. "I do tats. Only tats, for pay. So if you've got a problem understanding boundaries, the door is behind you. There's another place a couple of blocks up that opens in a few hours."

Taz reached over and shoved Ramsey. "I told you not to piss her off." He shook his smartphone in the air between them. "She's the best in the nearest three cities—checked her out." He turned to look at her. "Your references rock. Why are you working in this dump?"

"Because my boss might be a prick, but he's also got twenty-five years' experience, and references to top mine. I want to learn from the best, and there are a few things you can't learn from anyone but a master."

Taz nodded. "True, even if some masters are egomaniacs."

"You didn't answer me." Jewel aimed her inquiry at Ramsey. "Who are you?"

"Ramsey, Taz, and I'm Syon," the blond answered. "We're members of a band called Toxsin."

She bit back the snide *Yeah, right* that tried to escape her lips.

No way.

But they were all standing there looking pretty confident. She reached over and tapped "Toxsin" into the laptop on the countertop. Their website was the first thing to come up. She clicked on the link.

"What the fuck are you doing roaming the streets?" She looked up from the screen at the three guys standing in front of her. It was weird, to say the least, to have the pictures from the screen living and breathing in her shop. "Don't you have people to deal with stuff like this?"

Ramsey eyed her from where he was lying on the counter. "I'm a hands-on sort." He covered her hand with his, stroking the back of it.

Jewel ended up taking that step back. Victory flashed through his eyes as she sent him a sharp look.

Taz punched him in the shoulder again.

"How's that 'hands-on' thing working for you tonight?" Jewel said. It was a barbed comment, a challenge. Hell, it felt like she'd smacked him across the jaw with a white glove and dropped it at his feet.

The way his eyes narrowed confirmed that he felt the same way. For one split second, she half feared he might just flip the counter out of the way or jump over it.

"Let's focus on the problem," Syon said. "We need this fixed—discreetly, quickly."

"No joke." Jewel happily changed thought tracks. She pulled one of the shop disclosure agreements up onto the counter. The tightly packed lines of legal mumbo jumbo didn't give her the same sense of comfort they normally did. Ramsey grabbed it and yanked the top off a pen before boldly scrawling his signature across the bottom line.

Taz was flipping the lock on the front door.

"Good idea," Jewel agreed. She didn't care for the fact that she had to take a breath before getting her feet to move.

Ramsey flopped down on her worktable, popping his pants open. They were custom-made, all right; the right side of them shaped perfectly to contain his cock.

The guy had an impressive package.

She ended up stopping halfway around the counter, earning a smirk from him.

"Don't let my fame make you nervous," Ramsey teased her.

"Typically, I worry about my clients taking their displeasure out on my hide." She made it to her stool and sat down. Her workstation was normally the place she felt most comfortable.

Today, she felt like the padded stool was full of spikes.

"So what's your problem with me?" Ramsey asked.

She wasn't going to answer that.

Nope.

Not a chance.

She turned half away from him and sterilized her hands.

"Cat got your tongue?" he asked.

Jewel turned back toward him and swallowed the lump that had formed in her throat.

What a man-animal.

She really needed to get a grip and enjoy the moment. She was pretty sure she was never going to get the chance to work on so fine a specimen again.

"I'm thinking you wouldn't think twice about filing a lawsuit against me, signature on a release form or not," she said.

His expression turned serious, his eyes narrowing, his lips thinning. "I don't get my kicks out of using my money to pin my mistakes on other people. I own my fuckups."

It wasn't what she'd expected him to say.

But she liked it.

A whole lot.

Integrity was something most people sold out on. Especially when it came to admitting they'd made dumb mistakes.

"I'm beginning to see why the gals at Spike didn't refuse to do your girlfriend's dirty work."

Ramsey leaned his head back. "She wasn't my girlfriend."

"I'm guessing that was the problem."

He'd closed his eyes but opened them and looked at her. "Guess it was. But I didn't lie to her."

He really did own his screwups. It was there in the flat acceptance on his face. He looked past her to his bandmates. "I'm good. You guys can shove off."

"Not a chance." Syon settled himself on the other work-table. "Those little pink flowers will take us all down."

"Yeah." Taz sat down behind the counter and claimed her laptop. "Besides, I don't trust you to be polite. Jewel is a lady."

Ramsey made a low sound under his breath. "I bet she gets naughty with the right company."

Jewel didn't look up from where she was cleaning the skin on his abdomen. She was no stranger to personal jabs, especially off-color ones.

What surprised her was the way her pulse leaped.

She needed to get a grip.

"That's what I'm talking about," Taz said. "She's an artist, like Kate."

"Yeah," Ramsey agreed. "Sorry, I'm still a little buzzed. Talking out of my ass."

Jewel warmed under the single word of praise. She got the impression Ramsey didn't hand out undeserving compliments. She ended up looking into his eyes because he was watching her.

"Kate made my pants." He gestured at his buddies. "She makes all our leather gear."

"She's good." Jewel picked up her sketch and began to position it. "I see my share of leather around here. The good, the bad, and mostly the ugly."

"She's the best," Syon added without opening his eyes. "Even has good taste in men."

Ramsey snorted. Syon offered him a single-finger salute.

"Aren't you guys cute," Jewel muttered.

"There's nothing cute about the part of me you're looking at."

She should ignore him.

Should, but she wasn't going to. Jewel looked up and caught Ramsey grinning at her. "Did you want this done sometime before Christmas?"

"You wouldn't let me go on stage wearing flowers… would you, Jewel?" He tried out his puppy eyes on her.

"The idea is growing on me."

He made a soft humming sound beneath his breath. "I like a girl who plays rough."

"I bet you do."

Which was just enough of a reality slap to get her focused. He was an animal, the prowling kind.

And she was already living on the edge enough.

She got the drawing into position and transferred it onto his skin.

Canvas.

Normally the word helped her tune out everything but the art.

Yeah, well, there wasn't much of anything that was normal about Ramsey.

"Do you want any painkiller before I start inking?" she asked. "You seem to have sobered up. This is going to feel like a cat scratching at sunburned skin."

He bared his teeth at her. "Scratch me, pussycat."

She ignored the word *pussy*.

Or at least she tried to.

"Okay. But you might reconsider, since you're a virgin—"

He curled up as he laughed. Taz was snorting, and Syon actually rolled off the other workstation.

"Cute," Jewel said as she pushed her hands into gloves. "I've *never* had that response before." She dabbed a bit of Vaseline from a tub and put it on the skin she was about to work on. "But you are a virgin, big boy, an ink virgin."

Ramsey straightened back out, his lips curved into an expectant grin. "Can't wait for you to pop my cherry."

Oh yeah, one hundred percent animal. Night jungle cat, unless she missed her guess.

She got the impression it was something she'd both love and hate. He was a study in extremes. Which was something that combined rather well with the dragon she started to ink on him. It was a potent combination that made her feel linked in to the creature taking shape beneath her fingertips.

She wanted to breathe life into it.

Needed to, actually.

It was an obsession, one she willingly submitted to. Inside her art was her personal haven, where things like doubt didn't penetrate. She knew she was good and made sure she worked hard at becoming better. The little needle gun in her hand was a way to express herself and share the wealth of dreams inside her with the outside world.

She ignored the way her neck stiffened up and the pain in her knuckles. Bringing the dragon to life was all that mattered. Through it all, Ramsey watched her. It was hypnotic in a fashion and deeply intimate in another, because he didn't turn his face away when he flinched. It was like he was mesmerized by her, which couldn't be true. Not a man like him. Maybe she had her cute factor, but he must be chased by hundreds of women daily.

Still, he watched her. It warmed her cheeks, and his lips twitched up slightly in response.

Oh yeah, he knew what effect he had on the opposite sex.

But that just seemed to be part of his charm.

⸺⸺⸺

Her entire back ached by the time she finished.

Jewel decided she didn't care.

Ramsey was looking at his tat, his face set into an expression of dark satisfaction. He turned slowly in front of her full-length mirror. His gaze shifted up until he was watching her through the polished glass.

Her breath froze.

She was kinda sure that something shifted between them.

The sun was just coming up.

He was a little too perfect. Part of her actually

expected him to dissipate as she woke up and realized she'd fallen asleep on the countertop because the night had been another dud.

"You rock, Jewel."

He wasn't teasing her, wasn't trying to get a rise out of her. The three words were sincere, and she realized she liked the glimpse of his serious side far too much. There was something inside him just as tempting as his animal persona. Something she got the feeling he didn't share very often, if at all.

"Keep it out of the sunlight for three weeks," she warned him as she handed him a printout of rules for making sure the tat healed. "And follow these instructions. Seriously, follow them."

He offered her a lazy smile as he came toward her. "Worried that I don't follow rules?"

"Actually, I'm pretty sure you view rules as things to jump over, but in this case, follow them or you'll end up with scarring or in the hospital with an infection."

Taz reached over and whacked his bandmate on the side of the head again. Ramsey jumped, looking like he'd been caught off guard, and flipped Taz off. The Asian member of Toxsin wasn't intimidated. He pointed a stern finger at Ramsey before reaching past him and taking the instruction sheet.

"Right, I'll follow them," Ramsey said.

He was opening his wallet, digging out a bunch of bills. She hesitated before reaching for them. Which was stupid, but she didn't want to let the moment end.

Of course it had to.

He stopped with his hand on the door. "I'll leave your name at the security desk tomorrow night. Come see the show. You should get a front-row seat to the unveiling of your work."

Ramsey, Mega Rock Star, offered her a wink before he walked out of her life. Jewel watched him go, enjoying the uniqueness of the moment. There was a soft sound of an engine as an SUV pulled up in front of the shop without a shred of regard for the red curb. A guy hopped out from the front seat and had the door open before Ramsey and his buddies made it across the narrow sidewalk.

Oh yeah…they had guys to do stuff for them.

Jewel didn't waste her time feeling jealous. She soaked it up. It was the adventure element her life had been lacking.

And a fine, healthy dose of it, too.

"Hmm…" Ramsey considered the list of rules. "Tight clothing is ill-advised."

Syon groaned. "Why do we have to suffer?"

Taz snickered but turned and looked out the window as Ramsey popped open his pants. Ramsey didn't care for clothing most of the time anyway. Having an excuse to shed it was welcome.

"She was cute," Syon muttered. "The artist."

"Yeah." Ramsey stretched out his legs and let his eyes close. But his brain was churning. Jewel's face was there, and all the intensity that had shown while she worked. It was sexy, but he was used to having sexy females around. There was something else snaring his attention, something he hadn't associated with a female in a long time.

Admiration.

That made him frown, because it might lead to things like respect. Sure, he respected a fellow artist, but the last thing he needed to do was think she was sexy too. He enjoyed his sex life the way it was—uncomplicated.

Jewel was complicated. Problem was, that was the thing about her that he liked best.

———

"You fucking bitch!"

Ted threw his hat toward the hat stand as he blew through the door of the shop just before noon.

"Ramsey of Toxsin was here, and you didn't let me do his tat?" Her boss was in top form, his neck and face red as he threw one of his tantrums. The man knew how to seethe better than anyone she'd ever met. In fact, she was pretty sure she'd never actually seen a human seethe before she'd met Ted. Because in toddlers, what her boss was doing was called a temper tantrum.

He was covered in tats from his shaved head to his feet, and wore only a tank top with a low, scoop neckline to better show off his tats and body.

Jewel rubbed her hands, her joints aching from the hours of work she'd done on the dragon. "The deal is walk-ins are mine during my shift."

"Not when it's a mega rock star," Ted argued. "And why is this place a pig sty? Cleaning is part of your job."

"I had a customer."

"That you should have called me in to deal with." Ted planted his foot on the stool at her workstation and kicked it across the shop. "Get out of my shop!"

"You're firing me because of a walk-in?" she demanded. "That was our arrangement."

"You bet your ass I am," Ted snarled. "No bitch is working under my roof who doesn't know who gets the lion's share of the meat! In case you don't understand English, it means mega rock stars are mine, no matter when they walk in. I built this place, not you."

Ted chucked a half-full coffee mug at her.

Jewel yelped as she jumped out of the way. Cold, day-old coffee splattered across her leg as the pottery shattered.

There was a blur of motion as she regained her balance. Then a gurgle, and the sound of someone struggling for breath. She looked up and stared at Ted's arms and legs flailing while Ramsey held him pinned against the wall, a full foot off the floor. It was more than impressive, because Ted liked to lift weights, and wasn't flabby by a long shot.

"I don't let pricks near me." Ramsey released Ted. There was a scuff of boots against the floor as he landed. Ramsey faced off with him, his stance ready.

"Throw something else at her…" Ramsey's voice was low and menacing. "I'd really love a reason to kick your ass."

Ted spread out his arms. "What's the big deal? She's a fucking ice queen. Won't give out a pony ride or even lip service. You want to fight over that?"

Ramsey shook his head and looked back at her. Jewel discovered herself standing in stunned shock. She'd never expected the look of protectiveness in his eyes. "Get your gear."

Ted started to move. Ramsey turned on him in a flash. A tingle shot through her as she realized his well-honed body was more than just a showpiece. The guy had training in more than how to use the local gym weight equipment.

"And you"—Ramsey faced Ted again—"shut up before I kick your ass for being too stupid to recognize the value of professional behavior."

"I'll sue you," Ted threatened, sounding like a weasel.

"And I'll tweet, at the top of my mega rock star bandwidth," Ramsey countered, in complete control and command of the situation.

The tension was tight, the two men settling into a staring war. She flipped open her case and started dumping her gear into it. The second she closed it and secured the metal latches, Ramsey reached over and grabbed the handle. He opened the door for her in a few long strides.

She was standing on the pavement before everything really sank in. Just shy of noon, the streets were fairly empty, because it was a Thursday.

"Which way?"

"Uh…" The guy was just as sexy by the light of day, which should have been against some cosmic law.

"Your place," Ramsey said, enlightening her.

"Oh." She reached out for her gear box. "I've got it."

He offered her a raised eyebrow and kept her gear box out of her reach. Short of chasing his right side around in a circle, she wasn't getting it back.

"I didn't expect to see you back here."

Ramsey shrugged. "I wanted to bring you some tickets, since I had only a first name. Your real name is nowhere on the website, a real jerk move by your boss to keep you from building a following, if you ask me.

Seems like the dude doesn't feel his own work can stand up against yours."

He raised his voice, and she realized Ted had followed them outside. Ramsey shot that last comment straight at him. There was a muffled word of profanity behind them before she heard the door of the shop slam.

Ramsey gave her a grin that melted her a little. Sure, he was sexy, but when he was being sincere, there was a relaxed set to his eyes that made him as adorable as a puppy.

And likely just as much trouble as one too.

"I thought you'd be sleeping," she said.

He shrugged and started down the street. "Just drove in from Los Angeles on the bus. That's enough rack time for me, unless there's some action between the sheets."

Oh yeah, trouble in spades. The guy was adorable, made her fingers itch to stroke him, but he'd jump right into her lap and have his way if she didn't watch out.

Her nipples drew tight, tingling with anticipation.

"Well, you shouldn't have risked a fight with him."

Ramsey made a low sound in the back of his throat. "Worried I can't handle myself?" He slid her a sidelong look that was brimming with confidence. "Don't worry, Uncle Sam made sure I know how to protect myself."

"Seriously?" The question slipped out before she realized she already knew the answer. It was in the way he moved, the way he positioned his feet when he stopped. She knew her share of loud, self-proclaimed badasses, and the difference between them and Ramsey.

"Navy, EOD, bomb patrol," he offered.

It was impressive, and she lost the will to ignore him. Her gaze slipped down his lean body. He had on just a

leather vest that gave her a teasing glimpse of his flat
abs when he moved. His pants were black and fitted
perfectly to his hips, giving her a glimpse of her work
along his side. Just the back spikes of the dragon. She
couldn't have placed it any better if she'd been working
with a blank canvas.

"Oh, crap." The slight sheen of lotion slapped her back
into reality. "You've got to cover that up. Right now."

His eyes narrowed for a moment. "Sunlight, right,
you mentioned that."

Her mind was on the dragon. She dug her keys out
of her purse and hurried ahead of him. She fiddled
with the barred building door, finally coaxing the rusty
lock to move. She pushed it in and waved Ramsey up
the narrow stairway. He paused on the first step as the
weathered floorboards creaked.

"Yeah, I know, it sounds ominous, but no one's fallen
through yet," she tried to reassure him.

"Yet," he said before following her up the stairs. One
of the stairwell lights was still clinging to life, flickering
on and off in a vain effort to keep the stairwell lit. At
night, it resembled a medieval castle that was lit only by
torchlight. The steps groaned under every footstep, the
sound bouncing between the peeling plaster walls.

She was suddenly self-conscious, noticing the scent
of moldy plaster more than she normally did. The door
that led to her tiny apartment was a mass of cracked
varnish. Normally, she shrugged it off and labeled it
"vintage." Today, she bit her lip to keep from apologiz-
ing for the condition.

Ramsey carried her case into the middle of her apartment, but he didn't put it down. He was taking a survey

of his surroundings. She got caught up watching him because of how sharp he looked. His exterior hadn't changed. He was still the lean, leather-clad man more suited to darkness than daylight.

Which made the way he looked over her apartment more interesting. He was staring at the single window that had a fabulous view of the rusty fire escape ladder. He reached out and ran his finger along the edges of the wood, where there was so much paint, the pane would require a crowbar to raise it.

"This is a fucking death trap," he said.

"Yeah, it is. Welcome to the Bay Area, excessively high rent zone extraordinaire," she said with a flourish of her hand.

He found the small emergency escape hammer she had bought in the event that she needed to get through the window. Its handle was bright orange, and she always kept it on the windowsill.

"You're no idiot, Jewel," he remarked with a touch of admiration in his tone.

She thumbed through her meager supplies for enough gauze to cover the exposed areas of his tat.

Actually, she felt like a mega fool for bringing him inside her apartment. She was practically going into heat with so much raw brawn so close to her fingertips. Getting him out of reach was a priority, or she might end up hating herself when she did something impulsive.

She got the feeling Ramsey knew exactly how to take advantage of "impulsive" moments.

"This will do the job." The paper wrapping crinkled, seeming excessively loud, because every nerve ending she had was on high alert.

Ramsey turned toward her, the case settling onto the worn floorboards. He popped open the top button of his pants, and she fought off the urge to run a hand across her chin in case she was drooling.

Boy, was he worthy of it.

But she wasn't going there.

Nope.

As in…*No! All you have is your pride, girl.*

It was a sad little truth. Jewel covered the new ink carefully.

Ramsey chuckled softly.

Warmly.

So very…male.

"Don't be intimidated."

She looked up, the cloth tape she'd planned to secure the gauze with still dangling from her fingers.

He cupped her chin and lowered his head until their lips were a single inch apart.

"Don't be intimidated, babe." He stroked her jawline, sending ripples of delight down her body. "Touch me."

She shook her head, recoiling as a warning bell went off somewhere in the part of her brain still functioning on a rational level. "I am going to cover this and…"

Her fingers were trembling.

Hell, she was rapidly turning into a quivering mass of overstimulated receptors.

But she got the gauze taped in place and pushed the button on his fly back through its hole.

And realized she'd been holding her breath the entire time.

She stepped away from him and drew in a deep

breath. As she blew it out, she heard the unmistakable sound of him chuckling.

"Yeah, yeah, yeah…" She discovered herself laughing along with him. "Like you don't know what you do to the opposite sex."

His eyes narrowed, his expression becoming insanely sensual. Her mouth went dry as she stared, transfixed by the glitter in his eyes. She wasn't sure when he moved, only that he was suddenly folding her into his embrace.

"Glad to know I'm not the only one turned-on." His voice was a husky promise, just a whisper against her temple that shouldn't have had the power to send a shiver down her spine in the bright light of day.

"Whoa." She flattened her hands on his chest, but pulled away when it felt like she'd grabbed a pair of live jumper cables. "We're not doing this."

He cupped her nape, the grip ripping through the fragile hold she had on logic. As in shredded. There was something primal about the way he handled her, taking control and tilting her head up so she got locked into his mesmerizing stare. But he held back, just enough to make her have to commit to the moment. If he'd kissed her, she could have labeled him an overbearing jerk. A spoiled celebrity. Instead, she was caught between temptation and the screaming warning from her common sense.

"We're not doing it…*yet*," he rasped.

Disappointment drew its claw across her as he spoke. There was a flash of iron-willed control in his dark eyes that frustrated her as much as it titillated.

"You're not nearly excited enough, Jewel."

Hell...

"What I'm *not* is into jumping clients," she informed him with what was left of her rational mind.

She tried to shift away, but he moved his hand into her hair, threading his fingers through the delicate strands before he massaged her scalp. The motion set off a crazy twist of awareness that went coiling through her until it set fire to her clit. Her hips jerked toward his, giving her a blunt, firsthand knowledge of just how hard his cock was.

"Better," he said. "But still not enough."

"I mean it, Ramsey. Back off." She hated how desperate she sounded, but there was little help for it. She was transforming into putty, just a hairbreadth away from losing all grip on what she should do, in favor of what she craved.

All those dark cravings no one really wanted to admit they had. For the first time, she feared him, because Ramsey wasn't afraid of those dark tidings. Oh, hell no. He danced into the center of the storm and let it consume him.

"Really—" She pushed away from him, taking a moment to touch his chest, getting a glimpse of what she was forbidding herself to experience.

Being practical sucked.

He let her go, but she didn't think for a second he was in agreement with her. No, there was something in his eyes that warned her this was just beginning.

"Well, I've got to find another job," she said, trying to get herself focused on real-world issues. Trying to keep a roof over her head was as practical as it got.

He snorted. "Let me take care of that."

She felt cold now that she'd separated from him, but

the chill going down her back came from her need to stand on her own two feet. "I don't need you to get me a job."

"Yeah, that's what I like about you. No handouts. That's not your style," he muttered. From another man, she was pretty sure she would have labeled that a line. Insincere words meant to weaken her resolve. But there was a flash of confidence in Ramsey's eyes that told her he'd meant exactly what he'd said.

He tossed his head, his black hair whipping through the air, looking like black rain. "Get some sleep. Your talent will get you another job as soon as I reveal this tat tomorrow night. I'll send a car around for you."

Relief surged through her. She got exactly three seconds to enjoy it before he moved, hooking his arm around her back and stepping forward at the same time. The result was being closed in his embrace. Not pulled to him or being crowded.

No, it was far more overwhelming than anything she'd experienced before. He truly enveloped her. A level of control she'd never experienced. He knew his body, knew how to use it for maximum effectiveness.

She was so ready for him to kiss her.

Except he didn't. He nuzzled against her head, inhaling the scent of her hair.

"You smell...delicious." He drew in another deep breath, shifting so she felt the hardening of his cock against her midsection. "I want to circle you for a good long time before we get to the jumping part."

She recoiled from the hard certainty in his voice.

And his body.

But once she was staring at him across a space of

several feet, she realized what she was reeling from was her reaction to him.

And boy, was it knocking her for a loop.

"I do appreciate the help in getting me another job, but I'd like to keep things professional between us," she said.

His jaw tightened. "Me too, but I don't think either of us is going to be able to ignore the other," he answered with what sounded like her own thoughts.

She heard a hint of distaste in his tone and thought she saw a flicker of uncertainty in his eyes before he turned and left. It felt like the damned temperature of the room went down several degrees with his departure.

Oh…shit.

Just…shit.

Exactly what she didn't need, an epic infatuation with a bigger-than-life rock star. She was going to end up like a discarded candy wrapper, one of those little foil chocolate-bar ones, crumpled and tossed aside when he was done devouring her.

And his sweet tooth wouldn't be satisfied. Nope. He'd move on to another treat before she forgot what it felt like to have his mouth on hers.

Well, she was just going to have to find the strength to say no.

It was really about self-preservation more than morality.

Really.

⁓⁓⁓

He was tired, but it was worth it.

Ramsey didn't lament the hours of sleep he'd missed out on. He finished showering and walked out of the bathroom nude, through a thick cloud of steam. He went into the bedroom of his suite to see Jewel's work in a full-length mirror.

It was badass.

The dragon was clawing its way toward his cock, looking like it was going to breathe fire on the appendage.

His cock twitched, beginning to harden as Ramsey started to turn, admiring the way Jewel had inked the reptile along his hipline. It was done in soft shades of blue and pewter, the shading a true mark of Jewel's skill level. The proportions were perfect too. Moving around the curve of his body to where the back of the dragon was on the flat of his lower back and the tail trailed down over the top of his right ass cheek.

He'd seen his share of ink and knew quality from shit. This was true art. More than that, she'd seen him.

He wasn't sure how he felt about that, except he knew for a fact that he owed fate a massive "thanks." The members of Toxsin had rules about sticking together when they were drunk, and he'd just had a head-on collision with the consequences of not minding that code. The tabloids would have shredded him, and that would have spilled over to the other band members. It was a lapse in judgement he couldn't allow to happen again. They'd all worked too fucking hard to let anything take them down even a small amount.

The tattoo was itching now that his skin was dry. He turned around and found some lotion. Honestly, he was avoiding thinking about Jewel. Someone knocked on the suite door across the hall.

"Room service."

The scent of hot chow made his belly rumble. Ramsey found a pair of pants and slid them on. He wandered across the hall to where Syon and his new wife, Kate, were eating. Breakfast was laid out on the table in their suite. Every sort of breakfast dish you could imagine, from pancakes to blintzes. It was close to four in the afternoon, but they ran on their own schedule when they were on tour. Heavy metal concerts were a night business.

Kate offered him a "Good morning" as he settled in and started rummaging around the grub. She was looking at his hipline above the leather pants he wore.

"Want to see the whole thing?" he asked.

Syon flipped him off but followed the obscene gesture with a grin.

Kate was curled up in a chair, cradling a cup of coffee. "Said the spider to the fly." She drew off a sip before continuing. "See…I do want to see it, but…" She held a slim finger up in the air. "You'll likely show it to me if I admit it."

"It's too early in the morning to deal with your bare ass, Rams," Syon interrupted.

"Marriage is making you soft."

Syon shot him a hot look. "Sure is, over, and over, and over again."

Kate made a groaning sound under her breath.

"I messed up last night," he said. "Won't happen again."

There was a moment of seriousness in the suite. Taz offered him a two-finger "peace" sign. Drake nodded before going back to his breakfast.

"Going to fill Sammy in on Tia?" Syon asked.

Ramsey shook his head. "I'm not going whining to Sammy. He's our producer, not my nanny."

"Tia will run right back to him," Drake stated.

"Let her. Sammy's not stupid. He knows what she is," Ramsey replied. "I'm the dumb shit who let her get me drunk." Ramsey finished up and tossed his napkin on his cleared plate. "Got to talk to Brenton about stuff."

Normally, hanging out with Syon was his morning enjoyment. Today, he was focused on making sure Jewel showed up at the concert they had in a few hours. He avoided thinking about how much he wanted her there. So he focused on the idea of her being around when her work was revealed, one artist to another, professional behavior.

Yeah, he was completely full of shit.

What he wanted was to get his hands on Jewel again.

But he took comfort in the fact that he would be helping her career. She deserved it, and he knew firsthand how unfair the universe was when it came to giving an artist a well-deserved break.

And right after he got finished doing the right thing, he could get on with doing what he really wanted.

Jewel's phone buzzed with an incoming text around noon. She thought about ignoring it, but even with limited sleep under her belt, she was wide-awake. She reached for it and swiped the screen to unlock it.

Your car will be there at five. Ramsey.

How had he gotten her number? She rubbed her eyes and looked at the screen again, but the text wasn't a dream.

Guess he had people to do the stuff he didn't want to deal with. It was a little unnerving.

Another text came in. We'll be backstage. Someone will bring you through security.

Backstage? Well, it was going to be a premium experience for sure. So long as she didn't chicken out.

Acknowledge.

She stared at the text, stunned by the formalness of it. A little tingle touched her nape, rousing a memory of how Ramsey looked when he wasn't hiding behind the bad boy he seemed to think the world believed he was. She got the feeling he was a whole lot more, and that whatever was hidden inside him was also responsible for his rise to fame. There were people who thought success just happened, but she knew it took more than raw talent to make it to the top. You needed a dose of luck and enough brainpower to fuel a solid business approach.

She texted him back. Looking forward to it.

Good.

She heard his raspy tone as she read the text, a tiny ripple of sensation moving along her skin in response.

Wow. Just…wow. The guy was so potent, she felt the effect a full day later.

And through a text message, no less.

Suddenly, moving back into her parents' home in Denver looked a little more like a good choice, because it would be a shield against her suddenly impulsive nature. Except it would mean tossing in the towel on her dreams of being an artist, and admitting she was a chicken.

Those ideas left her feeling hollow.

So, she'd hang on a little longer. Sometimes things happened for a reason.

—᷾᷾᷾—

Keeping a car in San Francisco was a luxury.

Rent was super high, which meant garages were income generators if you were lucky enough to have one, willing to compromise on your personal freedom, and willing to use public transportation so you could rent your garage out to someone who needed it.

In many cases, using public transit was easier than trying to drive through the congested streets and find parking when you got to your destination.

Still, there was something about having a car to herself that Jewel admitted she liked and missed.

A whole lot.

She missed it even more keenly when she pushed open the metal security gate and a tinted-window sedan pulled up in the street. It was smooth. Judging the timing was tricky, but the driver was out of the car and opening the door for her without a care for the blares of horns from other drivers caught behind his double-parking job.

She stretched out in the backseat of the sedan as the driver hightailed it back into the driver's seat and pulled back into traffic. There was a privacy screen between her and the driver, a control panel on the armrest for her to use at her will, and a small selection of beverages, including ice. But what caught her eye was the little box sitting on the armrest between the seats. It was bound with a scarlet ribbon she recognized. The box was from her favorite bakery. A name tag was affixed to it.

Joan Marie Ryan.

Oh yeah, he had people, lots of folks to dig up her personal life. She didn't care for the slightly off balance feeling the name tag left her with, so she opened the box and smiled at the two chocolate-dipped strawberries resting inside. The scent rose up, teasing her nose.

It was her normal order. Her indulgence when life was too frustrating or she'd found a moment to celebrate. A little shiver went through her body, but what actually made her the most apprehensive was the idea that he'd set someone to looking into how to please her.

It had been a really long time since someone had spent much effort on trying to make her happy.

She lifted one and bit into it, savoring the combination of strawberry and chocolate. Dark chocolate. Like Ramsey. She hummed softly.

Get a grip, girl. Or he's going to toss you into the air like a Frisbee.

Well, that could be fun too.

Ha! Only if you want to suffer through the emotional meltdown tomorrow morning.

Truth was such a sharp-edged little bitch. She drew blood with every bite.

The car inched along, going slower as they got closer to the downtown area where the arena was located. Cars jammed full of long-haired fans were blaring Toxsin's music with their windows down. The sidewalks were full of more fans who had taken the underground trains from their hotels. Summer hadn't lost its grip on California yet. Even as the sun was setting, it was over eighty degrees, thanks to an end-of-summer heat wave.

The city police had intersections closed down. Officers stood out in the middle of them, directing everyone toward the entrance to the underground parking lot. But her driver cruised through, drawing the attention of those stuck in traffic. The driver knew what he was doing, pulling the vehicle past the "Road Closed" signs and the "Private, No Entrance" warnings. A couple of uniformed officers stepped up to the driver's-side door. The driver flashed a card at them and was waved through.

It was pretty cool.

They drove up the backside of the huge arena and onto the roof. Jewel climbed out without waiting for the driver, because she was curious. There was a whole staging area on the roof. Three black SUVs were backed in, waiting for a getaway. Hell, there was even a helicopter.

"You came."

She turned around to discover Ramsey standing behind her. He'd obviously come through the tinted glass doors that led into the area.

And he was very obviously a rock star tonight. His hair was teased and gelled into spikes. There was a sheen to it that caught the light and made it flash black with undertones of blue. Someone had done a brilliant job on his face with foundation and eyeliner.

He voiced what she was taking in. "Performance makeup. Can't be a blur on stage."

"I don't think anyone will miss you, eyeliner or not."

He closed the distance between them, moving with a fluid grace that was a whole lot more like a prowl than a stride. The guy was off the scale when it came to sheer presence. Her damned toes were curling as he took the last couple of paces.

His dark eyes were full of anticipation. It made her breath catch and her lips tingle when his gaze dropped to them.

He wanted to kiss her.

Hell, she wanted him to do it.

But he left her hanging in that moment, suspended between breaths as she waited to see what the next second would bring. He reached out for her, slipping his hand along the side of her jaw. It was a delicate touch. Like a promise of control when he looked so wild. He was tempting her, teasing her. Although maybe the best way to put it was…baiting her.

"Come on inside."

"Ah…sure." Her tongue felt like a wad of half-responsive tissue in her mouth.

Ramsey had started to turn away. He reversed course, sweeping back around and capturing her against his body.

She was suddenly surrounded by him, immersed in sensory overload as his scent filled her senses and the heat from his skin warmed her.

"I want to." His voice was muffled against her temple.

Jewel shifted back, recoiling as her brain fried and left her at the mercy of her emotions. "Want to what?"

He followed her again. Turning her around in a tight circle to control her attempts to escape—not holding her, just moving so she ran into him as she tried to avoid him. It caused her head to spin. She looked up, seeking out a stationary spot to fix her gaze on.

It ended up being his eyes.

And once she locked gazes with him, the remains of her thoughts scattered.

"I want to kiss you…" He cupped her head, gathering her hair in his hand and pulling the strands just tight enough to send a spike of sensation through her.

A wild, untamed spike.

"Umm…well, that's not a very good idea," Jewel managed to force out.

His lips curved softly. "Agreed." There was a mocking sound to his tone as he snorted. "And that is a first for me."

His gaze dropped to her lips, his expression tightening; she saw the desire glittering in his eyes. She ended up quivering, pushing against his chest, only to discover she was very much his prisoner.

"But I don't want you like this."

She was free before his words sank in. He'd turned away from her, and she realized he was hiding from her.

Don't ask.

Really, she needed to heed that warning, but she reached out and cupped his bicep, yanking him back as she stepped forward so she could see his face.

She ended up sucking in her breath.

Ramsey chuckled at her, turning all the way to face her and taking one long step to loom over her. "So you want to see? Sure you can handle it?"

His tone was rough.

But what she heard was the challenge in it. "You don't intimidate me."

"Yes, I do." He lifted his hand, reaching out to touch her. She stood her ground, unwilling to let him see her retreat. He ended up tapping her lips with the tip of his index finger.

The connection was electric. She shivered, her eyes

sliding closed as she lost all control of her thoughts and just slipped into a bubble of pure reaction.

"Okay…" She stepped back, fighting the urge to pant as her heart raced. "I'm not sure I can handle it."

"Neither am I." His eyes narrowed, surprise flickering in them before he captured her hand and turned toward the door.

The doors opened as they approached, and he took her through them as she was caught in her own moment of surprise.

Ramsey, the Mega Rock Star. She expected a fair number of things from him, but uncertainty wasn't anywhere on the list.

He was a beast.

An animal.

A creature carved out of midnight.

He was so far out of the realm of normal, and yet, she discovered herself drawn to that crack in his shell. The one she was pretty sure he wasn't happy about her seeing.

It struck her as special.

Maybe "intimate" was a better word. Even if using it set off another warning bell. It made no sense and was really a far-fetched idea altogether. Mega rock stars didn't play by the same rules as the rest of the world. Feeling connected to him on any level was going to end badly.

Very badly.

Still, she found herself looking at the way his fingers were curled around hers. A tender touch, innocent, and yet her heart rate accelerated. When was the last time a guy had held her hand? Before he'd made a move on her?

Okay, well, Ramsey had made a move on her. He'd embodied exactly what she'd thought he was: cornering her within minutes, laying waste to her morality with the force of his persona in a few polished moves that lived up to her image of him. Yet he hadn't taken her. No, it had been far smoother. He'd stepped into her path, unnerved her, baited her, teased her, tempted her, and made sure she was the one tumbling into his embrace.

It was a blast.

A total high.

The only problem with that was the fall to the ground when she came down.

Mega rock stars didn't leave the sky.

Nope. She'd end up looking up at him from the broken heap she landed in.

Alone.

Chapter 2

TOXSIN'S FANS WERE VORACIOUS.

The arena sounded alive, groaning and straining as showtime neared. It was like a tangible pulse floating through the air. It was a hundred times more powerful than static electricity.

Ramsey pulled Jewel down a series of hallways, past a couple of intense-looking security posts, and right through doors that had large warnings: "Performers Only. Violators Will Be Prosecuted." Inside was a huge ready room of sorts, with makeup chairs and mirrors, rolling costume racks, and even a complete set of instruments for warming up.

"This is Brenton, our road manager."

"Ah, the lady of the evening." Brenton offered her his hand. Jewel reached out and shook it. He was wearing a black polo shirt with "Toxsin" embroidered over the left bicep. There were several other men wearing the same thing. Some of them had on headphones that covered their ears completely, while others had only clear pig-tail communications devices stuck in their right ears. It was far more organized than she'd expected. Which was a tad shallow of her, because she realized she was judging Ramsey without knowing very much about him. There was an attention to detail that was, frankly, almost military in nature.

"We've got your seat reserved. Kate will show you

the way when showtime hits," Brenton continued.
"Here's a little pass to make sure no one stops you.
Keep it hidden. Some of the regulars know what it is
and might try to snatch it."

He handed her what looked like a hotel room key
card hanging on a lanyard. It wouldn't be hidden with
the V-neck of the dress she'd worn, so she stuffed it
into her bra. The road manager was somewhere in his
early fifties, with a receding hairline he hid by keeping
his brown hair clipped short. He clearly lifted weights,
his shoulders and back having that bulky, muscular look.
But his grin was easygoing, and there was a twinkle of
happiness in his eyes that told her he really loved his job.

It was quite a job though, along the line of dream-
come-true ones.

"You remember Taz and Syon?" Ramsey pointed
toward a line of makeup stations, where the two rockers
were sitting as their faces were touched up.

"I think you missed Drake," Ramsey said as he
pointed at the fourth member of Toxsin.

"Evening." Drake unleashed a very British accent
on her and winked from where he was inspecting his
overall look in front of a full-length mirror.

"And Kate, our leather artist." Ramsey pointed toward
a redhead standing by a rolling clothing rack that had
leather pants and vests hanging on it. "Syon's her bitch."

"And happy to be so," Syon Braden, lead singer, sang
out. He hopped out of the makeup chair and went over to
his wife. There was a smack as he landed a hand on her
bottom, her leather skirt popping.

"Don't start something you can't finish," she chastised her husband.

"Oh, I can finish it alright," Syon cooed softly to her. "And I will."

But he moved over to where a guitar was hanging from a stand. He picked it up and started fingering the strings.

"Got to go to work," Ramsey said.

He moved over to where Syon was and picked up another guitar. Syon Braden was a legend, but Ramsey smoked him when he started to play. There was a sharp edge to the notes he coaxed out of the strings. His expression became raw while his whole body moved with the music. It was erotic, and she was mesmerized by the sight, suddenly realizing that she'd never seen a true music legend at work.

Drake started up on the drums as Taz joined in. The staff in the room started nodding with the beat as they finished up their duties. Jewel ended up leaning against the wall, enjoying the private glimpse of Toxsin. Without a doubt, it was a privilege.

At least she saw it that way.

Ramsey opened his eyes, catching her gaze. Her breath stopped, time freezing, and she felt suspended between moments, waiting for the next note, unable to move forward until the music carried her. It was incredibly intimate—that thing she'd seen a glimpse of in his eyes on full display now. Her gaze lowered to his lips, and her own tingled.

God, she wanted him to kiss her. And just for a moment, his lips curved, making it clear he wanted to do exactly that.

In the next instant, his eyes slid shut and he looked like he was pushing the music straight out of his soul.

He was letting loose completely. Something most

people didn't have the guts to do. At least, not in front of others, and he was going to do it in front of thousands of fans.

He rocked.

It was that simple.

She felt it seeping into her, washing away her better judgment and leaving her nothing but a pile of receptors, just waiting for him to stimulate her.

Rock star.

He was definitely that and something more, something that hit her as polished and trained. It was a heady combination, because she could have ignored someone who had just gotten lucky and was pushing out decent music with a show to tantalize the teenagers. Now, an artist who had earned everything he had? That was intoxicating on an epic level. She watched the way his fingers moved on the strings; the skill was unmistakable. He was watching a flat screen, looking at the notes the computer program picked up to make sure he was hitting them right.

That was skill and dedication. As well as respect for his art.

Hell, she was totally impressed now. The car was great, the strawberries a treat, but seeing him and his bandmates focused and determined to excel, well, that sent a whole different sensation through her.

Respect.

—⁓—

She had a seat.

Not that Jewel stayed in it.

The moment the members of Toxsin took the stage,

the fans near the long catwalk surged to their feet and crowded the edge of the stage. The temperature felt like it was going up from the frenzy the crowd was working itself into.

Ramsey seemed to know exactly how to push their buttons too. He took the stage. He didn't walk onto it. He fucking stormed it and claimed it as his domain. There was no just watching him. The audience was captivated, held in a grip that was nearly hypnotic. Ramsey and his bandmates were putting out such high levels of energy, everyone in the arena was moved to screaming.

Jewel was no exception.

Nor did she want to be.

She surged to her feet and smiled at the pulsing in her blood. It warmed her like alcohol and was just as devastating to her wits. Thinking was completely out of the question as Toxsin finished one song and rolled into another one that punched up the level of frenzy surrounding them. The fans were like desperate disciples who reached out for their idols. The reason was clear. The members of Toxsin embodied what everyone fought for.

They were truly free.

What they were was on display, along with all of their inner demons. The music was an outpouring of all the emotions everybody tried to ignore as they went about being respectable, civilized people. The cravings they had and were too self-conscious to admit having.

Tonight, they all roared as Toxsin gave them permission to embrace those feelings, the seedy and the oh-so-often labeled immoral sexual passion. Jewel screamed with the rest of them, feeling freer than she ever had. She got it, really got it. Inside her was a person who wanted to be accepted for what she was. It wasn't always decent, and it certainly didn't fit into anything that might be termed "civilized," which was why she and everyone around her kept that part of their souls bottled up. The day-to-day grind made them all contain their cravings; Toxsin showed them how to embrace them.

Ramsey was a true badass, because he wasn't afraid of what the world would say about him.

She realized he was the most honest man she'd ever met.

"Oh. My. God! Look at the tat!"

Ramsey arched back, playing a solo on his guitar. His lean, ripped abs stretched out, his neck corded as he pushed the instrument and filled the arena with a perfect blending of sound. His leather pants slipped lower; his vest rose higher, baring his waist and the top of the dragon. There was a hint of the head and tail, tantalizing glimpses as he moved.

"It's a dragon!"

"I want one!"

"I have to have one!"

She lost track of all the comments, feeling the praise wash through her. That dream she'd so carefully nurtured for the last few months suddenly surged back to robust health like a drowning victim who'd received CPR. It was no longer limping along as she fought for enough morsels of strength to resist tossing in the towel and falling into line with the rest of the world because it was the sensible thing to do. The thing that would help her sleep at night, because she wasn't wondering how she was going to scrape together the rent.

Ramsey was a mythical creature who had defied the odds and won.

She let out another scream, enjoying the high of the moment. When the concert ended, she melted into the crowd, leaving the VIP pass in her bra. She made her way onto the pavement and followed a huge bunch of people toward the underground BART trains.

She was wrung out, but happily so.

And you're a chicken...

Well, it was a necessity, self-defense at its best. One kiss, and her self-control would be a goner. Poof! Up in smoke for sure.

Chicken...

Oh, she was guilty as charged. No argument. Just a twinge of regret kept her company on the train ride back to her end of town. Okay, a little more than a twinge. More like a bucketful, leaving her sexually frustrated and kicking herself for walking away from a prime opportunity.

Which was why she'd done it.

Ramsey was a lot of things, but she didn't want to see him as an alley cat. She wanted to hold the memory of him being an artist. Keep him on a pedestal. Let him be a panther, a creature with nobility.

Whimsical.

And she wasn't even drunk.

No mere mortal man could claim to have intoxicated her.

Only a god.

So she'd leave him in the heavens and hold on to her worship of him.

―――∿∿∿―――

"I'm sorry, sir. She never came this way."

Ramsey considered the doorman before shrugging. But he turned and caught Syon watching him. His bandmate knew him. Really knew him.

Syon carried a beer over to him, handing it to him as he sipped from his own longneck.

"Don't worry about it," Ramsey said.

Syon only took another long sip. Ramsey twisted the cap off and indulged, but the beverage didn't taste right. He ended up setting it aside. He was unsatisfied, and beer wasn't what he wanted.

Brenton came into the performers' backstage room. "Great work, gentlemen. I have some opportunities for promotion, if you're interested."

Their new road manager didn't try to control them, always making suggestions instead of demands. Brenton read off a few clubs that had issued invitations, along with two trendy restaurants that promised epic meals if the band wanted to drop in.

"Your wife looks like she wants to go eat at the place with the view of the bay," Ramsey said.

Syon grinned at him. "Think I can't spot a decoy from you, Rams?"

Ramsey shrugged again. "I'm fine. Just don't feel like drinking. It didn't end too well a couple of nights ago."

"I don't know about that." Syon looked down at the top of the dragon tattoo.

"Okay, it ended well. But in an ass-backward sort of way."

"Yeah, you almost got a reputation for liking flowers," Taz said from a few feet away. "I can just smell the dressing room in Portland now if the fans had caught sight of those cherry blossoms."

Ramsey snorted. "Exactly. I think I'm going to be on the wagon for a bit."

"So, come to dinner." Syon was already moving away before Ramsey got the chance to answer.

"I could do dinner," Taz agreed. Drake gave them a thumbs-up.

"I'll call and let them know you're coming," Brenton said as he pulled his cell phone out of his pocket.

Her electricity was off.

Jewel used her cell phone to light her way into her apartment and find a candle. She held it to the burner of her gas range to light it before setting it on the pub-style table. The golden, intimate glow fit her mood. The sketch of the dragon was on the table, drawing her to it. She sat down and picked up her pen, pulled to the image and the memory of working it onto Ramsey. Sometime later, she sipped a glass of red wine as she surveyed the finishing touches she'd put on the drawing. If she'd been smart, she would have had him sign it so she could have sold it for enough to pay her utility bills.

But she knew she'd rather be homeless than part with the drawing. It was too personal. Too much a part of something that had been created inside her soul.

So she savored her last glass of wine as the candle burned low and she finished the dragon.

———–✺–——–

Someone laid their fist on her door at nine in the morning.

It was the building door, at the street level, and the iron gate was making a huge racket that echoed up the narrow stair corridor. Jewel groaned, but she'd be lying if she said she'd been sleeping. She ran her fingers through her hair and slipped her feet into a pair of shoes and headed down.

"Good, you're up."

The woman at the door had a rose tattooed on the left side of her neck. Her forearms had ink as well. She was also wearing a spiked dog collar around her neck with a little metal tag that had "Pony" inscribed on it. "I'm Pony from Spike Collar."

"Hi. What can I do for you?" Jewel kept the key to the outer door in her hand.

"It's what I can do for you," Pony said with a snap of chewing gum. She propped one hand on her hip, the short, lacy skirt she had on flipping with the morning breeze. "Heard Ted booted you to the curb for doing the tat on Ramsey. Casey sent me over to tell you we've got a spot open for you."

Or more precisely, for her ten seconds of fame as tattoo artist to the stars.

"You know I was covering up your guys' work?" Jewel asked pointedly.

Pony snapped her gum again and smirked. "Sure do."

There was a gleam of enjoyment in her eyes. Jewel decided it was pretty ugly. "Sorry, but I don't roll that way."

"Like what?" Pony demanded. "The dude got what

was coming to him. Even if you're straight, you know men like him are massive pricks. About time he found out what it feels like to be on the business side of being used. You'll make a lot more money working for Spike."

"I'm a professional. I don't do drunk tats or vengeance ones," Jewel said firmly.

Pony snorted. "Don't judge it, bitch. At least I don't live in an armpit like this. Your morals aren't going to keep you from getting evicted tomorrow."

Jewel stiffened. Pony snapped her gum again. "Yeah, we know the manager of this building. He heard you got canned. Already has someone lined up to move in. Casey can make it right for you. Show up if you don't want to be on the street tomorrow night. It's a dog-eat-dog world, baby. Better get with the program."

She turned with a flip of her torn skirt hem and started off down the street.

Jewel leaned against the wall, feeling like the world was making ready to beat the crap out of her. She had options; she just didn't like any of them.

Something shifted, and her jaw dropped when Ramsey appeared in the doorway next to hers. It was all of three feet away. He had a T-shirt on today, to cover his new ink. But the thin jersey material stuck to him, sending a ripple of awareness through her.

God, he was lickable.

"Are you getting evicted tomorrow?" he asked.

She drew in a stiff breath and decided to roll with the facts. "Ted claimed my pay as rent due on my slot at his shop. So, I guess so." She tried to shrug it off but felt like she didn't quite pull it off. "Like you said, this place is a death trap. I'll be well rid of it. I'm sure not going to go to work for Spike to keep it."

"Did you mean that?" He pointed toward Pony making her way up the block.

She opened her hands, slightly confused. Okay, slightly dumbfounded, because he was there, messing with her thought processes again.

She was pretty sure she liked that best about his personality.

Glutton for punishment.

"Yes, I mean it," she confirmed. "It's a no-brainer. I'll go home first."

His lips curved. It was the real McCoy too, a genuine smile.

"Why'd you leave last night?" he asked.

She shrugged, but it was a chicken answer. He knew it, too. She saw the flicker in his eyes. Heat teased her cheeks, and she realized she was actually blushing.

Brain-frying time.

She ended up offering him a half bark of laughter. "I was worried I'd get caught in your gravitational pull and end up on a one-way trip into the sun. It would be a blast, no doubt, but I'd end up frying in the end."

He snorted at her.

"What? You think I'm buttering up your ego? Like you don't have scores of women flinging themselves at you? And not just the desperate ones. I Googled you on the train ride home. You tend to run with some tight girls. Why are you here? I mean, it's not like you have to go chasing anyone."

"Aren't you glad to see me?" His lips twisted into the cocksure grin she found far too irresistible.

Oh yeah…undermining.

She caught herself returning the grin. "I'm going to claim my fifth amendment right and refuse to answer that question on the grounds that it will incriminate me. And encourage you, which you definitely don't need."

His eyes narrowed as his lips curved. For a moment, he basked in the glow of the amusement her comment had provided him.

"Part of me was glad you took off last night," he said.

"Sure," she said to cover her shock, deciding on a change of topic to keep from looking too lame. "Thank you for the car and strawberries. It was a blast of a show."

"You still left."

Jewel drew in a deep breath and decided to level. "I don't do drunk tats, or vengeance ones, and I wanted to keep my memories of you in the area of 'he's an awesome dude, not a prick who's trying to get into my pants.'"

He contemplated her for a long moment, all hints of playfulness gone. A tingle touched her nape as she realized she was facing him. Just him, the person he kept locked behind a shield.

"Okay. Fair enough. I do like to party."

"I'm not judging," Jewel said.

"Didn't have to." He reached through the bars and plucked the keys from her grip. "Everything you think shows on your face. That's part of your allure. It was all I could do to resist kissing you last night when you looked at my mouth. But I wanted a bit more privacy for our first kiss."

"There isn't going to be any kissing," she told him flatly.

He pushed the key into the lock and gave it a turn,

completely ignoring her. The lock stuck, as usual. "Pony had one thing right. This place is an armpit."

The lock gave with a groan. Ramsey pulled the gate open and stepped inside. He was too large for the space.

Or at least his persona was.

Her belly tightened, the reaction surprising her. She was fascinated by how extreme it was.

"I wanted to see that look on your face last night." He slid a hand along her jawline, knowing exactly how to touch her. For a moment, she soaked it up, savoring it. The guy had talented fingers.

But her belly growled, long and deep.

He chuckled. "Come on, let's get some chow."

He was up the stairs before she realized he still had her keys.

"You're going to take me to breakfast?" she asked.

He sent her a wink so roguish, she felt her belly do a little flop. "Gotta work on the 'being more than a prick' thing, because I do want to get into your pants. That part's not changing."

"Not sure if you're honest or brazen to say that point-blank," she confessed as she fought back a smile. Damn, the guy oozed charm.

He offered her a steady stare. "I'm not a liar."

She liked that. It kept him on that pedestal she'd decided she wanted him on. "Fair enough."

"Need anything?" he asked as he started to lock her door.

She choked on what came to mind. Ramsey raised an eyebrow at her. His blunt honesty was catching, though. Her lips curled up into a naughty grin as she answered him.

"Underwear. I need…underwear."

She'd struck him speechless. And she got the impression that didn't happen very often. There was a flash of savage enjoyment in his dark eyes.

"That is completely a matter of opinion." His gaze slid down to her breasts. He looked like he was in pain for a long moment. "Yeah. Definitely underwear, or you'll be on the menu. I will eat you up."

It was her turn to feel her tongue stick to the roof of her mouth. He caught his lower lip between his teeth and growled at her.

Part of her wouldn't mind.

A large part of her.

Her clit was already throbbing with anticipation.

Crap. Did a guy like him even go down on a girl? It wasn't like he had to in order to get laid.

Danger. Danger. You really do not need to know the answer to that question.

Oh, but she wanted to know!

He hooked her arm as she tried to pass him once again. Doing that thing where he stepped toward her but around her and managed to turn her in a tight backward circle that made her feel like she was completely surrounded and the one running into him.

"I do." His voice was a raspy promise against her ear. He was cradling her head, his fingers threaded through her hair, taking her instantly to the edge of reason.

"Do…what?" She was pretty sure she'd never sounded so breathless.

"Give as much as I receive." His grip tightened, pulling just enough to send a jolt of sharpness through her scalp. It never really became pain, which only turned up the heat another notch, because his control was so mouthwatering. "But you're not a fangirl, Jewel. You're an artist. Get dressed before I forget how much I admire you in favor of how good you smell."

He released her, and she felt like they'd been jerked apart. His eyes glittered with the same need she felt pulsing through her.

She was torn.

Right, wrong, immoral…maybe.

So very true, though.

He was leaning casually against her wall, but looked a whole lot like a giant cat contemplating its next kill.

It wouldn't be an altogether bad fate.

She made it into her closet and flung off her yoga pants and T-shirt. She could have sworn she felt the air sizzling. Her tiny loft apartment was too damned small for someone like Ramsey.

In the time it took her to climb into her only pair of good jeans, he'd wandered to her kitchen table-slash-desk.

"You added to the dragon." He inspected the drawing of his tattoo.

"You put on a hell of a show. I was too amped up to sleep." She came out of her closet and enjoyed the way her work was keeping his attention. "I was just…"

"Thinking of me." He pulled his attention away from the dragon and locked gazes with her. "I like these details."

"They're subtle, just refinements really. A little separation anxiety. I never want to let my art babies go completely." It really was a confession, an intimacy, and she wasn't too sure why she was sharing with him.

"The additions. I want you to do them."

"It would be best to let the work you have healed before adding them. About three weeks." She smiled as she looked at the design.

He nodded before looking around the apartment. "How much of this stuff is yours?"

"Ah…" The question caught her off guard. "Not much, actually." She didn't care for how exposed she felt admitting it either. Church mice had more than she did.

"I thought that might be the case when Pony made that crack about your landlord already having someone lined up." He scanned the bare walls and the two-decades-old sofa.

"I just got out of school." She started to defend herself and then bit her lip when she realized she was feeling inferior. She'd made her choices and wasn't going to apologize.

Ramsey flashed her a grin that warmed her chilled insides. It wasn't arrogant or presumptuous, just knowing. "It wasn't so long ago that everything I owned fit into my duffel bag."

"No way." Just went to show she had no clue about his life. "Sorry. That was a little judgmental."

"Part of it's deserved," he surprised her by saying. "I live wild now because I can. Kind of like letting my inner kid run crazy in the candy store."

The images she'd pulled up on Google came to mind. "You do like to indulge."

His eyes narrowed. For a split second, she glimpsed his annoyance before he tapped the drawing. "I'm serious. I want you to do these additions." That businessman she'd glimpsed inside him was staring at her now. "Pack up your personals. Ditch this armpit. Ride along with us for a few weeks. It will give you time to hook up with a new studio. You can make sure I remember to keep this covered."

Oh man. It was the option she hadn't had when Pony had been there, slapping her with reality. That longed-for escape from doing the sensible thing and holding tight to her dream.

"Just hop on the tour bus?" It sounded ludicrous and amazing at the same time. "What will your bandmates think of that?"

"Don't care." And his tone told her he didn't. "There are forty-six members of the crew with us. Room, salary, and board. You don't have a better offer."

"I don't," she agreed, but crossed her arms over her chest. "But that doesn't mean I'm going to just roll over. I've made it this far on my own two feet. What would you be paying me for? I don't take charity. My parents paid for my education so I can earn my way. If my art doesn't pan out, I will use my degree."

"In marketing," he answered, a little too easily for her comfort.

Yeah, he had people to do stuff, all right.

"I may like to party, but Toxsin is what it is because we all pull our own weight. You'll be expected to do the same. I don't pay groupies."

That both reassured her and set her back on edge. There was something in his tone that made it clear he planned to be in control. She chewed on her lower lip as she contemplated him.

"Don't like me telling you what to do, Jewel?" There was an undertone in his question that set off a warning bell.

But she still shook her head. There was a flicker in his eyes like lightning, a white-hot bolt of pure electricity. She ended up rolling her lower lip in because it had gone dry. His attention shifted to it before he returned to looking into her eyes.

He had his hands pressed down flat on either side of the drawing. "Finish your dragon."

"Are you asking me or telling me?" It probably wasn't the wisest question to voice. He looked a lot like he was baiting her.

"I'm challenging you," he said flatly. "I make you nervous."

Touché.

His lips curved, victory glittering in his eyes. "You're not stupid, Joan. The wind has changed. Set a new course."

"You're right. And…not so right about starting the name game…" He crossed his arms over his chest and faced off with her, but she wasn't done standing her ground. "Matthew Brimer. You looked adorable as an acolyte," she said pointedly.

He winced but lifted his hands in mock surrender. "Three minutes for a phone call. Then chow. And I'll have an official offer to present to you by the time we get back to pack you out of here. Jewel."

He extended his hand. She took it. He closed his fingers around hers, pumping up and down two times in a formal handshake before he tugged her forward. She tumbled into his chest, a moment's distraction becoming her downfall.

She was plastered against him because he'd stepped forward when he tugged her, ensuring she ended up flattened against his hard body. It felt like a thunderclap ricocheting through her system. Her senses were suddenly full of his scent. Her hands pressed against his skin where his vest ended and left his shoulders bare.

"And then…I'm going to kiss you, Jewel."

———

His promise rang inside her head.

Maybe it was more of a threat.

Honestly, her system was in full anxiety mode as she tried to focus on packing up her gear and moving on. At least the fact that she had few possessions helped keep her from making a complete fool of herself. There wasn't that much to forget.

Ramsey disappeared outside and made his call. It gave her time to call her landlord.

"You're not getting your deposit back," he sneered at her. "Not with a day's notice."

"I hear you already have the place rented."

"Can't prove it," her landlord countered.

Jewel decided to cut her losses. "It's been nice knowing you."

She ended the call and found Ramsey back inside the loft, watching her. "He'll get a surprise when he discovers the electricity is off. Bet his new tenant won't be so thrilled about having to deal with that right off the cuff."

She'd meant it as a strike back but winced when she realized how pathetic it made her circumstances appear.

"Getting started is tough," Ramsey surprised her by saying. "There were a couple of times we all slept in the piece-of-crap van we had because we had to scrape together gas money. If I never eat another cold hot dog straight from the package, I'll die happy. No one gets to the top without learning how to tough it out."

There was a note of sincerity in his tone that warmed her. It made it so much easier to pull her two roller bags out of the closet and dump her clothes into them. She hadn't lied to her mom. She really didn't have much to speak of.

"You've been putting your money into your work gear." Ramsey had pulled her roller case out from where she'd stashed it against the wall. It was a hard case with heavy latches.

"Of course," she answered as she emerged from the closet. "That's a no-brainer. Bet you had a top-of-the-line guitar before that van was replaced or you indulged in hot meals."

He nodded. "Even a race-car driver is going to lose if he's driving a three-cylinder rice-burner." For a moment, she was envious of him, but in a good way. She saw in him confirmation of what she could accomplish if she stuck to her goals. There was a rap on the street-level gate.

"Troops are here." Ramsey disappeared out into the hall as she plucked the few things from the kitchen that belonged to her.

She heard him returning, the sound of heavy footfalls on the ancient stairs bouncing up to fill the apartment.

"You remember Brenton?"

The road manager offered her a hand that she shook before he opened a folder and laid out several sheets of paper. "I'm looking forward to having you on the team, Ms. Ryan."

The easygoing demeanor evaporated. Once again, she was struck by how sharp Ramsey was beneath his public image. The contract was general, but still tight enough to have her reading through the clauses with a critical eye.

Ramsey knew business as well as any tycoon wearing an Armani suit.

It was also a dream come true. The thing she'd set out to achieve. A job that centered around her art. The contract listed her salary, which made her mouth water, a private room clause, access to meals at the hotels they would be lodged at, and even a budget for supplies, based on how much work she did. They reserved the right to set a schedule for her with clients of their choosing. It curled her toes with excitement because somehow, she'd gone from expecting life to kick her ass to being a private artist with Toxsin. Four weeks wasn't very long, but it was the lifeboat she needed to escape the ship that was sinking beneath her feet at the moment. And a damned fine lifeboat it was, too.

"What the fuck is all this?"

Jewel looked up to find her landlord in the doorway. He looked between Ramsey and Brenton and then back to Ramsey. "I know you, dude." Her prick of a landlord was suddenly grinning, offering Ramsey a hand to shake, trying to schmooze him.

"Yeah?" Ramsey said as he shook the hand, but there was a tightening to his body. "Glad you came over. It will save me the trouble of having one of our people bring the key by and pick up the security deposit."

Her landlord didn't miss the implied threat. He bristled. "I've got to check things out before returning the deposit."

"Make sure you check the fire-code violations on the window," Ramsey said pointedly. "How did you get the local inspector to sign off on this place? That window is painted shut."

"The Bay Area weather just makes it look that way," her landlord hedged.

Ramsey picked up the emergency hammer she had by the window.

"I'm just making ends meet," her landlord defended himself. "Like everyone else in this town. It costs a fortune to keep these apartments rental-ready. Damned lawmakers are always passing some new law I have to deal with. She didn't give me any notice, and now, I'll get stuck with a rush fee if I don't want to lose income on this place."

Ramsey gestured around. "Take a good look and write her a check. Jewel is going on tour with Toxsin. She needs her business affairs here closed."

"That right? Going on tour with Toxsin?" Her landlord offered her a smirk. "Not too bad." The innuendo wasn't lost on anyone in the room.

Her landlord had on designer sportswear, with a pair of insanely expensive sunglasses hanging from a leash around his neck. A Rolex watch winked at her from his wrist, and she knew his Lamborghini was double-parked on the street.

He was a prick who had inherited his property from his grandfather and lived off the fact that San Francisco was one of the highest rent districts in the nation.

"Are you done looking over the contracts, Jewel?" Ramsey had been watching her landlord, but he proved he was very aware of what she was doing. He snapped his attention toward her. "Anything we need to negotiate?"

"No. I'm satisfied." She scrawled her legal name across the last page before Brenton gathered it up and pulled a phone from his jacket pocket. He pressed a couple of keys before there was another set of boots on her stairs.

Two polo-shirted crew members appeared. They looked at the three cases with questioning expressions.

"That's it." She bit back an explanation. They didn't hesitate, but took the cases and disappeared. Ramsey exchanged a look with Brenton. The road manager of Toxsin proved his expertise by changing places with Ramsey and facing off with her landlord.

"I'll be happy to go through the place with you and listen to any concerns you have that might impact the security deposit. My associates want Ms. Ryan's affairs settled today."

There was a slicing edge to Brenton's words, along with a warning. Brenton reached into his suit jacket and withdrew a cream-colored business card. "Our lawyer."

Her landlord didn't care for the way he was being verbally strong-armed. His expression darkened before he shot her a hard look. Ramsey stepped between them.

"Yeah, yeah. Everything looks in order," her landlord conceded. "Checkbook is down in the car."

"I'll follow you down," Brenton said as he gestured toward the door. Ramsey tossed him the keys. Brenton caught them and kept them when her landlord opened his hand. There was a soft sputter from her landlord before he turned and disappeared, Brenton on his heels.

"I could have handled that." It wasn't the wisest thing she could have said. In fact, keeping her mouth shut would have been a really bright idea, all things considered. She needed the money and position with Toxsin. But her pride refused to let her stay silent.

Ramsey turned to face her. There was a look on his face that touched off a shiver in her, a reaction to the ruthlessness glittering in his eyes. Sensation rippled along the surface of her skin, his strength feeling like it was coating her and seeping into her very pores.

Still, she pushed her chin out and stood her ground. Ramsey's lips curled, his expression menacing.

"I lied to you," Ramsey said.

Her belly did a little flop as he stalked her across the floor.

"I said I was going to feed you…"

He stepped up close, lowering his arms around her and trapping her arms beneath his. "But I'm going to kiss you first."

His voice was a raspy promise, setting off alarm bells as well as anticipation.

"Bad idea—" she managed to push past her lips before her brain fried.

"I'm all bad, Jewel," he informed her a split second before he claimed her mouth.

If that was a kiss, then she'd never been kissed before.

Nope.

Never.

Ramsey sealed her lips beneath his, clamping her arms to her sides with a hug as he pressed his lips against hers. It was hard but not brutal, skimming that border and pushing her into a realm of dark desires that lay beyond the controlled, safe dating she'd participated in before. Civilization faded into the distance as he moved his lips over hers with a touch of savagery no one had been bold enough to try on her before. She moved away, pulling back out of a need to maintain some sort of sense of herself.

He didn't allow her to keep the distance between them. Ramsey reclaimed her mouth, pressing a kiss against her lips that stole her breath. A soft sound escaped her, betraying how deeply she was affected. He lifted his head, just an inch, watching her as she forced her eyelids up. She felt unmasked, every weakness on display. His eyes shimmered with the promise of so many things, her mind reeled as she tried to take it all in. She tried to squirm free. He held her for a long moment, his eyes narrowing as he made sure she felt his strength. It was more than brawn; it was his will he was trying to press on her.

That sparked a need to rebel. She snapped her jaw closed, her chin jutting out in defiance. "Back off."

His lips twitched, a glow of enjoyment lighting his dark eyes. It was savage, primitive, and completely in tune with his nature.

She pulled her hand up, found the silver bar piercing his nipple, and twisted.

He snorted before lifting his hands in mock surrender. But it was only play, because there was nothing even close to submission in him. He was just enjoying her spunk.

Playing with his food.

The air felt cool as it rushed between them, frustrating her with just how much she wanted to be back against him. It was wrong, or had to be. Where was the modern woman who wanted to follow her dream quest into a future that involved art and being the captain of her own ship?

At the moment, she was a quivering mass of nerves, all because of the man standing in front of her.

"Let's roll, Ramsey!" Brenton called up the stairs. "Portland awaits."

Ramsey curled his lips back and flashed his teeth at her through a grin of victory. "Ready?"

She looked around the apartment, and it was just as depressing as always. Everything in it was threadbare, just holding on as it struggled to squeeze one more day out of life. She wanted more than that.

Ramsey was pulsing with life. She could feel it in the air between them. Like heat coming through a front door on a frozen winter day. Getting wrapped up in it was the only thing on her mind once she felt it.

"Ready," she replied, turning her back on the apartment.

It was time to stretch her wings and see what was over the next hill. Ramsey stood there, looking like a massive challenge between her and the wide-open expanse of opportunity.

Well, no guts…no glory.

Chapter 3

Toxsin traveled in style.

The band also proved why it was topping the charts and selling out arenas. Beneath the spiked hair, leather, and party-animal personas were professionals.

The sedan Brenton had arrived in took them through the streets of San Francisco and back across the bay to the location of the concert. It was a very different scene by daylight. Two big rigs were being loaded. The members of the crew Ramsey had talked about all performed their duties like well-trained soldiers, moving pallets into the trucks while supervisors watched through mirrored shades with headphones on and microphones sitting in front of their lips.

There were also three huge motor homes. As in bus-sized.

"That's the music coach." Ramsey pointed at one. "Band members only. It's a work zone."

Kate Braden was standing near the door to the second coach. She looked up as Ramsey brought Jewel into the loading area. The afternoon sun lit up her head of red hair. She had on a leather corset top and a skirt that had her hallmark of superior leather workmanship. Jewel couldn't help but admire them.

"It's going to be nice having some female company," Kate offered. "We can have corset parties."

Ramsey made a low sound under his breath and

smacked his lips. Jewel itched to ram her elbow into his side, but she wasn't close enough to land the blow. She settled for a narrow-eyed look.

"Don't mind him," Kate said. "We used to keep him leashed, but he was costing us a fortune when he chewed through the leather."

Ramsey leaned down and set his teeth into the side of Kate's corset. She squealed and shoved at him. Her husband turned around from where he'd been conferring with a polo-shirted crew member.

"My wife"—Syon Braden stressed the word "wife"—"isn't *your* chew toy, Rams." He grinned.

"Yeah, yeah." Ramsey flinched as Kate slapped his shoulder, but it was clear he was only playing along. "I hope you remember Jewel."

Syon crossed the concrete with a stride just as untamed as the one Ramsey used. The singer was wearing a pair of worn jeans today. His hair was a mass of golden highlights that fell just below his shoulders. It wasn't spiked-out today, his face free of makeup.

"I would never forget the girl who popped your cherry, Rams."

Ramsey stuck his arm out and flipped his bandmate the bird as the crew in hearing range laughed. As soon as he was finished being profane, he reached down and clasped her wrist. The hold startled her, striking her as some sort of public declaration.

She wasn't entirely sure she was ready for that.

"This is the lovebird nest." Ramsey pointed at the bus-sized motor home. "Don't come a-knockin' when the motor home is a-rockin'…"

Kate rolled her eyes. Jewel offered him a dry look.

"I'm getting the feeling personal boundaries are something you struggle with."

He stepped to the side again and then forward, so her arm was pulled around his body and she was forced to move into him as he turned her in a small circle. "Hands-on." He bit out the two words, oblivious to how many people were watching.

"I recall that." Jewel stepped back. Her heart was racing, but there was a sour taste in her mouth. She didn't like an audience. Ramsey didn't miss it. He reversed course and tugged her along behind him toward the third RV. They climbed up into it. There was a separate compartment for the driver and a privacy wall.

"But hands-on is a problem for you," Ramsey stated.

She turned back to face Ramsey and found him leaning against the wall between the living space and the driver's cockpit. He was far from happy.

"I'm not changing to suit you," he said.

She propped a hand on her hip. "I didn't ask you to."

His expression was tight. "You flinched out there."

"Just because I'm not into public displays doesn't mean I'm demanding you do anything," she said. "It's not like we're in a relationship."

"You want me to touch you."

It was the truth.

And he was arrogant, which she latched onto. "That doesn't mean I'm going to let you paw me whenever you get the urge. I do tats for a living. Every day I deal with hard-asses like you who think it's permissible to grab a little sex with their ink. Well, let me explain something to you: my body, my choice. I don't do casual sex."

His expression had become unreadable. He was

contemplating her; that much was clear from the glitter in his eyes.

Jewel made her position clear. "Feel free to tear up that contract if you don't like it or somehow think you've contracted more than ink."

She was disappointed. Like someone had punched her in the gut and she'd lost her wind. But she kept her chin level and sent him a determined look.

"The contract is binding. You signed, you stay," he said, then turned and was down the stairs before his words registered.

He'd always used his physical strength to capture her. Now, she felt the constriction of the business side of his persona. She might have read through the contract quickly, but she'd caught the penalty clause if she left the tour before finishing the dragon tattoo.

It was only a month.

She snorted as she sat down on the couch that faced the stairs. The doorway was right there, but she'd be a fool to go through it. There was no way she could pay the penalty fee, and there was also the reality of not having anywhere to go. Ramsey could even bury her, refusing to name the artist who had done his ink. She'd be out in the cold and on her way home to her parents' place inside of twenty-four hours.

Maybe she needed to do that.

Her pride rebelled, bristling and rearing its head as she felt her dream burning in her gut. She wanted to make it, which meant she needed to stick it out. She loved her parents, loved them enough to want to make them proud. Sure, they'd be proud of her if she went home, sent out resumes, and secured a job in an office building.

But she couldn't shake off the feeling that she could be more. At least, more unique. More…herself. Her parents had given her that spirit too, along with a large enough dose of practicality, teaching her to take a moment to look at the big picture before making snap decisions. Well, signing that contract with Toxsin had been a hasty choice if ever there was one.

Was she sorry?

There was a full-length mirror mounted on the wall between the kitchen and the back of the RV. Jewel took a moment to look at herself. Worn jeans hung sort of loosely off her hips, due to her budget being tighter since she'd graduated. Her tunic top had a few faded spots from stain remover. Her hair was longer now, having grown out over the summer. She had it in two chubby pigtails at the back of her head, her natural curl making it almost impossible to keep it neat. The kindest word to describe her hair was "disheveled." But she most often thought of it as a brown mess. She'd chopped it short while at the university, to make life easier, a choice that had made doing tattoos a bit of a challenge until her hair grew out enough for her to keep it out of her face when she was leaning over a client. It was either a buzz cut or long enough to pull back.

Her attention dropped to her fingers. The nails were clipped short, ink staining a couple of her nail beds. There were numerous puncture marks that were also stained with ink from doing drawings in her sketchbook.

She wasn't sorry she'd signed the contract. Even dream jobs came with requirements. Holding onto her personal standards was obviously going to be her problem. After all, it wasn't really fair to blame Ramsey. He was sex on a stick, and she did want to eat him up. But she also wanted more, always had when it came to sex.

That was the reason she was still a virgin.

———

"Stop smirking," Ramsey said.

Syon only raised a golden eyebrow at him before he went back to tuning his guitar. The music RV was built for the band to rehearse in. Drake was tinkering with his drum set sitting at the back end of the RV. Taz had taken over the right-hand side of the coach. Ramsey and Syon tended to stay close to each other. Today, Ramsey felt like he was crowded.

"I need the chick to finish my tattoo."

"You need her for something, alright," Syon replied.

"Is Kate on the rag or something?" Ramsey demanded before he let a squeal out of his guitar.

Syon stared at him the whole time, unimpressed. "Could ask you the same about Jewel," he countered when the noise died down.

"I don't need Jewel to get my kicks," Ramsey shot back. "Just my ink."

Taz snorted. Ramsey jerked his head around to glare at him. Taz wasn't intimidated. He considered Ramsey with a cool demeanor. Ramsey laid into the strings on his instrument. His insides churned. His blood heated. He funneled it all into his music, his bandmates joining in as the miles began to fall behind them.

———

Portland was wet.

Jewel emerged from the RV to find it raining.

California had been locked in the grip of a massive drought for the last few years. She smiled as the little drops hit her skin, skipping out into it while stretching her legs. She was full of energy, having curled up in one of the bunks in the RV and slept for most of the ride. There were puddles on the ground that she jumped into, making water splash up and onto her ankles. It was cold, but not enough to make her stop.

The drivers had pulled them up in the back of a massive resort-style hotel. Crew members already had the luggage bays on the underside of the RVs open as porters came out with rolling carts. Brenton was talking to a suited man who looked like a manager. Two more men stood waiting for commands as full luggage carts were pushed into the hotel lobby and toward the elevators.

———

"Thought you said you could get your kicks anywhere," Taz said from inside the music coach. "So why are you watching her?"

"None of your fucking business," Ramsey snapped. He headed down the steps of the coach and onto the ground. "I'm going to go get laid."

Taz didn't want to drop it though. "You better wise up. Before you mess up your chance with a quality girl."

"Is that some sort of pearl of wisdom?" Ramsey turned on him. "Because I don't fucking want it. You need to stop jerking off in the shower over a girl who doesn't think you're good enough for her little virginal snatch."

Taz wasn't intimidated. "Nailing everything that crosses your path hasn't made you very happy either.

Maybe you need to try a few shower jerk-offs and get an idea of why you're so pissed off."

Ramsey snorted in response.

Taz's expression stayed steady, too knowing for Ramsey's comfort. "No, what you are is uncertain," Taz said. "That's uncharted territory for you, and it scares you."

"Bullshit," Ramsey snapped. "I love my life."

"It's making you sick," Taz responded. "You're too proud to admit it. You've poisoned yourself with excess."

—⁂—

The sound flesh made when it connected with other hard flesh was unique. Jewel raised her head, recognizing it instantly. The tattoo business was full of drama. That little fact led to fights more often than not. She turned around to see Ramsey fighting with the Asian member of Toxsin. The crew watched them from a distance as they swung at each other. She was fascinated by the fight, because it was proof of a few things she'd suspected about Ramsey.

He was trained.

Taz danced out of the way with practiced martial arts moves, and Ramsey followed up with some of his own. Syon and Drake were close, while Yoon kept Kate at a safe distance. She wasn't happy about it either, her face as red as her hair.

Ramsey lunged at Taz again. This time they locked up, rolling into the shrubbery that surrounded the entrance to the hotel. Flowers went flying, along with huge amounts of mud. Ramsey was half out of his shirt, rolling through the landscaping with Taz going right along with him.

Dirt. It was sticking to the lotion on his tattoo. Her eyes widened, warning jolting through her.

"Get out of that dirt!" Jewel was in motion before her brain processed completely what she was charging into.

Syon turned and lunged at her. Ramsey jerked toward her. Syon tackled her to the ground, and there was a hard smack when Taz landed a blow on Ramsey because he was distracted. Pain went through her like a bolt of lightning as her head slammed into the asphalt. She blinked—she thought her vision had gone sparkly, but her eyes widened in horror when she realized it was camera flashes. The paparazzi snapped shots of Syon on top of her as the lead singer cursed and rolled away.

"What the fuck are you doing, Jewel?" Ramsey hissed at her. "Are you an idiot?"

"Me?" She blinked because her brain felt like it was stuck on hold. The rain was making the dirt stick to Ramsey, coating his bare torso. "You're the dimwit! You're going to get a massive infection!"

He was on his haunches but looked at the part of the tattoo above his waistband. Dirt covered a good bit of it. She struggled to get on her feet, her legs feeling clumsy as pain swirled around in her skull.

"That's got to be cleaned out right now," she declared to cover her lack of grace. Taz showed up from somewhere, she wasn't exactly sure because she had been so focused on Ramsey. He scooped her up from beneath her arms and stood her on her feet.

"Thank you." The polite response was misplaced but instinctual.

Brenton was suddenly sliding between her and Taz.

Ramsey reached out and captured her wrist. The connection was explosive again. It should have been impossible to have such a reaction to bare skin, but when it came to Ramsey, it seemed she was hypersensitive.

Or maybe allergic was a better way to look at it. Reactions just flared up when she came into contact with the guy.

He'd pulled her through the doors while she was busy being dumbfounded by how his touch affected her.

She pulled back on his grip when her brain started working. He looked over his shoulder at her.

"I thought you said this needed cleaning?" he asked as he tugged her into an open elevator. The staff of the hotel held the door for him, clearly ignoring the fact that he'd just been fighting in their flower bed and was trailing chunks of dirt across the marble floors.

"I did," she answered.

The doors shut, and the car jerked as it started taking them up. Ramsey leaned back against the hand-rail and rotated his neck until it popped.

He seemed to think everything was fine. She was left chewing on her lower lip as the elevator made it to the top of the hotel and the doors opened. He reached out and captured her wrist again.

"It isn't necessary to pull me along," she said.

He looked back at her, contemplating her for a long moment. There was a flash of something in his dark eyes before he released her wrist.

"Necessary…no." He'd turned back toward her, and before she realized what she was about, he'd leaned over and put his shoulder into her midsection. One solid motion, and she was hanging over his shoulder as he started down the hall. "But I like it."

There was a chirp. She looked around his body and saw him shoving a key card into his waistband before twisting the handle of a door and carrying her inside the suite.

"Ramsey...put me down," she insisted.

He tossed her onto a sofa. She bounced before righting herself. He dragged a chair over from a dining room table and straddled it, his back to her.

"So...clean me."

His pants were open.

That thought was white hot and completely distracting. It disabled her thought process as she caught the scent of his skin.

The man had musk.

"What are you waiting for?" He turned his head and looked over his shoulder at her. "You were so hot and ready a few minutes ago."

"Well, you were acting like an idiot, so you're lucky I was ready to do something to slap you back into reality." She leaned forward and looked at the tattoo. His skin was healing well, but the lotion he'd put over it was caked with dirt.

"You got hurt," he chastised her. "Taz and Syon are going to feel bad about that. You should have stayed back."

"Have you ever seen an infected tattoo? You could end up in the hospital with a staph infection. It could scar," she snapped. "You need to take a shower. It's a massive mess now."

"Okay." His tone had changed, hinting at gloating. He stood up, swung his leg over the back of the chair, and kicked off his boots.

And then, he dropped his pants.

Her mouth went dry, and she was pretty sure her heart was going to break through her chest wall because it was thumping so hard.

His ass was perfect.

And mouthwatering.

"Come on…Nurse Jewel," he taunted her on his way into the bedroom section of the suite.

"Uh—"

He turned his head to look back at her and started to turn around.

"What are you doing?" She squeezed her eyes shut, only to hear him laughing.

The damned man was laughing so hard, the sound was bouncing off the walls. Her cheeks heated, but she kept her eyes shut.

"Aren't I your…canvas?" he asked smoothly. "Come on, Jewel…dig deep. Find that professionalism you were so busy telling me about when we pulled out of the Bay Area."

"I can," she snapped back, losing the battle to keep her eyes closed. Part of her was really, really glad she did, too.

Magnificent.

He was raw, lean, sculpted, hard, and her tattoo fit him perfectly. She had placed the dragon to appear to be breathing fire onto his cock.

Now she knew it was spot-on.

"You're being a turkey," she accused him softly, trying desperately to ignore the pulse of need throbbing in her clit. His cock was huge, and even if she'd never tried one out, she'd seen her share of them in the tattoo business. Guys and gals had fascinations with getting their bikini lines inked but what was sending her into overdrive was the confidence he displayed. A confident man was sexy, no matter how you sliced it.

"And you're being…chicken, but hey, leave if you can't handle finishing what you started," he said.

Direct hit.

She bristled and braced her hands on her hips. Honestly, she should walk away, but her pride reared its head. "I can handle anything you dish out."

He raised an eyebrow. "Shower is that way." He gestured behind him with his thumb.

He turned and walked across what was a premium suite, the likes of which she'd seen only in magazines and on television shows. It passed in a blur, because she was focused on the fact that somehow, she was following Ramsey into a shower. He was buck naked, and she was doing it to prove a point.

Whatever that was. Honestly, she was pretty sure thinking was overrated.

The bathroom boasted a huge walk-in shower tiled with stone from floor to ceiling. There was a double-long seat at the far side of it, and three shower heads. He flipped on the water as she fumbled with the selection of soaps and body washes displayed artfully on the vanity top.

"You might want to strip down," he said.

Said the pirate to his captive maiden…

"So not happening." She pulled open the wrapper on a bar of soap. Her brain was working again, at least until she turned and looked toward Ramsey, in nothing but his gorgeous skin.

He flashed her a smile from inside the shower. A menacing, challenging curving of his lips. Damn, but the man was so devil-may-care, and it was sexy. As well as tempting.

She suddenly understood the core concept of bra burning. It was about grabbing freedom with both hands and flinging the rule book aside. Utter abandonment of all the rules society surrounded her with, confined her with as it tried to mold her into what it wanted her to be.

If ever she'd encountered a man who made her believe he'd be worth the trip down guilt lane when reality caught up with her, Ramsey was it.

He lifted his hand and crooked his finger at her. "I'm ready for you to have your way with me, Jewel."

"I'll bet."

"Sure you don't want to take your clothes off?" he asked.

"Real sure," she responded a little too breathlessly for her comfort. She was really, really sure it would be a bad idea.

"Won't hurt my reputation any to have you leave my room…wet." He opened his eyes and caught her looking at him. The water must have been cold, because his nipples were puckered, but it didn't seem to affect his cock. The thing was still standing straight up.

"You have a one-track mind." She busied herself with taking her shoes off, trying to scrape together some composure before getting close enough to touch him.

"With you…yeah."

She snorted. "Damned if you didn't manage to make that sound like it's my fault. You're the kid in the candy store, remember?"

Steam started to rise from the water, surrounding him in wispy fingers of vapor. "Maybe I'm waiting for someone who won't take my shit."

"Maybe you're just trying to get me to say something that will give you a reason to be pissed off at me," she said. "Sure sounds like you're looking for justification."

"You're the one projecting expectations onto me," he said. All hints of teasing were gone, leaving her facing that person inside him whom she'd gotten only a few glimpses of.

She crossed into the shower, able to do it because he had his shields lowered. The water soaked into her clothing, making her realize it had been foolish to leave it on, because when wet, the fabric molded to her body.

"I'm really not judging you, Ramsey." She moved behind him and started to gently wash the tattoo.

"So why the constant brush-off?" he asked. "I know I turn you on."

"You do," she agreed.

He made a soft male sound that bounced around the stone-tiled interior of the shower.

"I already told you…" Touching him was practically euphoric. It was like they were standing in a bubble, removed from the rest of the world and its rules. He was naked, and she might as well have been. It was surreal and more intimate than any experience of her life.

"Told me what?" he asked.

"That I like the way I think about you. The way I see you, or saw you, on stage." Her voice lowered, because she realized she was confessing something very private. The dirt washed away, leaving the dragon clean.

He turned and cupped her chin. "That's what I mean…you're projecting onto me."

She shrugged but smiled. "Can't help it. That's how I see you."

"It's how you want to see me."

She nodded, feeling the bite of defeat. He didn't like her view of him. "Don't worry about it. There are plenty of people who don't like the way I think."

"I didn't say I didn't like it," he growled. "That's the problem."

She started to pull away, but he caught her by the wet waistband of her jeans. He held her fast as he pressed his mouth down on top of hers. It was ludicrous and wild, the water raining down on them as he kissed her until she was completely breathless. There were just so many things about the moment that were contrary to logic. It felt like the world was off balance, and the only thing left to do was reach for him. Ramsey was solid, something to cling to while she reeled. Like a kid sitting in a tire swing, twisting up the rope and letting go, twirling around and around and around for the joy of the ride while they battled the urge to throw up.

He felt amazing too. Once she'd given in and locked her hands on his shoulders, she was in complete bliss. Her fingertips became amazingly sensitive, letting her know exactly how smooth and hot his skin was. How hard the ridges of muscle on his chest and shoulders were. Time felt like it had stopped, because she was able to feel every tiny second as she traced his shoulders, fingering the definition of each muscle before moving across more smooth flesh to the next ridge.

"I like the picture you have of me," he said, his tone

husky and torn. He cupped the back of her skull and angled her head so their gazes met. "But I didn't choose to be that man."

The conflict in his dark eyes was extreme. It touched something in her heart. She wanted to hold him, felt like he needed it. She rose up onto her toes and kissed him, just a soft pressing of her lips against his, before he stiffened and pulled his head back.

But the effect was colossal. He jerked, stepping away from her as he shook his head. What sent a shiver down her spine was the conflict in his eyes. His expression tightened, sealing his feelings behind a facade. The one he gave to the world.

"The crew will have brought your luggage up by now. Might as well strip and shower before you come out." Then he was gone, leaving her behind in the shower. She leaned against the tile wall, feeling lonelier than she ever had in her life.

And there was nothing overly dramatic about that thought either.

It was plain fact.

A harsh one.

―᠊ᜠᜡ᠊―

Brenton was surprised to see her. He covered it well, fishing out an envelope with her key card in it. Her cheeks heated as she took it and made some vague, polite response before hightailing it down the hallway and around the corner to seek out her room. Her exit was less than unnoticed, because she was dragging her luggage. The crew had delivered them to Ramsey's suite, just as he'd said they would.

Her face burned, and she ended up banging her fore-head against the wall a few times once she made it to the sanctuary of her room.

Presumptuous.

The entire lot of them.

Well, you're the one who wants to see him in a dif-ferent light...

Yeah, that was where she needed to focus her energy. On getting her thinking ironed out. Ramsey was an animal, a prowling, prey-seeking man-animal.

But he wasn't happy.

Like it's any of your concern? He doesn't seem to want saving.

She huffed at herself and walked farther into the room. It was a little nicer than she'd expected. There was a small sitting area with a comfy-looking chair and love seat clustered around a coffee table. Through a doorway, there was a king-size bed with a small mountain of pillows. The bathroom was nice too, but she only stayed in it long enough to take off her wet clothing and pull on the robe that hung on a hook. Her imagination was humming, ideas forming inside her brain. She opened her bag and pulling out her sketchbook. What she needed to focus on was using the time she had to work up new art. Normally when she was drawing, her mind was absorbed with her forming creation.

Today her thoughts kept shifting away from the paper.

Okay, it did bother her, the fact that he wasn't happy. The man was a musical genius. He moved his fans with his work. It seemed so unfair that he wasn't happy.

Well, he was making his own choices.

That much was for sure, and so was the fact that she wasn't his choice tonight.

She refused to wallow in self-pity, so she laid her pad aside. Actually, if she did, it was going to be a mandatory self ass-kicking time. After all, the suite was a major step up from her loft apartment. There was a minibar and a room service menu. She took her time selecting something from the mini-fridge, because it had been a really long time since she'd seen a full refrigerator.

She needed to savor the moment, because her time with Toxsin was going to be limited.

That was the way it had to be.

———

"Are you done being a dick?" Syon asked when Ramsey wandered into his suite.

Ramsey scowled at Syon, but his bandmate didn't back down. Syon was set up in the corner of the suite, near the windows that showed them a view of the downtown Portland area. Syon had his guitar and laptop there. The screen displayed the music Syon had just been playing on the guitar. Ramsey plugged his guitar into the system while ignoring the question hanging in the air.

"Taz—"

"And I are fine," Ramsey said, cutting Syon off. Ramsey started fingering the strings, but the music wasn't flowing.

"And Jewel?" Syon wouldn't relent.

"What about her?" Ramsey made his string squeal. "She took care of what she's here for, and can't do the rest of the work for a few weeks. I only brought her along as a convenience for me."

"I'm pretty sure we all figured that out," Syon said.

Ramsey sent him a hard look. "I'm not screwing her."

"Obviously her idea."

"What the fuck does it matter?" Ramsey demanded. "I don't need any chick who has ideas about relationships. That's how I ended up with cherry blossoms on my skin."

"That answers my question," Syon said.

"How so?" Ramsey asked. He reached over to hit the pause button on the laptop when Syon aimed his attention at the screen instead of answering. Syon sent him a narrow-eyed look.

"Lumping Jewel into the same category as Tia tells me you aren't finished being a dick," Syon answered.

"So what are you getting at?" Ramsey demanded. "Because you're playing house, I need to settle down now? I'm a dick if I don't? Is that it?"

Syon shook his head. "You're a dick for being pissed at the girl for not seeing you as a sex toy."

Syon punched the enter key and laid into his strings. The notes appeared on the screen as he played. Ramsey joined in, but his attention wasn't on the music, and it showed in electronic black and white. His timing sucked, the computer program displaying his efficiency rating.

"Guess you'll be glad to know there's plenty of work to keep Jewel busy and away from you."

Ramsey looked at Syon. "What kind of work?"

Syon reset the program. "Seems word is already out that she's on the bus with us. Kendra called and said they've got scores of requests for appointments with her."

"She's not here to do tattoos for other people." The words were past his lips before he realized how possessive he sounded.

"Seems to me it would keep her out of your path," Syon said. "A few of those requests come from our VIP box ticket holders. Kendra thinks it would be a boost for publicity if we gave away a session or two with her. We *are* paying her a salary."

Ramsey fingered his strings, feeling like the lump in his throat was going to gag him. The idea of Jewel being requested by their box ticket holders irritated him. The boxes went to men with enough money to hire a private jet on show day. Sometimes the boxes held trophy wives or spoiled kids of billionaires. A lot of the time, there were business tycoons who used the concert as time to hook up in wild abandonment under the cover of going to a concert.

He didn't want Jewel near them.

As soon as the thought passed his mind, he grinned. Seeing Jewel hold her own against those balding, pudgy bastards, who thought they owned the world, would make his day.

She'd do it, too. Keep them in their place or refuse to share her art with them. She had grit and spunk. A spirit that wasn't going to surrender to being shackled, no matter how hard life became as a result.

He fucking loved that about her.

And it scared the shit out of him, too.

He transmitted his emotions into his music as he thought, tipping his head back as he dissolved into the notes. Syon backed him up, letting him take the lead. It was like letting a piece of himself be ripped off his chest. It stung, and that just made him feel more alive.

Like Jewel did.

The thought refused to be pushed aside. It sat on his mind, lingering as he and Syon played. Sometime in the early hours of the morning, Kate appeared, her hair clipped on top of her head as she came in from checking on their wardrobe. She cast a look toward her husband, one that Ramsey was certain warmed Syon. The connection between the two was palpable. Syon set his guitar down and followed her into the other side of the suite, where their bedroom was.

It was far from the first time he'd watched them retire for the night.

Tonight, it was different.

He ignored the sensation, refusing to name it as he wandered down the hallway. Drake was entertaining. Music spilled out of his suite, mixed with the sound of laughter. There was a top lying on the floor of the hallway, making it clear Drake was partying.

His cock didn't even stir.

Ramsey gritted his teeth and made his way to his suite. It was huge, as well as decked out. The cost for one night equaled Jewel's monthly rent on the armpit loft. There had been times when he'd just enjoyed the extravagance, for the sake of knowing he could afford it. Tonight, he felt hollow. Like a rich kid with a pile of toys and no one to play with.

Syon was right; he wasn't happy.

Normally, he ignored it. Popped the top off a beer and numbed his wits enough to enjoy being played with by the fans who wanted to score with Ramsey of Toxsin. Tonight, he fell asleep, convinced he could smell the scent of Jewel's hair lingering in the bedroom. His cock stirred at that, keeping him from true oblivion.

———

Before noon was considered early on a concert tour. The top floor of the Hyatt wasn't really stirring when Ramsey reached over and plucked his cell phone off the bedside table. He was tired but not really sleeping. He slipped his fingertip across the screen to unlock it. The display filled with emails, but he tapped on an alert that had come in. He kept tabs on his name being used on the Internet. Even if most of it was wildly exaggerated gossip, he wanted to know who was talking trash about him. It made life so much more interesting when those same people tried to kiss up to him in person. They were just trying to use him to get their twenty seconds of fame and they'd never think twice about playing him for a fool if he didn't watch his back. So yeah, he wanted to know who was talking smack about him. Becoming famous had taught him to be very careful about whom he considered a friend.

And that really stank.

The normal websites appeared. Road Kill was boasting a fuzzy photo of his new tattoo. He scrolled through the images of him on stage, sitting up when he found one of him fighting with Taz. What snared his complete attention was the headline attached to it.

The romance is over for Syon of Toxsin… Band members brawling in Portland over lead singer's infidelity.

There was a full-color shot of Syon on top of Jewel.

He reached over, grabbed the hotel phone, punched in Jewel's room number. It rang and rang before going to voice mail.

"Shit." He dropped the phone and tried her cell from his. Her voice mail picked up.

Ramsey rolled out of bed, landing on his feet as he typed in a line of commands on his phone. He cursed again when the tracking chip on Jewel's phone came back as nonfunctioning.

She had no idea the paparazzi were hunting her.

It was his fault for not cluing her in, too. He'd been too distracted to focus on the business and personal details of having her on tour. In short, he'd dropped the ball the second his cock got hard. He dressed and went down the hall in the hopes she was still in the hotel. He pounded on her door, but there was no response. He laid his fist on it again, and kept at it long enough that a couple of doors farther down the hall opened to investigate the racket.

"Come on, Jewel," he said.

Brenton appeared in the hallway, a little less polished looking than normal. He'd clearly rolled straight out of his rack. "Problem?"

"A picture of Syon on top of Jewel is plastered across the Internet," Ramsey said.

Brenton stared at Ramsey in disbelief.

"They will eat her alive," Ramsey growled. "Give me that override key."

Brenton was already digging into his pocket before he decided what he wanted to say. "I can handle this."

"As soon as I find her, I expect you to." Ramsey pushed past Brenton when the door to Jewel's room was open. It took him exactly thirty seconds to confirm she wasn't inside. He paused for a moment, distracted by the sketch pad on the table. Damn, her art was spellbinding, just like her, and he needed to find her fast, before some of their more unstable fans cornered her. It had been a hell of a long time since he'd cared about anyone except his teammates. Sure, they were bandmates now, but they'd forged a bond in Afghanistan; that was the foundation of their relationship.

Jewel was merging across that line, doing something no one else ever had, and he wasn't sure what he thought about it.

Bullshit. It's got you off balance.

Fine, whatever.

Brenton was waiting for him at the door, his expression blank, but Ramsey caught the hint of disgruntlement in the man's eyes.

"Sorry," Ramsey said. "I'm a little charged. When I find her, let's discuss security details."

Brenton nodded. "Sounds like a plan."

Taz was leaning against the wall in the hallway when Ramsey started toward the elevators. There was a look on his face that stung when Ramsey passed him. But Ramsey only made it a couple of steps before he turned on his bandmate.

"I just don't want the paparazzi to rattle her," he said. "I haven't explained their piranha personality to her yet."

Ramsey flipped his phone up, showing off a snapshot of Syon lying on top of Jewel in the hotel entrance. Taz straightened.

"That's not good," Taz said. "Did you try calling her?"

Ramsey rolled his eyes as he walked into an elevator and Taz followed. "No, I decided to try the bloodhound approach first, because I've always wanted to be a hound dog."

"You do act like a dog...sometimes...well...to be

honest…a lot of the time." Taz shrugged when Ramsey flipped him the bird.

The elevator doors opened, and Ramsey headed toward the security desk. The manager stood up inside the glass-enclosed office and came out when he recognized the hotel's VIPs. Ramsey changed the picture on his phone to one of Jewel. "She left sometime in the last few hours…give me details."

—⁓—

Portland was a lot like San Francisco. Jewel stopped at a corner and considered the gray clouds keeping the city wet with a soft sprinkle of rain. Instead of a bay, there were hills covered in tall trees. What helped make the city seem like San Francisco was all the bicycles. People were happily pedaling their way through the streets, making the cars stick to the center lanes. All along the inner-city sidewalks were bike racks. The hotel even had bikes for their guests, an amenity she'd happily taken advantage of.

A distraction was a distraction. Besides, life was short. Any day, she might have to pack it in and start toeing the line in a more…stable career. The nine-to-five grind, complete with boring wardrobe and a nice little cubicle. She cringed at the mental image. Until then, she was going to enjoy every moment of her wild, carefree days. Or at least she'd decided that the opportunity to see Portland was one she wasn't going to squander. Ramsey might wake up and decide she was way more trouble than she was worth.

You're totally worth it.

She smiled at her own comment. At least her

confidence was still holding up. Considering the guy reeked sex appeal, she was going to score a point for herself for not folding under the pressure of being in contact with his very decadent body.

Contact? He'd been naked...

Yeah, he had been, and honestly, worthy of being in the buff. So, make that two points. He was an extreme circumstance. She deserved bonus points for not jumping his oh-so-delectable bones.

Her cheeks heated, but she enjoyed the sting. If nothing else, it warmed her face. Her nose felt like an ice cube.

Jewel looked at the street signs at the intersection and waited for the light to change. When it was green, she pushed off the curb and joined the bike traffic. A car buzzed by too close, spraying her with water. She recoiled, her grip on the handlebars of the bike tightening as she tried to control it. The wet conditions of the road made it impossible. The bike slipped and tilted, dumping her. At least she landed on the sidewalk. It was a hard landing, sending a jolt of pain through her hip, but it beat becoming roadkill.

The car pulled over, skidding to a halt in front of her.

"Are you okay?"

Jewel struggled to her feet, feeling clumsy while trying to pull the bike off the street as other bikes rang their bells and shouted at the car blocking the way.

"Stellar," Jewel said. "Better move your car before—"

A flash went off about a foot from her face. It was so bright, it blinded her. She blinked as another couple of flashes went off.

"What are you doing?" she demanded.

"How long have you been Syon Braden's lover?" the

driver of the car asked, holding a recording device in her face. "The fans want to know if his wife is letting him have an open marriage."

"You're…wrong…" Jewel said. She wanted to say "sick" but dug deep for professionalism. She stepped around her bike and used it as a barricade. "Leave me alone, please."

The woman only pressed forward, the bike little protection as she shoved the recording device closer to Jewel's lips.

"Tell us about the tattoo you did. Does Ramsey have a mega cock?"

The hell with polite, politically correct comments, she needed space.

"Get away." Jewel released the bike in favor of scrambling back across the sidewalk. There were cars in the road and businesses open all around her, but no one seemed to notice she was being attacked. It was surreal and more than a little frightening. The camera was still flashing away, two of them circling her, caging her between them and the woman asking questions.

"Please…leave me alone…" Jewel said.

"You heard the lady." A man slid up to her and pointed her toward an open coffeehouse door.

Jewel went for it, letting out a sigh of relief as she stepped into the warm air of the shop and heard her rescuer warning the camera crew that he'd call the cops if they didn't clear out.

The shop smelled like rich, fresh coffee and scones. She drew in a deep breath and turned to watch the camera crew crawling back into their car and taking off. She was a hairbreadth away from panic, and gulped down a bunch of deep breaths as she tried to regain her composure.

"Coffee?" her rescuer asked kindly. "Looks like you could use a cup. Me too."

The guy was middle-aged, with silver hair that had only hints of black left in it. When he smiled, there were wrinkles around his eyes, making him look like her grandfather. He took off his glasses and wiped the lenses with a napkin before putting them back on.

"Actually, I think I should be offering to buy you coffee," Jewel said. "Thanks for the rescue."

He extended a card. "Bryan Thompson." He gestured toward the counter where a young woman was waiting to take their order. Jewel tried to pay, but Bryan had cash in hand, and the woman made change before Jewel finished protesting. Her hand was shaking anyway, so she stuffed it into her jacket pocket.

"Let's have a seat. Your friends are back." Bryan gestured toward a booth on the other side of the store, away from the window. Through the front of the store, Jewel gained a glimpse of the camera-wielding dude and his driver/reporter. They were eyeing the door of the coffee shop, but a pair of uniformed police officers stood on the sidewalk, sipping hot java as they talked.

Jewel slid into the booth. The espresso machine was going in the background, and a moment later, a woman delivered their coffees.

"Thank you, Ronda," Bryan said.

"Thank you," Jewel said before she took a sip from her coffee.

Bryan left his on the table. "I'm glad we could meet today, Ms. Ryan. My employer is interested in making

you an offer for exclusive rights to your artwork."
He pushed something across the table to her. "A very
lucrative offer."

She'd been taking another sip from her cappuccino,
and it went down the wrong tube. She ended up sputter-
ing as she put the cup back on the table.

"What kind of setup is this?" Jewel demanded.
Her cheeks turned red as she gestured with her thumb
toward the two paparazzi on the street. "Did you
arrange for them?"

He shook his head.

"Then how are you here?" she asked, feeling like the
seat she was on had just turned to stone.

"I was waiting in the lobby of the Hyatt for you to
come down."

Her mouth went dry. It was a surreal moment that
froze her brain, because things like being sought and
stalked just didn't happen to her.

Except that the camera dudes and the reporter were
still eyeing her from outside the shop.

"When I noticed you leaving without an escort,
I decided to follow. I hope you'll consider it a good
thing," Bryan said smoothly. He took a moment to lift
his coffee up and take a sip. At least it gave her time to
grab her composure.

"Okay," Jewel said. Her heart felt like it was going to
burst through her breastbone. "Okay…"

Bryan lifted an eyebrow.

"Just fine," she sputtered before realizing he hadn't
asked the question. "I mean—" She'd started to lift her
coffee but put it back on the table. She so didn't need
any caffeine at the moment.

"Thank you for the help," she managed to get out in a tone that was somewhat collected. "I shouldn't have needed it."

Bryan offered her a soft smile, the sort you gave a child when you knew they had no fucking clue. "If I might be so bold, Ms. Ryan, your life has changed dramatically in the last few days. I suspected you might be unaware of that fact when you departed the Hyatt alone. On a bicycle."

He was wearing a kind expression, but all that did was drive home the feeling that she'd acted like a Twinkie-brain. Fresh from a backwater, three-horse town in North Dakota.

"Morcant Industries can take you to the top of the art world. Mr. Morcant has a unique interest in your talents," Bryan continued. "Mr. Morcant is committed to signing you as an exclusive artist."

"Except that she's under contract with Toxsin."

Jewel jumped. Ramsey was suddenly there, his expression dark. "Tell Morcant to back off."

"Toxsin was a good launching pad, but they can't do for your career what Morcant Industries can," Bryan went on. He pushed his business card right under her hand resting on the tabletop.

"She's mine," Ramsey declared. His tone was hard, and more than one female in the store glanced their way. When they took in Ramsey, they sent her withering looks.

"Take a meeting with us, Ms. Ryan. You won't regret it."

Ramsey hooked her bicep and pulled her out of the booth. She let him, only because Bryan had stalked her.

Talk about being between a rock and a hard place. The camera jockeys lifted their hardware when she neared the door of the coffee shop, surrounding her with flashes as the reporter moved in.

"Ramsey, could you tell us more about your fight with Taz?"

"That's Toxsin-style play," Ramsey replied smoothly. "My bandmates are my brothers."

"Is that why Syon Braden was on top of your new girlfriend?" The woman followed them toward the curb and the car that was sliding up smoothly. "Brotherly love? Sharing all around?"

Taz opened the door of the car for her as Ramsey turned and blocked her with his body, shielding her from the paparazzi.

"Wait…the bike…I have to return it." Jewel pointed at the bike where it was leaning against the coffee shop. Without missing a beat, the man in the passenger-side front seat was out and striding toward the bike. He hopped onto it and started away.

"That's not a good idea—" she called out to him.

The damaged front wheel wobbled, and he ended up crashing into a tree.

"How did you ride that thing?" Ramsey demanded.

"It worked fine until she almost hit me with her van," Jewel defended herself. Ramsey had turned to look at her. His expression darkened, rage flickering in his eyes. He spun around, but the reporter was scrambling backward, stumbling into people who had stopped to watch.

"It was an accident," she claimed.

The two police officers had taken notice of the bike

hitting the tree. They frowned at the reporter as Jewel reached out to stop Ramsey.

"Let's just go," she said. "It's only a bike. I'll pay for it."

Ramsey snapped his attention back to her. "I don't give a shit about the bike."

That much was true. She slid into the car, mostly in an effort to get away from the smoldering glare coming from him. Ramsey ended up following her, but not before Taz gave him a shove. The door slammed shut before she realized Taz had taken up a seat in the front with the driver and copilot. There was a soft whine as a privacy window slid up to seal her in the back with Ramsey.

"You don't fucking need this…" He reached out and plucked the business card from her fingers. He crushed it in one hard motion before chucking it across the car.

"That's not for you to decide," she countered. "I thought the idea was for me to find another position."

Her words brought him up short. She watched them sink in as he bit back a word of profanity.

"Not with Morcant. He's looking to use you against us."

"Why would he do something like that?" she asked.

Ramsey looked like he didn't want to tell her but his resolve weakened under her glare. "Because we didn't sign with him." He blew out a breath and shook his head. "Look, I know I sound like a colossal jerk."

"You're acting like one too. Why are you so hot on my tail? Did I miss clock-in time or something?"

"I forgot to tell you about the paparazzi," he answered her sharply. "There are pictures of you and Syon all over the tabloids today. I should have warned you last night about them. Why did you go out so early? And what's up with your cell phone? The location chip doesn't work."

"It was noon," she said. "And what do you mean about my cell phone?"

He gave her a bored expression. "EOD. I can hack a civilian phone in moments."

The information was unsettling. Hell, it should have pissed her off, except she discovered herself battling that respect she'd felt for him on the night of the concert.

Get a grip, Jewel!

"I wanted to find Voodoo Doughnut. They're a Portland-area highlight."

Jewel realized her head was spinning. She lifted her hand and suddenly felt like her right hip was on fire. Obviously her landing had left a mark.

"Shit." He shot to the end of the bench seat they were on and turned so he was facing her. Her chin was suddenly cradled in his hand as he held her head level and studied her. "They ran you off the road? And Bryan sat there pushing Morcant's offer on you instead of getting you checked out?"

There was raw fury in his tone.

"I'm fine," she said as she tried to lift her chin out of his grip.

"Your eyes are dilated," he said as he reached down and clasped her hands. "And your hands are like ice. You're in shock."

He leaned forward and banged on the privacy window. It lowered instantly. "Those pricks ran her off the road. She needs treatment."

"I do not," Jewel protested. "I just landed hard."

"You hit something too," Ramsey said. "Or the bike wouldn't have been damaged."

His tone was softer now. Caring. That freaked her out when she coupled it with the mental image of the bike as the Toxsin crew member tried to ride it.

"I don't remember hitting anything." But she did feel like she was ready to hurl. The few sips of coffee she'd swallowed felt like they were ripping the lining of her stomach off. "This is stupid. I was fine. Just… really…fine."

Ramsey still had her hands. He was rubbing them, the heat from his fingers making her sigh.

Taz held up his cell phone for the driver to see.

"I'm not going to an emergency room," Jewel insisted.

Taz cast a look over his shoulder, but at Ramsey, not her. She pulled her hands from his grip. "I mean it."

"Private clinic," Ramsey countered.

"Voodoo Doughnut," she demanded.

Ramsey's lips twitched, betraying how much he enjoyed her stubbornness. She pointed at him. "You smiled. I win."

She leaned back against the seat. She was still cold, but her thin jacket was already zipped up. She tucked her hands into the pockets and tried to will herself to warm up.

"Come here."

Ramsey, Metal Rock God, was suddenly folding her into his embrace as though she were a fragile baby bird. He had on a T-shirt to cover up his tattoo, the thin jersey warm from his body.

"Put your hands between us," he whispered from where he was resting his chin against her head. She thought she heard him inhale against her hair, his solid frame shuddering.

"On my chest…"

She wiggled as she pulled her hands free of her pockets and flattened them on his chest. Her senses were full of him, setting off the mind-numbing intoxication he always seemed to knock her into.

Heck, bike accidents were a breeze compared to being in contact with Ramsey.

And that was what scared her.

Really, really bad.

———

There was more work to do than Jewel would have given rock stars credit for doing. Their arrival back at the hotel was brief, because the Toxsin crew was in full swing, preparing to depart for the arena. There was a neat line of black SUVs lined up to ferry the crew. Syon and Drake were waiting inside the lobby as hotel security stood in front of the huge revolving doors to keep the paparazzi outside. They were camped out on the sidewalk like a flock of pigeons.

Actually…they were far more aggressive than pigeons, Jewel decided. More like the flocks of sulphur-crested cockatoos in Australia. Brenton slid up as they climbed out of the car.

"Everything alright?" he asked.

"No," Ramsey said.

"Stellar," Jewel replied at the same time. Ramsey scowled at her, but Taz snorted behind her. Ramsey gave his bandmate an open-hand gesture that Jewel was pretty sure meant "What the fuck?"

"Can you make the sound check?" Brenton asked.

There was a definite business demeanor in the air. Ramsey looked at her. He felt responsible for her, and she could see that it wasn't sitting too well.

"I'll be here…when you're finished," she offered, not entirely sure why she was feeling the need to smooth out the road. The impulse was just there, and the words passed her lips before she realized what she intended to do.

Ramsey nodded. "Stay inside the hotel. I need to clue you in on how we roll. So you don't walk into trouble."

"Got it."

The line of SUVs had been making steady progress. Pulling up, filling, and departing. Ramsey whistled at Syon, Taz, and Drake before the four of them fell into step together and left the lobby. They were lean and covered in leather. Even without their eyeliner, their personas were raw and over the top. The flock of waiting paparazzi surged forward, lifting their cameras and recording devices. Some of them were even perched on top of their parked cars to get a better camera angle. Questions were shouted out, the hotel security pushing people back who tried to step into Toxsin's path. Private security held open the doors of the SUV as the band members climbed in.

"Now that is the way to go to work." She turned, making her way to the elevators.

But she stopped two steps inside her room. There was an easel set up with a chair and a spotlight. Her sketch pad was resting on it, the unfinished piece just begging for attention.

She didn't ignore the call. It was like it was bottled up inside her, trapped behind her fascination with Ramsey.

Only today, things were slightly different; she felt everything shifting and merging. She flipped the page and started a new piece, letting the extreme passion Ramsey triggered in her flow through her hand and onto the page.

"That's a wrap, mates!"

Ramsey set his guitar down, but not before he wiped the face of it off. The one-of-a-kind instrument was his prized possession, his drug of choice.

The arena was full of union workers, securing the seats as others hung curtains around the walls for better sound acoustics. There was a team above them in the lighting, taking notes on the rehearsal.

Ramsey let out a whistle. Syon did an about-face and came back toward him, Taz following. Drake crawled out from behind his drums to join them.

"Quinn Morcant is already trying to contract Jewel."

Syon snorted. "He doesn't waste any time."

"Is that who ran her off the road?" Taz demanded.

"What the fuck?" Drake exclaimed.

Ramsey shook his head. "Morcant's a lot of things, but he knows business. He wouldn't take a risk on Jewel being injured in something like that. Artists need their fingers. But the man's reputation as an iron fist tends to drive those attempting to impress him to extreme lengths."

"You can bet he's made good use of the time we've been here," Syon said. "Bet he's had a proposal delivered to her room."

Ramsey scowled. Brenton had joined them. "We should think about getting that art copyrighted. As it stands, Jewel has the rights to sell it. I'll get Carl Pearson on it."

Brenton stepped back and pulled out his phone. It was the wise thing to do. The business-minded one. Logical.

Jewel wasn't going to like it.

Ramsey tried to brush the thought aside, but it clung like static electricity, crackling when he tried to wipe it free and shocking him. But he got it, deep in his gut. The dragon was her baby, her creation. He knew what it felt like to push something out of his soul and see other businessmen like Morcant try and lock it up in legal mumbo jumbo.

"You good with that?"

Ramsey had to look at Syon for a moment before he shifted gears enough to respond to the question.

"Yeah. Makes sense," he replied. Not liking it didn't mean he was going to let the dragon go. She'd made it for him. It was going to stay between them. She'd have to agree to joint custody. Because there was no way he was letting her do another one of them for anyone else. The thought pissed him off.

"You look a little unsure," Syon pressed.

Ramsey shrugged. It was a habit, shrugging off inquiries he didn't want to answer. His bandmates knew him well enough to recognize it.

That served only to make him feel unmasked. It was unexpected. His gaze shifted back toward his guitar as he polished it to avoid the knowing looks of his buddies.

Hell, they were so much more. They were the only ones on the face of the planet who understood him.

And then, there was Jewel. With her desire to see him as something more than who he put out to the masses.

It should have been pathetically simple to dismiss her
ideas. Hell, he should be immune to caring about what
people thought of him. His entire childhood had been an
ongoing litany of lectures on his shortcomings. Tossing
in the towel on giving a shit had saved what was left of
his sanity and likely kept him out of a psychiatric ward.

"It's interview time, lads."

Brenton was back, the road manager performing his
function of keeping them all on task.

"Just enough time for a little makeup before the local
stations get a crack at you for preshow publicity."

They filed off the stage, heading for the performers'
room behind it where the makeup stations were. Brenton
fell into step with him.

"Carl will have an agreement drawn up by the end of
the week."

"Make it good," Ramsey said, "for her. I don't want
to put the thumbscrews on her. No artist deserves to be
tied up too badly."

"In the case of the dragon, it would be best if Toxsin
controlled it," Brenton argued. "Since it's part of your
public persona."

"Agreed," Ramsey said. "But pay her what it's worth
to us."

The problem was, he wasn't too sure how Jewel was
going to react. The dragon was her baby. Asking her to
sign away custody was asking for trouble.

Isn't that what you fucking want?

*A way to keep her from painting you like some
damned hero?*

Sure. It was what he wanted.

So why did it make him feel like puking?

———

Someone knocked on her door around dinnertime. Jewel looked up from her sketchbook, and her neck popped.

"Delivery, Ms. Ryan."

A uniformed employee was on the other side of the door. Once Jewel opened it, she spotted the security guard standing behind him. A wave of fragrance hit her as the employee pushed a cart through the open door, with a huge vase full of flowers. There were pink and white star lilies, long-stemmed yellow roses, purple tulips, and all sorts of greenery. The employee moved it to the dining table, along with a covered plate and a letter-sized box.

"Enjoy, Ms. Ryan."

"Oh…" Jewel went dashing to where she'd left her bag slung over the side of the sofa.

"The gratuity has been provided," the employee said before slipping through the door while Jewel was still fumbling with her wallet.

The flower arrangement must have cost a fortune. At least in her budget zone anyway. She reached for the card nestled in the arrangement.

I hope you will consider my offer.

Quinn Morcant.

The box had a lid that lifted off easily. Inside was a quarter-inch-thick contract offer. She lifted it out, reading through it as her curiosity grew. There was another knock on the door, and she opened it before looking. Her thoughts were on the contract.

"Guess you're enjoying Morcant's offer." Ramsey was looking past her at the flowers.

"Ah…well, I mean, it's the first time someone's ever noticed my work on such a level," she explained lamely.

Ramsey reached out, and his hand stroked her chin. "I let you ink my skin. Put your mark on me."

His tone had deepened, becoming sensuous. His sudden appearance satisfied something inside her she hadn't realized she'd been longing for. He looked past her at the easel and let out a low whistle.

"That's epic." He moved closer to her work, studying it. She ended up smiling, because it wasn't fake admiration.

She knew the difference.

"Come on." He reached down and clasped her hand. She followed him down the hallway, her door closing with a bang before she managed a protest.

"I don't have my key card," she said as Ramsey pulled her around a corner.

"I'll get on that," Brenton said.

She blinked at the number of people in the main hallway of the top floor. Crew members were carrying stuff around, wearing their black polo shirts embroidered with Toxsin Crew on the chest. Each of them had an identification card with their picture on it dangling from their shirt pocket. Along with the suites, there were large meeting rooms on the floor. One of them had the double doors open wide, music spilling out of it. Drake was sprawled out on a sofa with two girls dancing on the coffee table in front of him, their spike heels making clicking sounds on the glass surface.

"Ramsey!" Female voices called from inside the room.

Ramsey waved them off as he tugged Jewel around

another corner and slid his key card through the lock on his suite's door.

He was being presumptuous, just tugging her along into his suite. At least, that was how she should have viewed it. The door closed, and the rest of the world was shut out, making her feel like she was in his private world, like he was sharing something with her.

You're really asking for it...

Oh boy, was she. Problem was, she couldn't seem to stop thinking of him the way she did. At this point, she might as well enjoy the ride.

"Come here. I want to show you something."

He continued on to the large desk, past the small kitchen and dinette set. His suite had three full sofas in it and a great view of downtown Portland.

Ramsey had stopped in front of the desk. There were three laptops sitting on it, their screens displaying pictures of Syon on top of her.

"Oh...snap." She leaned over to stick her face closer in some vain hope it wouldn't be as bad up close.

No such luck. All she gained was a good look at the headlines.

Toxsin members brawl when Syon Braden cheats on new wife Kate...

Marriage is no boundary for Heavy Metal Rocker Syon Braden...

The honeymoon is over, Kate, make room for the new flame in Syon Braden's life...

"As you learned this morning, the paparazzi are voracious in their appetite for more," he said from behind her.

Jewel forced herself to take a deep breath and blow it

out. She straightened up and turned to face Ramsey. "I haven't given you enough credit."

"How so?"

She blushed. "I saw this suite as an extravagance to feed your inner child. Truth is, you need a sanctuary."

His lips twisted. "My music is my sanctuary. I don't give a shit about those camera jockeys. They can print whatever the hell they want, the wilder the better. There's no one I care about impressing."

He was blocking her out again.

Ha! Try shoving you out with a steel-toed boot to the ass.

"Yeah, you've been making sure I know how little you care. Should have let me get my Voodoo doughnuts," she said as casually as she could.

"I didn't keep you from them. That's what this is about," Ramsey fired back at her. There was a serious note in his tone that cut through everything else in the way that only reality could.

Jewel cast another look over her shoulder at the laptop screens, making herself look at the reality of the world she was part of. At least for the moment anyway.

"Got it," she said as she returned her attention to Ramsey. The sight of him, with an open leather vest and nothing but lean, rippling abs, was counterproductive to rational thinking.

But, well, truth be told, she liked that about him a whole hell of a lot.

He raised an eyebrow at her. She realized her lips had twitched up. "It's just the sight of you…and hard, cold facts…don't…well…" She pushed her fingers together so they were interlaced. "Don't really mesh well."

He grinned. That cocksure, devil-better-worry grin that set her blood on fire.

"I promise, no more sightseeing on my own."

She started toward the door. Forcing her feet to move was damned hard when all she wanted to do was look at the silver bar piercing his right nipple.

"Chicken."

A challenge. She felt it as much as she heard it, just as she felt him watching her with those midnight-black eyes.

But she turned around and faced him. Ramsey stopped short, surprised by her about-face.

"I don't play games, Ramsey," she said firmly. "You're the one who doesn't like the way I think. So stop toying with me. You brought me in here."

His expression tightened, becoming guarded, but there was a flicker of hope in his eyes that made her hesitate. "I want you to stay."

She scoffed at him. "I'm not willing to play by your party rules."

His lips twitched. "Damned shame."

She shook her head. "I disagree."

His eyebrows lowered. "How so?"

"I think it's a shame you don't realize you are the man I think you are." Counterchallenge issued.

Her words hit him hard. She watched the impact, was pretty sure she felt it too. Their gazes locked, the moment frozen.

He burst the bubble, lifting one hand and crooking his finger at her.

He'd kiss her if she went to him.

Hard, slow, and deep.

Hell, I'd kiss him…

The desire raged in her. His features softened with it. She'd never before been so aware of what another human being was thinking.

Ramsey moved toward her, closing the distance, and she felt sure her feet were stuck to the floor. Her skin rippled with awareness of him, her heart hammering inside her chest as he stepped closer, closer, and finally stopped a single inch from her.

"Don't take Morcant's offer. He's going to use you like a captured chess piece. Nothing more than a prize with point value at the end of the game. That's his world. The only thing that matters is winning."

His tone was husky but edged with hard warning. There was something there, some dark emotion that made her shudder, because she knew it revealed an old wound. The raw truth was in his eyes, a scant second of vulnerability flickering in his dark gaze before he cupped her chin and joined their mouths.

It was a slow kiss. Ramsey took his time, tasting her as he teased her lips with his own. She felt herself melting and didn't give a rat's ass about what it meant, only that she was dissolving beneath his kiss.

Shivering.

Shuddering.

Her damned nipples tightened. The intensity was off the scale. She rose onto her toes, seeking more. The moment her fingertips landed on his chest, he pulled away.

He didn't want to.

Or maybe that's just what you want to see…

It probably was. And it was going to hurt a whole hell of a lot when she was disappointed. She turned around and pulled the door open. Fine, she was a chicken. But she suspected wearing the label would be better than trying to glue the pieces of her shattered heart back together.

Ramsey punched the door, hammering it a couple more times before laying his head against it.

Chapter 4

SOMEONE KNOCKED ON HER DOOR THE NEXT DAY.

Jewel rubbed her eyes and laid her pen down. The contract offer from Morcant was spread out all over the table. She'd taken to sketching again as she tried to decide what to do about it.

It was impressive.

But Ramsey's words were stuck in her mind. Getting caught in a crossfire wasn't her idea of a good time. The moment Morcant realized she wasn't going to be the right bait, he'd leave her to wither and die without a second thought. A contract was only as good as the marketing backing it.

She looked through the spy hole in the door, surprised to see the drummer of Toxsin standing on the other side.

"Morning," Drake said as she opened the door.

"Hi."

He had warm brown eyes with amber flecks, and a square chin. He was thick through the shoulders and sported a leather jacket made from a deep, port-wine-colored leather.

"Voodoo doughnuts," he said.

"Excuse me?" Jewel asked, trying to decide what he was getting at.

"I understand you were denied your prize yesterday. Drake is here to help you bring it in."

She smiled. "Oh yeah? Would that be Sir Francis Drake, by chance?"

"None other." He wiggled his eyebrows. "Get some shoes on."

"You're on." She turned and went back into her room. Her shoes were under the table, and she grabbed her bag as she swept up her key card. They were in the elevator before she remembered the horde of camera jockeys waiting below. Her belly did a little flip as the elevator neared the ground floor.

"No fear," Drake said.

"Ah…sure," she answered. "I'm getting right on that."

He winked at her before looping an arm across her shoulders as they went through the lobby. "Let's confuse them completely by being seen together."

His tone was so properly British, but the gleam in his eye was most definitely wicked. She was snorting as he took her through the doors. Cameras flashed and questions began sailing at them over the heads of the Hyatt security.

A polished Harley was sitting outside, a polo-shirted Toxsin crew member standing beside it. Drake lifted his leg and swung it over the seat of the machine. The paparazzi enjoyed every second of it, leaning over the barrier tape the hotel had placed outside the main driveway. He revved the bike, his features contorting with enjoyment.

"Let's take a ride, Jewel."

She slung her bag over her shoulder and slid on behind him. Her skirt rode up, making her eternally grateful for the leggings she'd put on. There were whistles as Drake pulled out of the circular drive in front of the hotel. Members of the paparazzi jumped on motorcycles and followed.

"Hold on," Drake advised as he revved up the engine.

But he didn't do anything stupid. A few of the camera jockeys kept up with them, but he didn't care. He pulled up in front of Voodoo Doughnut.

"My lady's pleasures await."

Jewel laughed as she climbed off the bike and Drake swung his leg over to join her. Voodoo Doughnut had more than one location, but he'd brought her to one of the larger ones. It was in a brick building, the doors opening out onto the sidewalk.

"Wow…" Jewel said as she stepped inside and took her first breath of the sweet-smelling air. "I think my blood sugar is going up just by the scent of this place."

There were cases of doughnuts, but not the sort she was used to seeing. All of them were over-the-top. Some were dipped in chocolate and then in candy or kids' cereal. There were oversized doughnuts and vegan ones too.

She was pressing her nose to the glass of the display cases, enjoying the variety, when Drake came up behind her.

"Please get the phallus-shaped one…" he cooed next to her ear. "I want to tell Ramsey I watched you eat dick."

She laughed at him.

"I'll take that as agreement." He straightened up and pointed at a huge doughnut shaped like a male cock and covered in chocolate. The kid behind the counter didn't miss a step as he used a paper sheet to cover the sweet and lift it off the tray before nestling it in the box he had balanced on his arm. Jewel realized he'd been filling the box with everything she pointed at.

"Ah—" She started to correct the clerk because her budget couldn't support that sort of excess.

"Don't worry," Drake said, cutting her off. "Got the whole crew to dispose of the leftovers." He wiggled his eyebrows at her. "What sort of pirate would I be if I neglected my crew?"

"A dead one. Or marooned," she said.

They'd reached the end of the counter where the register sat. Drake tossed down a hundred-dollar bill without blinking. "Keep the change."

The kid flipped him a thumbs-up and handed over the box.

"I can pay for my own," Jewel protested.

"Not a chance," Drake said. "I'm working you over because a couple of guys in the crew are begging me to hook them up with you for some of that amazing ink you do." He pushed the door open with his shoulder as he cradled the box of doughnuts. "You wouldn't want them to think I roll over for nothing, would you?"

"Oh, please, send them my way," she said as a camera flashed. "I am bored off my gourd."

"Hey, Jewel, is Drake a good lover?"

Drake smirked at the reporter before he handed the box of doughnuts off to a Toxsin crew member who had somehow appeared. Drake winked at her before he looked at the crew member.

"Go get another box. That one's for the band."

The crew member was in motion the second Drake finished. Jewel looked at Drake. "My image of you taking me away just shattered."

Drake mounted the Harley and crooked his finger at her. "Had to have someone hold the doughnuts," he said in a deep tone. "You're going to be busy holding on to me."

The reporter whooped as Jewel choked on her laughter. She slid onto the back of the bike and wrapped her arms around Drake. The drummer was solid and smelled like leather. He was fun too. When he peeled away from the curb, her insides tightened, making her laugh. He took her through the streets of Portland, taking the scenic route back to the hotel. Her nose was cold by the time they made it back, but she didn't care. She followed Drake into an elevator, laughing with him as it took them to the top of the hotel.

But the doors opened to reveal Brenton waiting for them. He was poised and congenial, but the hairs on the back of her neck stood up. There was something in his eyes that hinted at a very serious conversation heading her way.

"Ms. Ryan, could you come with me?"

"Sure." She was already falling into step with him as she caught Drake watching them with a frown.

But Brenton didn't give her time to dwell on it. He turned around a corner and took her through a set of double doors that led into a conference room. It had a long table in it with padded rolling chairs.

"This is Carl Pearson, our solicitor."

"Nice to meet you." Carl offered her his hand. When they finished shaking, Carl indicated a chair. "Have a seat. We have a little business to work out."

She was suddenly glad she hadn't eaten any of the doughnuts. Her belly knotted as she took a seat.

Carl had a neat stack of paper sitting in front of him. Brenton had departed, leaving her and Carl alone.

"Toxsin's image is vital to the band's success," Carl began.

"I believe I've experienced that in the form of doing a cover-up to avoid 'image' damage." She was on the defensive. Every muscle was drawn tight.

"Yes." Carl took back control of the meeting. "The tattoo you applied to Mr. Brimer is now a part of his stage persona. We would like exclusive rights to the artwork." Carl was spreading out a contract in front of her. "We are prepared to pay for controlling rights, of course."

Fresh from the stage, the members of Toxsin were still pumped up. Now that the concert was done, beer was flowing backstage. Makeup artists were touching up the band members' faces as Brenton looked at his watch and made a "wrap it up" gesture with his fingers.

"Press is waiting, gentlemen."

They left the backstage room, moving through the arena as fans squealed. Security lined the walkway, keeping the enthralled crowd back.

"Eat them up," Brenton said with a firm pat on Ramsey's shoulder.

The road manager was looking through the one-way glass in the doors at the horde of press waiting for the band to come out and talk to them. They were packed in behind security rope barriers, minding their places, because they knew the celebrities wouldn't come out unless they behaved.

Ramsey opened his mouth and acted as though he were

taking a bite out of the air between him and Brenton. It earned him another pat on the back as Brenton snickered softly, said, "That's why they love you."

Brenton fell back as Drake and Taz moved up to join them. The stadium staff pushed the doors open, and the cameras started flashing. They knew how to fall into place, each one hitting their pose for a long moment so pictures could be snapped. Once the frenzy died down, they each took one of the director chairs waiting for them. The interview questions started coming fast and furious. Every answer was being recorded, but there were still reporters scribbling down notes.

Each band member had a microphone, and they took turns answering. They ignored the more outrageous inquiries.

"Ramsey...the tattoo...who's the artist? Why is she on tour with Toxsin?"

"Jewel Ryan," Ramsey answered. "If you've got to ask why she's on tour with us, you must need glasses, man. Her work is off the charts."

There was a round of laughter.

"So, Drake, what is Jewel to you?" another reporter queried.

Ramsey snapped his head around, his calm stage face sticking in place only because of years of experience. Drake offered the reporter a wink.

"She's a lady. What sort of a pirate would I be if I didn't try to get her on the back of my bike?" Drake answered smugly.

The crowd of reporters laughed again. Brenton finally appeared, putting an end to the press conference. The reporters all scrambled to snap a last few shots before

Toxsin disappeared behind the tinted windows of a black SUV. The trip to the hotel was short.

Security was thick, guiding them toward the elevators and making sure no one slipped in. Still, there were a good number of girls hugging the walls and peeking through the planters. They squealed and sent the band members suggestive looks, more than one flashing them. Taz eyed Ramsey and joined him in the elevator when he passed the rest of the band, making it to the elevator first and bypassing the girls for the first time in a very long time. Taz offered an approving nod as he joined him in the waiting car.

But the moment they made it to the top floor, Ramsey caught Drake in the hallway. The drummer had his arm draped across the shoulders of a giggling blond. She looked up at Ramsey with a little sigh.

"Get on in there and make yourself at home," Drake said as he gave her a smack on her very delectable ass.

She jumped and turned to shoot them both a hot look. "Don't be too long…" She fingered the straps of her dress, pulling them over her shoulders so more of her breasts were revealed, and her nipples were hard, poking out against the soft jersey fabric. "I don't have very much to take off."

Drake blew her kiss before turning back to look at Ramsey. "What's up?"

"Why did you take Jewel out on your bike?" Ramsey demanded.

Drake blinked, his British demeanor solidly in place. "The woman had a craving… I fulfilled it, mate. Can't help it if you're slow on the uptake when it comes to satisfying her."

"Fuck off," Ramsey snarled.

Drake opened his arms wide as he took a step back. "Exactly my plan." He turned and made his way into the open suite. There was a husky giggle before music started blaring.

"You're better off," Taz said from behind him. "Not going in there, I mean."

Ramsey rounded on Taz. "Virtue might work for you, but I'm not going to be mind-fucked by some cultural dictate about morality being tied to monogamy. No one is heeding it anyway."

"Plenty of people keep their word," Taz argued. "Lots of couples keep their vows."

"And double that number are boinking in their offices or limousines the second their spouse is out the door on a business trip. So don't fucking tell me it's the way to true happiness, or any shit like it's good for my soul."

Taz didn't take offense at the way Ramsey was trying to poke holes in his beliefs. It was worse than that. His lips pressed into a hard line of disapproval. "Jewel is good for you because you want to be better for her. She brings out a better part of you."

"I'm not trying to please her," Ramsey said. "Know why? Because she isn't interested in what I have to offer."

Taz slowly shook his head. "That's what I said. She won't take your crappy party-animal relationship. She can see there is more inside you. Better wise up before you lose her. You should be grateful she doesn't see you as a toy. What has that life gotten you? Take a good look in the mirror—you don't like who you've become."

Taz turned and left, leaving Ramsey fighting the urge to hurl a comment at his back.

He could tell 99 percent of the people on the face of the planet to fuck off, but not his bandmates. They were his family, and as such, shrugged off what they thought didn't work very well. He knew they meant well, even when they pissed him off.

Besides, Taz was right, and to tell him he was wrong would be to say principles were something Ramsey saw no value in at all. Well fuck, he wasn't going to do that, even if there were times he wondered if there was a single redeeming glimmer left alive inside him.

Jewel thought there was.

Hell, the way she looked at him, the way her eyes always lit up like he was some kind of hero—it stripped him bare, reducing him to a pile of need to be everything she believed he might be. A need he couldn't ignore because it made him feel incredible, and Taz had nailed it.

Ramsey didn't like the person he'd become.

—⁓⁓—

Jewel woke up sometime after midnight when someone pounded on her door. She was sacked out on the sofa, where she'd fallen asleep looking out at the Portland skyline. Her cell phone vibrated with an incoming text.

I know you're in there, Jewel.

It was Ramsey.

Well, I know you're standing in the hallway she texted back. It wasn't the most mature message. She heard him snort on the other side of the door and smiled.

"Alright." She rolled off the sofa, walked barefoot across the dark mini-suite, and undid the security latch before opening the door.

"You didn't come to the show," he said.

"I had a business meeting with your lawyer and was pinned in a boardroom," she shot back, but she didn't like the sound of her voice. Didn't care for how rattled she was. If she wanted to play in the big leagues, she was going to have to pull up her big-girl panties. "Not that I couldn't handle it."

"You're mad," he accused her.

"Okay, fine. But not because of the contract. I get that part," she answered.

He opened up his hands, looking at her for an explanation. She chewed on her lower lip as she contemplated clueing him in. His attention dropped to her mouth, his eyes narrowing with hunger. She jumped at the chance to change the topic back to something nonsexual.

"You should have asked me yourself, not had your lawyer and road manager corner me. I drew the dragon for *you*, Ramsey. I never would have done another one—I have integrity." She sounded hurt, and she hated the fact that her emotions were bubbling over while he was there. She felt on display, like she was standing there naked.

She heard him snort.

"Does that mean you won't be accepting the money?" he asked. "I don't think so."

She rolled her eyes. "Did you knock on my door just to start a fight? I know what I do. Are you a sell out for signing with a music producer? Would you rather be strumming your guitar on a street corner for change?"

Ramsey opened his mouth to say something, but he shut his jaw and considered her for a long moment. He pushed away from the wall and closed the distance between them. Her belly twisted, her body coming alive.

He kept her in the grip of anticipation as he reached out and stroked his fingers down one side of her face.

She shuddered. His touch unleashed a rush of sensation that crackled through her.

"You need to understand…" His voice was rough from the concert. "Being around me means dealing with my fame."

She pushed away from him, back into her room, but he followed her, the door hitting his shoulder as he came right in after her. But there was a very resounding thud as the door shut behind him.

"That's a chickenshit answer," she said. "You didn't want to ask me because you knew what it meant to me. And then, when I tell you that, you're just going to say I'm projecting onto you again because I see you as more than a dick."

She was suddenly so frustrated, she wanted to yank her hair out.

He was overwhelming her as usual. She backed up, moving to where the room opened up. She'd never turned the lights on, and when the outer door closed, there were only the city-skyline lights to illuminate him.

"You sell your art, Jewel, " he countered. "Why should I worry about your feelings of attachment? No one's ever paid you what I have."

"That's not the point." Her voice was a mere whisper, as though she was out of strength.

"The point is, you want me to care about you," Ramsey said. "You want to make things personal between us. Not going to happen, sweetheart."

He was exasperated, frustration edging his words. The sight quelled her temper.

"Why does that bother you so much?" she asked, throwing her hands into the air and turning her back on him. "Why do I care? I'm such an idiot."

She actually grabbed a handful of her hair.

He was suddenly there, against her back, his arms locked around her, pushing her arm down, keeping her in place as she jerked against the overwhelming stimulus of being in contact with him.

"Don't...don't...stop caring." It was a dark whisper from the blackness surrounding them. A flicker of need deep inside him she'd known was there, despite his denials.

"Just...don't," he rasped out.

He was kissing her hair, nuzzling her temple. She shivered, the skin-to-skin contact flashing through her like an explosive. It blew her common sense to bits, leaving her with nothing but yearnings.

She turned to him, slipping her hands up his neck. His skin was smooth and hot. So hot, she felt like her clothing was too much to suffer. Ramsey seemed to think the same thing. He slid his hands down her sides until he found the hem of her tunic top. His mouth captured hers as he rolled the fabric up her body, breaking away from their kiss to tug it off her.

She gasped, a little sound that betrayed how vulnerable she felt. He was so confident, so much in his element. She felt helpless by comparison.

"You're beautiful," he rasped, reaching out to finger the lace-edged cups of her bra.

"You mean a pirate's dream, a sunken chest." She closed her arms over her breasts as her confidence deserted her completely.

"I mean beautiful." He scooped her off her feet, cradling her as he carried her into the bedroom. "And your body is smokin' hot too."

Somehow, she was on the bed, and Ramsey was shrugging out of his vest. He reached down to work the fly of his pants without missing a beat.

"Look… I'm not sure I'm ready for this."

He stopped, his fingers still on the laces of his pants.

"I'm not trying to be a tease," she sputtered as she struggled to sit up, unbearably conscious of the fact that she was on a bed. "I know it seems like I am…and I'm sorry… I'm just not ready."

He was suddenly there with her, surrounding her, embracing her, kneeling in front of her as he pulled her between his knees.

"I'm being pushy"—he cupped her chin and raised her face so their eyes locked—"and callous…"

He was only shadow, illuminated in silver lights.

He trailed his fingers along her jawline, raising gooseflesh across her skin.

"Let me…try." His voice was a rumbling whisper. A promise of something she craved. All she had to do was trust.

She wavered, undecided, as he found the two hair ties in her hair and popped them like they were nothing. She trembled. The strength he had in his fingers was amazing.

"Let me try…seducing you, Jewel."

"Okay…" She wasn't sure when she decided to mutter the word, only that it came across her lips as she shuddered. God, he smelled good. Her senses were on overload.

His lips were next to her ear. Her breath caught as

he stroked her arms from shoulder to wrist and then back up her sides and across her back until he found the closure of her bra. There was a snap as he undid it, and then he was slipping the straps down her arms and off her completely.

"Don't compare yourself to other women. You're perfect."

He cupped her breasts, sending a jolt of awareness through her. "Perfect handfuls."

He brushed her nipples with his thumbs, his lips curving as those sensitive peaks drew into hard points beneath the contact. She wanted to close her eyes but was mesmerized by the look on his face. The pure fascination displayed as he palmed her breasts. Saying they were pretty was one thing; the way his features were set made her believe him.

"So…perfectly responsive." He lifted his attention to her face. "But I wonder, will they taste as good as they look?"

Her breath caught again, this time harder, feeling like a rock lodged in her throat.

"Do you want me to try them?" he asked.

She'd never pictured herself in a moment when he waited on her whim. It filled her with a confidence she'd never felt before.

"Yes." Her voice was a husky whisper.

His lips thinned before he leaned over, and she felt the brush of his breath against one nipple before he closed his lips around the tender point.

She shuddered, her eyes closing as she slipped into the moment. It swamped her, covering her as he supported her descent onto the surface of the bed. There

wasn't any further thought about what she wanted.
Need ruled.

So did the desire to offer herself to him. He sucked
on her nipple, pulling it, stretching it until she gasped
before he released it. He claimed it again, lapping it
with his tongue before kissing his way down the side of
her breast and up to the peak of her opposite breast. She
arched, offering it to him.

Ramsey purred as he claimed it, his hair teasing her
bare skin while he pulled and sucked on her nipple. He
released her with a little pop before laying a trail of
kisses down her body. He held her, slipping his hands
along her sides until he grasped the waistband of her
leggings and pulled them down.

The bed rocked, and she lifted her hips as he
dragged the garment free. He ended up on his feet
again, standing at the foot of the bed, her leggings
dangling from one hand.

She hugged her knees, completely bare, once
again vulnerable.

"Trust me." He let her leggings go before placing a
knee on the bed again. He didn't reach for his fly, but
slipped his hands up her legs instead.

The skin-to-skin contact was amazing. She felt
doped, and like any addict, craved more. He stopped at
her knees, his gaze locked with hers.

"Trust me not to take what you aren't ready to
give me."

It was a promise dearer than any declaration. It also
stabbed into her heart. There was no way to shield her
feelings from it. He could have overwhelmed her in
about two kisses, leaving her his to devour at will.

She knew it.

So did he.

But he was waiting for her to answer him, slowly rubbing his hands down the outside of her thighs and back up to her knees.

She relaxed back until her elbows were supporting her weight. "I do trust you."

There were certainly reasons why she shouldn't. The only problem was, she couldn't think. Her brain was operating on a different level now, registering everything as pure sensation. Ramsey cupped her knees and spread them, threatening to fry her senses, but honestly, she didn't give a shit.

But now, nothing mattered other than the way his body felt against hers.

He spread her thighs. It was exhilarating as well as more exposing than anything she'd ever experienced. With anyone else, it would have been an impossible thing to do. She'd have died of shame.

With Ramsey? It felt like destiny. As though they had been heading for this moment since the second they met. She'd known he'd bend her, always sensed that he'd push her to total submission.

"God, you smell hot…"

He hovered over her spread sex, his breath teasing her wet folds.

"Ramsey." She started to sit up, curling away from him.

He pressed her down with one forearm against her belly as he locked his fingers around the curve of her hip. "What? You don't think I like the smell of your pussy?"

She flinched and heard him chuckle. He massaged her hip but didn't move even a millimeter.

"I do," he rasped out. He looked up her body, his eyes glittering. "It smells hot and delicious."

"Bullshit," she bit out, feeling like the effort to form her thoughts into words was beyond her.

He chuckled again. "You don't know how glad I am to hear you don't like pussy, baby. That means I won't have to share you with a girlfriend."

He teased the bare mound of her pussy, fingering the smooth skin. "Seeing this bare cleft made me wonder if you're bi."

"I like to swim," she explained in a breathless whisper that she had a little trouble identifying as her own voice. "It's just…cleaner."

"It's hot," he bit out with a rasp in his voice.

He leaned down and lapped her, throwing her into a torrent of responses that wrung her like a dishrag. Maintaining any sort of composure was impossible. Her eyes closed as he licked her cleft, his tongue so hot, she was fairly sure it was going to leave a burn.

She writhed beneath him, arching against the sheets and clenching handfuls of the smooth fabric as he spread her labia and tongued her clit. Her cry hit the ceiling, pleasure running like a coiling live current up from her clit to the deepest part of her core. It tightened with every stroke of Ramsey's tongue. Perspiration popped out on her skin as she arched up, seeking more pressure.

"I'll take care of you, baby…"

His tone was arrogant, hard, like he was, and she wanted him just that way. He leaned down and sucked her clit into his mouth, applying his tongue to it while he held the tender flesh between his lips.

She cried out and then moaned low and deep as pleasure

exploded inside her. It jerked her into a swirling whirlpool of rapture. How long it lasted, she couldn't say, only that when it ended, she was nothing more than a quivering mass lying on the bed. Lifting her eyelids was too much effort. All she wanted to do was let the lingering delight carry her away into darkness. But she couldn't be so selfish.

"You...you didn't...enjoy—" She fought to open her eyes and found Ramsey crawling up the bed to lie beside her.

"The hell I didn't." He gathered her close, cupping her head to keep it against his chest.

His pants were still on. She tried to think about why that impressed her, but the sound of his heart was filling her head, lulling her back into slumber. Sleeping in his embrace was by far the most perfect thing she'd ever experienced.

She smelled good.

Better than good. His cock was throbbing, on the border of pain. He curled his lips back and stroked Jewel's hair again.

He wanted to fuck her.

But it seemed trivial compared to the privilege of holding her.

———∽∿∽———

Ramsey was sleeping in her bed.

Jewel didn't have to wipe the sleep from her eyes, and she wasn't longing for coffee. Nope. Two seconds after waking, she realized she wasn't alone in the bed. Ramsey wasn't exactly the sort of guy one overlooked, after all. She ended up looking down at him because she'd sat bolt upright the second her brain absorbed the situation.

He was stretched out on his back. The morning light

made the bar piercing his right nipple gleam, and it made her more aware of the fact that she was nude.

"The sunlight makes that sheet transparent."

She jumped as he spoke. There was a male sound of amusement as he opened his eyes and sat up so he was facing her. She settled back onto her knees, but couldn't make herself release the sheet. The feel of the fabric between her fingers was too tangible.

"You still have your pants on." It was a stupid thing to say. She felt her cheeks burning the second the words were past her lips.

He smiled at her, flashing his teeth. "Don't sound so surprised."

The bed rocked as he rolled over and landed on his feet beside it. "I'm not such a dick that I insist on having an even exchange."

He meant it. He was six and a quarter feet of raw male. Hard, leather-wearing badass, and his words charmed her. Her eyes burned with unshed tears.

"Don't take that as any sort of declaration," he was quick to add. "I'm just…not a complete dick."

There was a glimmer of something in his eyes that she had to think about before she realized what it was.

Fear. Maybe she could be kind and label it uncertainty.

"Got it," she said. "And don't get the idea that I trust you because I let you…"

"Suck you off?" He was taking cover in his persona once more, only this time, she recognized the tactic.

"Tantalize you?" he pressed when she didn't give him a rise.

"Hold me," she said softly. "If I wanted sex, it wouldn't be too hard to find it. You don't have an exclusive on that."

Surprise registered on his face. Jewel seized the moment, releasing the sheet, and it fluttered down and left her bare. She kept her chin level, realizing she didn't feel exposed by her nakedness, only by the way he made her feel so deeply.

"Excuse me. I think I want a shower before we clear out. Seattle next?" She stood up, marveling at her new-found confidence level.

He nodded.

She left him standing next to the bed. He watched her go, and she was pretty sure she felt his dark gaze singeing her back as she went toward the bathroom and disappeared behind a wall.

The moment she did, her knees turned to jelly, and she ended up leaning against that same wall as her heart beat at a frantic pace.

What the hell did she think she was doing?

Well, that was it in a nutshell, wasn't it? With Ramsey, she lost the ability to think.

But at least he wasn't being a dick about it.

That thought warmed her. It burst inside her chest like a tightly condensed bundle of happiness. She was partially giddy as she flipped on the shower, brushing her hair out while she waited for the water to warm up.

He'd held her.

She was surprised and awed.

And on the brink of trusting him to introduce her to passion.

—◇◇◇—

Seattle, Washington, had the Space Needle.

Jewel Googled the city highlights as she sat in the

motor coach. She was getting better at reading while the vehicle was in motion. She made it an hour before nausea claimed her and she crawled into the bunk for a nap.

Ramsey's comment about getting enough rack time on the road suddenly made sense. There wasn't a whole lot to do, since she wasn't driving. But it was the only way to move the stage equipment. She was gaining personal insight into the workings of a major concert. It was fascinating and far more work than she'd ever realized. Rock stars worked hard, like the rest of the world.

Ramsey also had a heart.

That revelation kept her company along the miles. She was happy and scared too. It drew her toward him while her common sense screamed at her to notice just how dangerous a road it was.

Hearts don't listen...

Ramsey wasn't any happier about that than she was.

She giggled at the thought and decided maybe, just maybe, she'd share it with him later.

―⁕―

"This so fucking rocks!"

Jewel sat back as her customer looked over his new ink. Tom was a veteran with Toxsin. He'd signed on to run the sound-mixing board years before the band had made it to the top of the charts. He turned his arm over, using a mirror to get a good look at the tattoo she'd done for him. This was a service one, with an American flag and an eagle.

"Drake, man...I owe you," Tom said as he passed Drake, who was leaning in the doorway of the meeting room the crew had set up as a studio for her.

"Keep it out of the sunlight for three weeks…and clean." Jewel stressed the last word.

Tom turned and gave her a mock salute. He disappeared, Drake falling into step with him.

"So, now that the work is done"—Kate appeared in the doorway—"is it girl time?"

Jewel grinned. "If there is food involved, you're on."

Syon's wife smiled. "Food and shopping."

Jewel grabbed her bag and punched off the lights on the way out of the room. Most of the crew was kicking back after a day of stage building and sound checks. Their work wasn't done. They'd be at it again in the morning. But there was music going at the other end of the floor, where one of the suites had been opened up as a party room. Hotel staff was arriving with food, and drinks were flowing.

Syon Braden looked up as Kate came into sight. He disengaged himself from the crew he'd been talking with and came down the hallway toward his wife.

"I'm going to spend as much of your money as possible," Kate informed him.

"Hmm…" he growled softly as he leaned down and pressed a hard kiss against her lips. She wiggled, but he held her and kissed her for a long moment before allowing her to get away.

"Buy something lacy," he said, looking behind her at Yoon. The bodyguard shared a look with Syon before Kate reached over and grabbed Jewel by the wrist.

"Come on… Let's make our escape. I think the testosterone levels in here might be toxic."

"Possibly," Jewel agreed.

They ended up in the elevator, heading down to the

ground floor. Yoon was with them, and another man who looked just as deadly as the Asian bodyguard.

"This is Steven," Kate said, introducing the stranger. He offered Jewel a nod.

"Ramsey and Taz are feeling protective of you after your little run-in back in Portland," Kate explained.

"What?" The doors opened, the two bodyguards exiting first.

Kate shrugged. "Trust me, you can argue, but you are never going to win, especially now that you and Ramsey are involved."

"We're not involved," Jewel said.

Kate shot her a questioning look.

Jewel felt her cheeks heat. "You guys are like some weird medieval clan who knows everybody's business."

Kate laughed as they made their way past the entry doors. Outside, the paparazzi waited.

"Kate, are you pregnant?"

"Jewel, are you Kate's lover?"

The cameras flashed as Yoon and Steven closed the doors of a limousine to give them privacy.

"We all live in one another's back pockets during concert season," Kate offered with a shrug. "So everyone knows Ramsey spent the night in your room."

"We didn't have sex," Her cheeks caught fire as her memory offered up exactly what they had shared. Kate didn't miss it either.

"I'm a virgin," Jewel spat out. It was a defensive move, and it backfired.

Kate's mouth dropped open. "Ramsey deserves more credit than I thought."

Jewel drew in a deep breath and let it out. "Well, he

doesn't like hearing anyone tell him he's got a good heart. Just remember, I warned you."

"Oh, that I know," Kate said. "The first month I was on tour with these guys, we tangled."

"Yeah?"

Kate nodded.

"How did you end up on tour with Toxsin?"

It was a safe topic and a fun one. Kate's eyes glittered with merriment as she launched into a tale of torn pants, a partner who was too scared of heights to get into a helicopter, and Syon Braden ambushing her into joining the tour to keep the band in leatherwear.

By the time she'd finished, the limo had slid quietly up to the main entrance of an upscale shopping mall. Kate happily bounded through the doors while Jewel hung back, sure there was a surcharge just for entering. But Kate's bubbly personality was infectious. Jewel was drawn into their expedition, even when it ventured to the top floor where the designer-label dresses were. Here there were plush chairs to sit in while waiting, and racks of unique feminine apparel that delighted the senses with their style and crafting.

Jewel indulged herself by trying on a sapphire-blue dress that gave her heart palpitations when she glanced at the price tag. The moment she left the dressing room, the style specialists brought over shoes and even an expensive leather purse that matched the dress perfectly.

"That makes you look like a million bucks," Kate said from where she was standing on a viewing box with three full-length mirrors surrounding her.

"You too," Jewel responded. Kate had on a cotton dress that complemented her red hair.

"It needs alterations." Kate pulled on the middle of the dress. "I wish I had your bustline. I always have to get a size bigger."

"Please…" Jewel responded. "I'm the girl stuffing tissues in her bra because I think I should look like you."

A tailor arrived, claiming Kate's attention. Jewel used the moment to escape to the dressing room. She took one last longing look at herself before she took the dress off and hung it carefully back on the hanger. She left it in the dressing room.

They made their way to an unmarked entrance that led them to a private Italian restaurant.

"Paparazzi-free zone," Kate said with a flourish of her hand. "Something I undervalued the idea of just a short year ago."

Jewel accepted a menu before answering, "They are insane."

Kate shook her head as she turned a page in the menu. "I ended up in a fountain once, trying to escape. Taz rescued me. Yoon is his cousin."

The bodyguard was seated at another table with Steven.

"Honestly, I think this is a little overreacting," Jewel said. There were no prices on the menu. That meant it was way out of her budget. The money Tom had given her was about to be yanked out of her "resettlement fund." At least the place smelled amazing.

"Good luck convincing the boys of that," Kate informed her with a hint of mirth in her voice. "Ramsey in particular."

Jewel had broken off a piece of bread and pointed it at Kate. "That's hitting below the belt. Where's your sister spirit?"

"I went through a fountain; you got run off the road," Kate countered. "Besides, I've got my hands full with my man-child husband. I'm sort of hoping you'll throw a saddle on Ramsey."

Jewel snorted at the mental image, but the look of expectation in Kate's eyes sent a shiver of anticipation down Jewel's body.

—◌◌◌—

The party was still in full swing when Jewel made it back to the hotel. The mood was changing though, the vibe shifting to something more along the lines of "Red Light District."

Somewhere down the hallway there was a different song being played. It was deeper, with more bass.

"The boys are working," Kate said.

Kate crooked her finger at Jewel and then laid it against her lips as they neared the side of the hotel where the presidential suites were located. Kate slid her key card through the door and opened one side of the double-door entrance slowly.

The music spilled out like vapors. It wrapped around them as Kate gestured Jewel inside. There wasn't any artificial light on in the suite. Instead, there were candles, their golden light illuminating Syon and Ramsey as they played near the open patio doors.

It was captivating. Ramsey was leaning back, the guitar across his groin as he fingered the strings. There was no denying how deep his music ran—she would have sworn she saw it flowing out of his soul in that moment. Kate kicked her shoes off, so her heels wouldn't disturb the moment. Jewel did the

same and moved closer as Syon and Ramsey continued to play.

The pair were connected somehow. Jewel wouldn't
be so arrogant as to say she understood it, only that she
knew she was witnessing a connection that ran soul
deep. It was Toxsin's foundation, that thing that so
many people didn't credit the rockers with having.

Dedication to their music.

Sure, it was heavy metal.

But in that moment, there was an undeniable beauty.

They finished and plunged the suite into silence.
There was a laptop on the table in front of them. Syon
punched something on it, and the screen lit up. It was
muted, but with only the candlelight in the room, it
seemed bright. Ramsey leaned over and looked at the
screen, both of them staring intently at whatever was
there before Syon touched a stylus to the screen and
made a change. Ramsey nodded in agreement.

They cued it up again, filling the suite with sound
once more.

Ramsey locked gazes with her. Her breath got lodged
in her throat as he pumped the music out while watching
her. A chill raced across her skin and down her spine,
leaving her nipples hard and her toes curled. She wanted
to sway with the tempo, let her hips follow along in time
with the rhythm. He was gauging her reaction, watching
her to see what her response was. She got the impression she was seeing a part of him very few people had
ever glimpsed. It was the thing she'd seen on stage, just
glossed over by his performance persona.

This was who he was. The demon he embraced
instead of fought.

It was fucking beautiful.

The music was reaching its finale. Kate moved closer, her body flowing with the melody. She stretched up and kissed her husband. He pulled out the last few notes as his mouth claimed hers. Kate was between Ramsey and Syon, in contact with both of them as she stretched up onto her toes to kiss Syon. Ramsey didn't move away—he was finishing up the last of the notes, still watching Jewel, still waiting to see what she'd do.

She realized he wanted her honest, knee-jerk response. *Isn't that what you crave from him as well?*

It was.

She was in motion without further thought. Moving toward him, letting herself be caught in his gravitational pull. He was waiting for her, his eyes glittering with anticipation. She smelled him as she got closer, the scent of his skin filling her senses. It drove her insane, and she was happy to dispense with sanity.

All she wanted was the madness he stirred in her.

She flattened her hands on his chest, slipping between the open fronts of his vest to connect with his bare skin. The nipple bar was warm, and she teased it, turning it with a gentle touch as she watched him.

He curled his lips back and bit the air between them. He cupped her nape, squeezing it just hard enough to send a jolt of awareness down her spine. But he didn't kiss her. He released her and set his guitar aside. The candle flames flickered as he turned and scooped her off her feet, carrying her through a doorway into one of the two bedrooms the suite offered.

The door closed behind them, leaving the candle-light behind. The darkness suited her. She wanted to do everything she'd always shied away from. All of the things the night was fabled to be full of.

She wanted those. All of them.

Immoral or not. Maybe even more so if there was depravity involved. To put it bluntly, she wanted to sin.

She slid her hands into his hair and gripped it before he found his way to the bed. He sucked in a harsh breath as she angled her head and kissed him. She was hungry and went after his mouth with the appetite of a starving woman.

Ramsey let her legs down onto the bed and captured her nape as he kissed her back, hard.

She purred with delight.

Not a soft, cat sound. More like a lioness. She didn't want to be petted; she wanted to take what she pleased.

And it was right within reach.

She kissed her way down his neck. His skin was hot and soft, but the muscles corded as he lifted his chin and stretched out to offer himself to her. She kept going until she found the bar adorning his right nipple. She licked it, drawing a word of profanity from him.

It filled her with boldness.

She reached down and found the ties holding his leather pants closed. She tugged at them and lifted her head when they didn't release easily. It took a moment before she loosened them completely and opened them.

His cock sprang out, hard and hot. She teased it with her fingertips as she slipped lower on the bed.

"Jewel—" He caught a handful of her hair, stopping her.

But it was the stress in his voice that pleased her. She teased his cock again, drawing her fingers from the tip to the base and then back up. He shuddered, his body responding instantly.

"My turn," she muttered determinedly. "And you're going to just take it."

His grip tightened in her hair, his features hard as he contemplated her. Jewel didn't leave the matter open to his opinion though. She leaned down, pulling her own hair until he released it. She heard him suck in his breath as she teased the head of his cock with her lips.

"Holy shit!"

He growled when she opened her mouth and took the head of the organ between her lips. There was a slight salty taste. She drew her tongue across it, suddenly finding a use for all the coarse suggestions her ex-boss had delighted in vocalizing.

With Ramsey, they suddenly lost their seediness. Became something she was eager to try. She wanted to drive him to the extremes he'd pushed her to. Wanted to know she wasn't alone in being susceptible to his allure.

So she opened her mouth wider and sucked more of his cock inside. The part that didn't fit, she clasped her fingers around and stroked.

"Jewel…" His voice was stressed. "Stop…"

She doubled her efforts instead, using her tongue on the underside of the head, moving up and down as she hollowed her cheeks and sucked. She pumped her hand down to the base and cradled his balls in her fingers.

He made a sound that delighted her, because she recalled feeling so strained when he'd been going down on her. He was close to orgasm, and she had every intention of pushing him over the edge. He fisted a hand in her hair again, pumping his hips toward her. She felt him straining to bury more of his length inside her mouth a moment before he started spurting.

Victory was sweet. She savored the way his grip tightened in her hair and the frantic motion of his body as he thrust toward her. She kept his cock inside her mouth, sucking hard.

He collapsed on the bed, his chest rising heavily as his eyes rolled back. "That was…fucking…awesome…"

He was spent, his body relaxing as sleep claimed him. She enjoyed the sight and sometime later ended up slipping into sleep next to him.

It felt right.

That idea conflicted with so many things she'd believed to be true until she'd met him.

Well, there was no arguing the feeling.

None whatsoever.

"You were proving a point to me."

Ramsey had been watching her sleep. Or wake up, as it were. The first thing she saw was his face when she opened her eyes the next morning. He was on his side, his head resting in his hand, his dark gaze on her.

"Well…" She blinked, trying to jump-start her brain and not sound like a complete idiot.

"Getting even with me," he continued, as though she was alert enough to follow the conversation.

She sat up and pushed her hair out of her face. "That's a little harsh."

He sat up, looking too big by far for her to handle so early in the morning. "Right on the money. You wanted to push me around the same way I did you."

"Look, it's too early in the morning for your

commitment issues." She crawled out of the bed and tried to pull her clothing into some semblance of order.

Ramsey was buck naked. His pants were lying across the back of a chair. He was so damned at ease in his skin, it actually pissed her off. She didn't like thinking about how often he woke up in the buff with women.

"Don't be a bitch."

"Then don't be a dick," she shot back before throwing her hands into the air. "You're looking for a fight, and I'm not interested."

"Because you still don't like what I have to say," he countered. "I'm not the guy you think I am."

She stopped with her hand on the door. It would have been wiser to keep going. But she turned around and stalked back toward him. He stiffened, but she reached down and locked her hand around his nape, pressing her mouth against his before he moved. His lips were frozen and stiff. She pressed a firm kiss against his mouth anyway before withdrawing.

"Don't tell me what to think." She flipped around, intending to make a clean getaway.

Ramsey hooked her around the waist and turned her back to face him. His eyes glittered with need. She got only a glimpse before he pressed his mouth against hers, threading his hand through her hair to hold her steady. It was a hard kiss, full of all the conflicting emotions inside him. He ravished her mouth, opening her lips and thrusting his tongue deep inside.

She retaliated by sucking on it, boldly meeting him, refusing to be intimidated by his experience. His cock pressed into her belly, the hard presence setting off a throbbing in her clit.

"Goddamnit." He suddenly released her, stepping away.

They stood there for a moment, both of them breathing heavily. The arousal was tangible, like a tension they shared.

"You're making me crazy."

Ramsey spoke, but Jewel felt like he was vocalizing what they were feeling. The need was growing, jerking at both of them. What bothered her most was how uncontrollable it was for them. He'd seemed so confident, so capable of rejecting her, that it had given her a false sense of security. She might fail, but it wouldn't matter, because he'd refuse her in the end.

That wasn't happening.

It scared her.

And there was no shame in admitting it, only a very frightening wisdom in looking it square on and acknowledging the reality.

She ended up back in her room, leaning against the door as she tried to quell the urge to call her mom and book a bus ticket home.

Ramsey was going to smash her world to bits. The problem was, she was more afraid of missing the opportunity than of the consequences. Scared she'd kick herself for years over the discarded opportunity.

She was an idiot.

But she was staying, because she couldn't hide from herself.

Show night had a vibe all its own.

Jewel started to feel it before noon. The crew was

moving around, their steps lighter. Brenton was flashing his smile. Kate was in her workshop, while Jewel
enjoyed having her own space. It really was a marvel
the way the crew transformed a hotel into a living space
while they were there.

Her workshop was empty today as the crew started
making their way toward the arena where the concert
was going to be held. Steven was hovering, clearly rest-
less as the afternoon stretched on into evening. Jewel
took the time to make sure her equipment was clean and
worked on a new piece for her sketchbook.

"That's wicked."

She jumped, her hand slipping. Her unexpected company grabbed her wrist, lifting it away from the sketch.

"Wouldn't want that piece to be ruined now, would
we, luv?"

Jewel twisted away and stood up. The guy was a
pistol, sharp and deadly. His eyebrows were slashes,
clearly professionally maintained. He had a head of
golden, honey-blond hair that was spiked up in front but
short on the back of his head. An earring winked at her
from his ear as he grinned, clearly pleased with getting
the jump on her.

"I'm Rage," he offered in a deep-timbered tone that
sent a little shiver down her spine. It was like liquid dark
chocolate, that voice.

"I said I'd introduce you," Kate said from the doorway. Her hair was held in a clip on top of her head,
which Jewel had come to recognize as her working
mode. "If Jewel lets Steven kick your tail for sneaking
up on her, you'll have it coming."

Rage offered her a short chuckle. "Bring it on. No

one lets me have any fun anymore. Not since Sammy got hot under the collar about the stitches on my chin."

Jewel considered the chin in question and found the faint pink line marking his skin.

"Hey…What am I? Chopped liver?" Another man appeared behind Kate. He had slightly longer hair, but it was styled to the extreme. "Hmm…" He made a low, rumbling sound in his throat. "On second thought… Nice score, Rage."

"That's Dare," Rage offered.

"They're known as Act of Fury," Kate supplied. "Samuel Moss produces them as well as Toxsin. Sam sent them over, since they don't know how to take care of their leather any better than our boys."

"I am definitely a bad boy, darlin'," Rage said, "but I'm also a real good man when it counts."

He'd turned his attention back to Jewel as he finished. She propped her hand on her hip and rolled her eyes.

Rage snickered. "I'm going to have to do better than that to shock you, aren't I?"

Jewel nodded.

"Come on," Kate said to Dare. "You're making me miss my husband's show. So let's make this a good fitting."

"We flew in. Isn't that worth missing a show you've seen over and over?" Dare asked as Kate left him standing in the hallway. He ended up following her.

Jewel faced Rage. He'd parked himself against the wall, but she didn't buy the relaxed pose for a second. He was gauging her.

"Is there something I can do for you?" she asked.

"Maybe. Since you're approved by the big man, I

can consider letting you loose on my skin." He pushed away from the wall and snatched the sketchbook from the table.

"Approved?" she questioned.

Rage nodded as he turned to the sketch she'd been working on. "As in, you signed the confidentiality agreement and turned over the exclusive rights on the dragon you did for Ramsey. Image is something Sammy gets possessive about. I can't have just anyone inking me."

He tapped the new sketch. "This is really dark. You're pissed at someone."

"Maybe I know enough about my business to know dark sells well," she answered. "I mean, you don't exactly look like the pony and butterfly sort, and a lot of my clients look like you."

He scoffed at her. "They wish they looked like me."

She had to smile, because that was true in more cases than she cared to admit. A few mental images rose up to torment her. What had been seen could not be unseen. "Point taken."

He was going through her book, but she felt like he was seeing the sketches differently than most of her clients. He was another artist. He didn't dismiss the personal element so many people were just blind to.

"I heard you did the dragon personally for Ramsey," Rage said when he'd reached the end of the book.

"Yes." She didn't go into details about the rescue necessity.

He set the book down and pegged her with a hard look. "What do you see for me?"

"I don't really know you well enough." She was hedging. There was something about him that was intense, like Ramsey, only she wasn't interested. In fact, her hackles were raised.

He suddenly grinned, like she'd presented him with an opening. "In that case, I'm taking you to dinner. So you can get to know me."

"Ah…" Her mouth hung open as he reached out and tried to claim her wrist. She lifted her arm out of his reach, at least until he decided to lunge for it.

And she got the distinct impression he wouldn't hesitate to do exactly what he wanted.

"Unless I make you nervous," he said.

He might as well have called her "chicken" straight out.

"Dinner is cool," she said slowly, relieved her voice came out even. "Holding my hand isn't. We just met, after all."

He pushed his lower lip out in a pout before he gestured toward the door. Jewel didn't care for how much she hesitated. It was dinner with a prospective client. She picked up her bag and turned back around to face him. It was what she'd wanted when she'd taken Ramsey's offer, after all. The chance to establish herself as a serious artist.

So why did she feel so hollow?

Chapter 5

STEVEN STUCK WITH THEM, AS WELL AS TWO OTHER bodyguards obviously attached to Rage. The three men had their hands full when Rage escorted her through the entrance of the hotel. The paparazzi surged to life, stepping past the barriers as they dispensed with civilized behavior.

"Jewel… Jewel… Are you dating Rage now?"

"Are you Ramsey's submissive? Is he sharing you?"

Rage laid an arm across her back as the cameras closed in, shielding her while half-carrying her to the waiting car.

"Jewel isn't the type of girl a man shares," Rage said, distracting the horde of press by giving them something to listen to. "A smart man knows she's the best there is and recognizes what a lucky bastard he is. Now if you'll excuse me, I'm going to wine and dine her as she deserves."

There were shouts of agreement and more than one thumbs-up before he dropped into the limo beside her and the door sealed the paparazzi outside.

"That was—" Jewel began to protest.

"Good for image," Rage cut her off. "As well as making it clear we hold you in high esteem. They'll be a little less likely to run you off the road when they realize they might catch hell from both bands over it."

"You heard about that?"

He sent her a serious look. "Security details need to be shared. You wouldn't want me to make the same mistake with a girl, would you?"

"I guess not."

He flashed her another one of those grins that implied he was getting everything he wanted. "But you're not too sure you like me knowing your personal details?"

"Pretty much," she answered.

He offered her a shrug. "Reality can be a real hassle from time to time."

She ended up laughing, maybe at herself, but it really didn't matter because it cut through the tension.

"I'm going to be really disappointed if you take me to a high-class restaurant." She mimicked a yawn. "Like a…nice guy."

"I see what Ramsey likes about you." Rage pulled his cell phone out of his inner jacket pocket and punched in a text. The limo turned a few moments later.

When he made eye contact with her again, there was a sparkle in his blue eyes—he was plotting.

Well…bring it on.

Ramsey wiped his face the moment he made it into the performers' room. His hair was full of sweat, and his chest was covered too. The crowd roared, and music started to blare outside in the parking lot as the fans made it to their cars and began the after-show party. It would go on until they were evicted from the property, only to be carried on to houses all over the city.

He seriously loved his job.

"Where's Kate?" Taz asked.

Syon took a long drink from a bottle of water. He lowered the bottle and sent Ramsey a disgruntled look. "Sammy wanted her to deal with Rage and Dare. Flew them in early so she could measure them." His tone made it clear he didn't care to know his wife was anywhere near the other rockers.

"And you didn't think to tell me that?" Ramsey demanded.

Syon drank again and sent him a confused look. "What's your problem? Kate's my wife."

"The problem is Rage better keep his paws off Jewel. He's a damned poacher, and you know it."

"Careful," Taz said, "it sounds like you give a shit. That sort of thing might ruin the perception that you don't care about her."

Ramsey flipped Taz off. Drake responded with a two-finger, profane English gesture.

"You two can suck my dick," Ramsey said as he found his cell phone and swiped the screen. The moment he did, it chirped to life, multiple messages appearing.

"That son of a bitch!" Ramsey exploded. "I'm going to kick his ass! And Sammy can fuck off for all I care."

Taz and Syon looked over at what had Ramsey pissed. There was a full color shot of Rage with his arm around Jewel.

"That's kind of bad," Taz agreed. "But you can't kick his ass."

"Watch me." Ramsey punched at the screen of his cell phone, scowling when he didn't get what he wanted from it. "Shit. Jewel's cell phone location chip doesn't work."

"Yeah, we knew that," Drake said.

"Brenton?" Ramsey called out. "Find out where Rage took her."

Brenton weighed the request. Ramsey snorted and turned around to sit in a makeup chair. Charlene was used to him, but she hung back for a moment, judging his mood.

"What the fuck?" he demanded of pretty much everyone in the room. "I'm jealous. So what? I'd think you'd all be happy."

Syon rolled his lips in to cover the grin he was fighting. Drake lifted a beer to his mouth to avoid the issue. Taz, on the other hand, gave him an approving nod that was salt in the wound. Charlene muttered something under her breath that sounded way too much like a prayer before she started removing his makeup.

He was jealous.

But there was no way in hell he was going to do anything about it.

—◆◆◆—

"I cannot believe this," Jewel muttered. "But then again...I can."

The place Rage took her to was full of king-size beds. The restaurant boasted dining and the opportunity to take to one of the large beds for lounging and horsing around. There were giggles and pillow fights going on as wait staff shuttled food to the booths ringing the beds.

"It's like a geek's dream. Getting the girl into bed on the first date," Rage offered as he watched her from where he was sitting across from her in their booth. "Want to try it?" he suggested wickedly.

"Isn't it sort of old hat for you?" she asked.

He chuckled and raised his tumbler to her. He had a double shot of something very fine in that glass. He appreciated it too, sipping from it as his features tightened with the bite of the liquor.

"I believe you're accusing me of being shallow." There was a slight slurring of his speech, a hint of Scottish accent coming out.

"Maybe," she agreed. "You did sort of ambush me into a date—"

"And now I'm asking you to bed," he added. "Bet it's already up on the tabloids."

She felt her mood change, like the fun was draining out of the moment. Rage's features became serious, his eyes hooded.

"You'll have to toughen up a bit if you're going to roll with Toxsin. Can't give a shit about what the vultures say, or it will eat you alive."

There was bitterness in his tone he covered well. It was the thing she saw in Ramsey and wanted to soothe. She suddenly missed him. Lamented not seeing the show. It was an opportunity wasted, and now she was keenly aware of it. There was a clock ticking in the background, her chances to be near him dwindling with the dates on her contract.

Rage groaned. "You're thinking about him."

"Excuse me?"

The singer rolled his eyes and took another sip of his drink before putting it down. "Ramsey's a lucky shit. He'd better know it, or I'll kick his ass."

"I think you've got the wrong idea about me and Ramsey—" Jewel started.

Rage sat up, abandoning his playfulness altogether. She got a glimpse at the very serious side of his nature, the one that had to be responsible for his standing as a rock star.

"Another reason to kick his ass."

It was a cryptic comment and didn't make a whole lot of sense. Not that she was doing very well with figuring out the universe lately. No doubt the problem was on her end.

"Rage." Brenton was in the suite with Dare when they made it back to the hotel. The road manager was on his feet, striding toward Rage as he offered his hand.

"I hear Kate has enough allure that she drew you two up here a few days early," Brenton continued as he shook Rage's hand.

"I won't miss being parked on the coach," Dare said from where he was sprawled across a couch.

"Enjoyed being in bed with Jewel a lot more than driving upstate," Rage remarked.

Jewel rolled her eyes, but the vibe in the room changed instantly. There was a tightening of expressions, and she was pretty sure she actually felt the temperature drop before she heard a grunt from Ramsey. He'd been in the far corner, out of her sight, but he came into view fast, his attention on Rage.

"Problem, Rams?" Rage asked pointedly, clearly enjoying baiting the other singer. Ramsey faced off with him.

"Oh, I don't think so," Jewel declared. She lunged between the two men, shoving them apart as Steven made a grab for her. She turned on the bodyguard and warned him back with a finger. She turned on Rage.

"Cut the shit," she said. Rage lost a little of his arrogance. "I don't do this game, and I sure don't do custom
ink for jerks who want to use me. Start your own fights."

She left just as fast, exiting the suite as her temper
sizzled. She didn't make it very far.

"Why the hell are you doing ink for Rage?" Ramsey
cupped her shoulder and turned her around to face him.

"He asked," she said.

"And you're going to do it?" Ramsey demanded.

"Not after that dick move." She pointed toward the
suite. "The dude takes me to dinner and then rubs your
nose in it? Screw him."

He liked her answer, smiling slightly. It didn't last
long. His attention lowered to her mouth, hunger glittering in his eyes. That damned current linking them
worked perfectly too, allowing the pulse she saw in his
gaze to jump right across the space between them and
set her on fire.

"I missed you," he growled a second before he
claimed her mouth.

That second felt too long. Like an eternity that she'd
been starving for the taste of him. Maybe it had been the
dinner with Rage. All of that time wasted on a man she
didn't crave. No, it didn't matter how hard-bodied Rage
was, she wanted Ramsey.

"My pants are coming off this time." He'd ripped his
mouth away from hers, looking like he was fighting to
control himself long enough to make his intentions clear.

"You bet your ass they are." She reached down, dug
her fingers into the waistband of the leather, and found
the lace that held the garment closed. She pulled it free
as he cupped her nape and kissed her again.

But it was a fast kiss this time. Ramsey scooped her off her feet a second later and tossed her over his shoulder. It left one of his hands free to slide the key card through the door lock. He let the door slam shut as he took her to the bedroom.

He was working the lace through the eyelets as she bounced on the bed, pulling the thin tie loose and letting his cock fall into view. She let out a little sound of approval before reaching for it.

"Oh...*shit*..." he growled as she closed her fingers around his length. "You're going to make me lose it, baby..."

She purred as she leaned down and licked his cock. "Good. High time I was the one pushing you around for a change."

He captured a handful of her hair, raising her face so their gazes met. There was a hard glitter in his eyes. "Payback is my specialty."

She shivered, excitement racing through her. She bared her teeth at him, unable to do anything but respond to him. At any other time, she would have labeled the behavior cheesy; with Ramsey, she felt like it was rising up from her gut. She cupped his balls and used her fingers to massage the sac. His eyes closed to slits, betraying just how much he enjoyed it.

"Suck me, baby...make me come."

It was both challenge and plea. She opened her mouth and claimed his cock as anticipation surged along her insides. Her clit was throbbing, driving her insane, but so was the idea of pushing Ramsey over the limits of his control. The opportunity was hers, and she took it, sucking his cock deep as she teased his balls. She judged the strength she used against the sounds coming from him. She could hear him sucking each breath through his gritted teeth, feel his cock hardening as she swirled her tongue around it and beneath the circumcised head.

"Christ!" he yelped.

So she did it again and again, as he leaned back, thrusting toward her, gripping her hair as he fucked her mouth in those final moments before his come started shooting out in a thick stream. She sucked it down, pulling every last spurt from his cock before his hand relaxed and he landed on the bed. It bounced and rocked, the springs squealing.

"Jesus…you made me…light-headed…"

"Like that's never happened before." She wasn't sure why her confidence was deserting her. But the words came across her lips, and she winced when she heard them.

Ramsey cracked open his eyes and looked at her. He rolled over, and she found herself scooting back against the headboard and a mound of pillows.

"Not since I was about sixteen."

Each word was sharp. He was suddenly on all fours, looking a whole lot like the night jungle cat she'd mentally likened him to so many times.

"That rocked my world, Jewel." He was coming closer, the mattress dipping under his weight. "And now…"

He caught her calves and pulled her toward him. The smooth cotton of the comforter made it easy for her butt to slide, and he had her on her back in two seconds.

Flat on her back as he loomed over her and pressed her thighs open. Her jersey dress ended up around her waist, leaving her in nothing but her panties.

"Now," he drawled as he settled over her spread body, "it's time for payback."

He caught her panties at her hips and pulled them down her legs. For a moment, he was on his knees between her thighs, letting her see that his cock was hard again. The sight set her clit to throbbing along with the slide of her last bit of clothing as it was pulled free. Her dress was next, ending up nothing more than a flutter on its way to the floor before he hovered over her once more.

"You smell good…"

He'd settled back down between her thighs, pushing her knees wide so the folds of her sex spread. It was almost unbearably exposing. Part of her shied away, but he held her still.

"Do you think for one second I'm going to let you grab me by the cock, turn me into a howling animal completely at your mercy, and not visit the same on you?"

His breath hit the wet folds of her sex, sending a quiver of need through her. Her heart was hammering inside her chest, the need to feel his tongue against her sex so intense, she was sure she'd climax at the first touch.

"Oh no, baby… I'm going to make you scream," he promised.

A second later, her cries were echoing around the room. There was no hesitation, no gentle exploratory touches. Ramsey lapped her open sex, pulling her folds even farther apart so he had full access to her clit. He claimed it and sucked it for seconds that nearly drove her mad, because she needed to climax so bad. Just as the torment felt like it was going to end in a spine-tingling orgasm, he released the little cluster of nerve endings and licked his way to the opening of her pussy.

She was writhing on the bed. He stabbed his tongue inside her, growling softly. The vibrations only added to the torment, making her squeal.

"Good and wet..." he muttered, teasing her pussy with two fingers. The wet sounds made her cringe, but she still lifted her hips toward him.

He worked his fingers in and out of her body, driving her insane with the need to climax. "Are you ready to scream for me?"

His tone was husky and demanding. She opened her eyes, the need to protest rearing its head, but his eyes glittered with determination. His face was drawn tight with his desire to push her over the edge. She recognized it as the way she'd felt when she'd been going down on him.

"Yes." It was submission and a challenge.

His lips curved up with enjoyment. A moment later, the room was full of her cries again. He claimed her clit once more, sucking and rubbing it with his tongue. He kept up the motion of his two fingers in her sheath, driving her over the edge into oblivion. She twisted and bucked, felt like her lungs stopped working as her entire body seized up and pleasure wrung her like a dishrag. The intensity was off the scale, and when it passed, the room was spinning from how light-headed she was.

"Perfect." He crowed with victory, but tenderly. His tone was soft as he smoothed his hands along her abdomen, gently massaging the tight muscles. He smoothed his hands up and over her ribs and onto her breasts, teasing the tight peaks of her nipples.

"Orgasm makes the nipples pucker," he whispered.

"Ahh…okay…"

He smiled at her confusion. "I know a bullshit partner."

The mention of his other conquests soured her mood, and she shifted, trying to slip away.

He caught her wrists and pinned them to the surface of the bed. She gasped, surprised by the sudden change.

"That was a compliment, Jewel."

"It sucked," she snapped back. "Want me to tell you about my dinner with Rage?"

"No." He shook his head. "I want to fuck you to another screaming orgasm."

She shivered, instantly reacting to him once again. He felt it, his lips curving in response. She was suddenly free as he lifted off her and grabbed something from the bedside table. She heard the crinkle of the condom packet, even if she couldn't see it in the darkness of the room. He tossed the open package aside and sheathed his cock in one efficient motion.

And he was back, pressing her into the mattress again, leaning down and kissing her. It was slow and unhurried this time, his mouth exploring hers now that the edge had been taken off both their appetites.

Shit, but the man knew how to kiss.

He cupped her cheek and slid his lips against hers, teasing her lower lip with his tongue while he pressed her mouth open. His hand slid up into her hair, tightening as he drove his tongue into her mouth, boldly invading. Her heart started accelerating again, her breathing ragged as she felt his cock teasing the opening to her body. It felt so right, so very necessary. She twisted, unable to decide what she wanted, only that lying still was impossible.

He thrust into her with a solid motion. It wasn't harsh, but she stiffened, her body protesting the invasion.

"You're tight," he muttered, groaning as he held still.

"More." It was the only thought in her head. She didn't want to start thinking; she'd feel the sting if she did.

"Yeah." He pulled free and pressed his length into her again, groaning as he buried his cock inside her. "Oh…*yeah!*"

The headboard was banging against the wall a few moments later. She strained toward Ramsey, desperate for each thrust. He didn't hold back either, thrusting into her again and again, driving the breath from her as pleasure speared through her with every penetration. She'd never realized her body could feel such a level of intensity. Every motion drove more of it into her core. Her heart raced, and she didn't care if it burst; all that mattered was meeting him, lifting her hips so his cock could plunge into her. She clasped her legs around him, pulling her to him as it all burst inside her. A pulsing, shattering explosion of rapture that made her scream.

Two thrusts later, Ramsey snarled as his body reached the same zenith. They clutched at each other, straining toward one another as pleasure cracked through them like a whip, both of them held in the grip of the moment.

―――∽∽∽―――

She woke up as lightning cracked across the sky. Gray light was coming in under the curtains, the sound of rain hitting the glass windows.

"At least it held off until after the show."

Jewel's eyes widened when Ramsey spoke beside her. The bed moved as he rolled over and considered her. He reached out and stroked one of her breasts. A soft touch, but she jumped.

"I love the way you respond to me, baby." His voice was still edged with sleep, lazy and unhurried.

Her heart started racing like a rabbit. The anxiety she'd expected to feel the moment she lost her virginity showed up at last.

Which sucked, because the moment was long past.

Get a grip, she ordered herself.

Someone pounded on the door. "Check out time in one hour."

The crew member moved on to the next suite and repeated the warning. It was the escape opportunity she craved. She rolled out of the bed, looking for her clothing. Ramsey chuckled at her abrupt exit. It was a damned good thing she'd turned away from Ramsey, because she made it only two steps before she noticed how sore she was.

"We've got time to play," he offered suggestively.

"Um… I want a shower before we leave." Her voice was tight, betraying her frayed nerves.

"I love your ideas," he purred, still sitting on the bed. "What the—"

Jewel turned around, the sudden change in Ramsey's tone cutting through her morning-after fluster. His expression shocked her.

He was furious.

His attention was on the surface of the bed, specifically, the dark stain left there. "You were a virgin."

Each word was clipped and short. He raised his gaze to her face, and it felt like he'd reached out and slapped her.

"Why the fuck," he growled, "didn't you tell me?"

"What are you so ticked off about?" she asked. "It's my body."

"And now you've made it my responsibility."

She felt like she had been shoved through an open door, out of an airplane. The long fall to earth had begun. "I know. I get it. You're not into anything besides casual sex." Her chest hurt, making her voice hollow. "Don't sweat it, rock star man. I'm not asking you for anything. That's why I didn't tell you."

Her bag was lying on the floor with her clothing. She shrugged into her dress without bothering to put on her underwear.

"Jewel—"

She yanked open the door as he was trying to formulate his argument.

"We're not done with this conversation," he said. She heard him stepping into his pants. Lace-up leather might be hot, but it had drawbacks when it came to chasing people.

"Oh, yes, we are." She left the suite. There was a smattering of crew in the hallway, packing up the gear and making ready to move on to the next town. Ramsey dove after her, capturing her wrist.

Jewel spun on him. "We are…*completely*…done."

"I never lied to you," he said, oblivious to their audience.

"Bullshit," she countered. "I told you I wasn't into casual sex, and you sweet-talked your way around the term. Laying guilt down on me for judging you. Well, who's got his panties in a twist this morning? Look at you, so damned worried you can't make your getaway. Well, I'll save you the trouble by giving you my back."

And that's exactly what she did, turning around and

heading toward the room Brenton had assigned her. At least the key card was in the front pocket of her bag, making it easy to grab and slip into the door. The lock chirped, and she pushed open the door.

She'd known it would hurt.

Bad.

But she was still in shock as she turned the dead bolt and slid down the wall. She hugged her knees, and tears streamed down her cheeks. Shock numbed her mind as pain sliced through her chest.

She'd known.

But that didn't change a damned thing.

Not one damned thing.

—✻—

Something tore inside him.

Ramsey snarled as he felt like the skin was ripped off his fucking back. The pain rushed up and slammed into his brain, knocking his judgment out cold. He lunged after Jewel, the need to drag her back to him overwhelming.

Syon caught him, their bodies colliding like two linebackers.

"Get the fuck out of my way!" Ramsey snarled.

"No way. You need a time-out." Syon pushed Ramsey back.

"Fuck you!"

"He's right." Taz joined the scuffle, locking Ramsey's wrist up as the two of them shoved him back into his suite.

"Assholes," Ramsey growled as he jumped back from his bandmates. They followed him right into his suite, clogging up the doorway. "It's none of your fucking business."

He cursed as he shook his hand. "And don't mess with my hand, Taz! You want our next show to be shit?"

Taz cocked his head to one side and shrugged. "I didn't do any permanent damage."

Ramsey flipped him off. He grabbed a beer from the minibar and popped the cap, but the scent turned his stomach. He chucked it at the wall. It broke, the sound harsh in the daylight, the beer spreading out in a huge splat on the wall before it started to run down the surface.

A virgin.

Hell.

"I'm a complete asshole," he muttered before walking toward the bathroom and turning on the shower. He walked into the cold water, hoping the sting would somehow lower his guilt level.

It didn't.

⌐⌐⌐

"Do you have a passport?"

Brenton was waiting for her in the lobby, watching as the Toxsin crew moved the personal luggage of the band toward a now-familiar line of waiting vehicles.

She felt like her belly flipped. "Yes."

"With you?" Brenton asked.

Jewel patted her bag. He nodded and reached inside his suit jacket to tug something from the inner breast pocket.

"Good. You're off to the airport. Flight leaves in two hours."

She felt like she'd been punched in the solar plexus. Shock held her silent as Brenton turned to address a couple of crew members who were hauling her gear.

"That's going to the airport with the artist," he told

them. They nodded and went through the open doors of the hotel to where a sedan town car was waiting.

Her mouth was dry, and it felt like moving was beyond her ability.

"You could have told her why, Brenton." Kate Braden had appeared, her face flushed as her bodyguard, Yoon, came up behind her, carrying two bags. "Men are insensitive pigs."

"Excuse me?" Jewel asked.

Kate brushed her hair back from her face as Brenton came over and handed her an identical envelope with an airline ticket in it.

"Sorry," Brenton said. "I thought you filled her in."

Kate rolled her eyes before Brenton started gesturing them toward the door and waiting town car.

"Come on," Kate said. "I'll explain on the way." She looked behind her. "Where's Steven?"

Brenton pulled his cell phone out of his pocket, but the second bodyguard came skidding around the corner, his dress shoes sliding on the polished marble floors of the lobby. He shrugged into his suit jacket. Yoon sent him a long look that made it clear the veteran found him lacking.

"Samuel Moss," Kate said as she slid into the back of the town car and made room for Jewel. "He's Toxsin's producer," she continued as Yoon shut the door and Jewel fumbled with the seat belt. "Pretty much a god in this business."

"Quinn Morcant is his competition?"

"Hell yes," Kate replied. "And someone the boys aren't too fond of either. So I wouldn't bring his name up if I were you. How do you know about Quinn anyway?"

"He sent over a contract offer. His man, Bryan Thompson, sort of stalked me in Portland."

Kate's eyes widened. "That contract is a grenade. Trust me. Quinn is a tycoon. He just made it onto *Forbes*'s most eligible bachelors list, and I'm pretty sure he plans on staying there, if you catch my drift. He'll use your talent to form another stair for him to climb up." She shook her head.

"You just described anyone with enough resources to get me where I want my work to be," Jewel countered. "You're an artist. You know how hard it is to pass out your business cards and hope for enough clients to keep a roof over your head. Ramsey told me about a van and cold hot dogs."

Kate nodded. "I wasn't with them in those days, but I hear you, sister. I'd have thought about a contract offer from Quinn Morcant too. Just be careful. The man plays for keeps."

"I noticed that in the contract language," Jewel confessed, feeling too overwhelmed from the lack of caffeine in her bloodstream.

"Anyway, Samuel is having one of his house parties. We're flying out to it. As usual, Sammy gave a couple of hours' notice, so there was no way to get us all on the same plane. The private jet seats only ten. Since Dare and Rage are here, you and I get commercial air, because we're less likely to be recognized. We've got Yoon and Steven though, in case things get dicey."

Relief swept through her. Pathetic but true. Jewel relaxed against the seat, feeling spent both physically and mentally. Now that her emotional dilemma was fading, her body was making sure she knew how abused it was feeling. Her insides felt bruised, like she'd decided to do two hundred sit-ups the night before.

Well, you were straining…a lot…

Her cheeks started burning. She opened her bag and rummaged around inside it so she didn't have to look Kate in the eye.

"Here."

Kate was holding out something. When Jewel looked up, she discovered it to be a single-serving package of painkillers.

Jewel debated protesting that she'd only been looking for lip balm, but the knowing glitter in Kate's eyes made it pointless.

"Thanks." Jewel took the package and reached for a bottle of water.

"All the cars come with the basic hangover kit." Kate lifted the armrest between them to reveal a compartment filled with all sorts of over-the-counter pharmaceuticals.

"Guess the company knows its business," Jewel said as she swallowed the pills.

"Do you have a swimsuit?" Kate asked.

"Ah, sure."

Kate held up a finger. "As in a knock 'em dead suit?"

Jewel shook her head.

"Well, we'll have to remedy that. Samuel is a magnet for gold diggers, who will be there in string bikinis as they try to steal our men," Kate explained.

"Ramsey isn't—"

Kate fluttered her eyelashes. "Save it. I'm not blind. I saw Ramsey when you left his suite. If you say he's not yours, it's because he hasn't worked hard enough to win you over."

She was wrong. They were pulling up at the airport, giving Jewel the chance to avoid the conversation. Jewel focused on the task of making it through airport security, which was surprisingly easier when one was holding a first-class ticket. She smiled at the unexpected luxury, happily settling back into the wide, plush seat.

She only wished it was so simple to sort out her thoughts.

It wasn't.

—◦◦◦—

"Sorry, guys," Kate said to the pair of bodyguards as they climbed into a waiting SUV. "But we're going shopping. Now."

The driver offered Kate a nod before slipping away from the curb and into the flow of traffic. Denver, Colorado, was picture-perfect, with a huge expanse of blue sky overhead complete with fluffy clouds. The driver took them to another posh shopping complex. The parking lot was full of sports cars and BMWs. There wasn't a reasonably priced sedan in sight. Jewel tightened her hand on her bag, but if it was a pool party, she did need a suit.

"I'm paying, too," Kate said as they climbed out of the car.

"Wait," Jewel argued. "I make my own way."

Kate shook her head. "This is a business function. It's all going on the expense account. You'll understand when we get there. The pool will be full of sharks and other flesh-eating vermin."

"Lovely," Jewel said. "I'm suddenly feeling sick."

Kate reached out and hooked her arm. "Not a chance. I'm not going alone."

Jewel laughed at the mock panic Kate flashed at her.

"Okay, so it's dress to defend our turf time. Lead on, sister."

"I knew there was something I liked about you," Kate said with a smile. "Now let's spend some money."

Kate hadn't been kidding about defending her turf. Samuel Moss lived in a mega mansion. It was a sprawling, twenty-room home that boasted a tennis court, indoor and outdoor pools, as well as a sound-recording studio. The entire estate was surrounded by thick stone walls. They entered through a huge double-wide gate that reminded Jewel of Jurassic Park.

She smiled at her mental image. Kate had said there would be creatures waiting to strip the flesh from her bones, after all.

"Pull up your bra straps," Kate said beside her as they drove up the long driveway. It ended in front of a ten-car garage. Two men in uniforms came over on the double to open the back doors of the car before Yoon and Steven got the chance.

The sun was warm, the temperature getting close to ninety, but it was near six in the evening, so the heat was waning. The second they crossed through the front door, Jewel was grateful to Kate for making sure they'd hit the shopping center.

"I owe you," she whispered.

"You're my wingman," Kate replied.

The house was built like a cabin. Huge exposed wood beams ran across the ceiling of the entrance. Music came through a sound system as they walked through the foyer and into a great room.

"Oh…crap," Jewel said softly as she got a glimpse of the other guests. "This really is Jurassic Park."

"Mm-hmm," Kate agreed.

The great room had lots of comfortable-looking furniture in it, in gold, blue, and cream tones. There were more than a dozen females in sight, all of them dressed to kill. They found a reason to turn and consider the newcomers, eyes narrowed, lips pressed into hard lines, as Jewel felt herself being rated.

"Oh boy," Kate said. "Tia's here. Should have guessed she'd run back to the hunting grounds."

"As in the girl who took Ramsey to Spike Collar?"

Kate nodded. Jewel looked over to discover a dark-haired woman considering her over the rim of a martini glass. She had almond-shaped eyes and had applied eyeliner to accentuate them. Her lips were glossed perfectly, with just a dark enough shade to match her complexion. She had on a vintage, pinup girl sort of swimsuit that made it possible for her to float from the deck to the great room without changing.

Tia took a sip of her martini and boldly started across the room toward them. Yoon started to step between them, but Kate shook her head. Tia's lips twitched in amusement.

"Glad you got an invitation," Tia started off as she took another sip. "Samuel can be picky sometimes."

"And yet you're here," Kate said bluntly.

Tia fluttered her eyelashes. Jewel got caught up in just how full and thick they were. The woman must have spent an hour putting on makeup. Eyelashes just didn't come like that in nature.

"Samuel's a friend," Tia said. "Obviously you forgot that fact."

"I heard he was Toxsin's producer," Jewel said.

Tia snapped her attention to Jewel. "As if you know anything about it beyond what information you managed to skim off Google. Who are you?"

Tia didn't wait for Jewel to answer. She started off across the room, sipping her martini like it was some sort of ambrosia endowing her with powers of immortality, putting her above the mere mortals in the room.

"Bet the boys are hiding outside," Kate muttered as she started for the far side of the room where the doors were.

"More likely, she's taking cover in here to avoid having her good buddy Samuel ask any questions that might lead to the story of my meeting with Ramsey."

"You're probably right about that," Kate said. "Samuel might like to have fun, but threaten his bottom line, and you'll see his teeth."

The entire back wall could open up, but it was closed to keep the room air-conditioned. Kate was right. The handful of people inside the house were nothing compared to the horde outside. The patio area was massive, with a huge oasis-style pool that had three sections and eight hot tubs. There were sitting areas under palm trees, and a barbecue section that was a chef's dream. Polished stainless steel gleamed in the summer sun as a man in an apron lifted the lids of the barbecues to turn the meat.

"There they are," Kate said.

The members of Toxsin were clustered around a man in a pair of Tommy Bahama pants. His chest was chiseled, and he clearly enjoyed having it on display.

"That her?" he asked as he peered over the rim of his designer shades.

He was coming toward her a moment later, distracting her from Ramsey, who was leaning against a palm tree, watching her.

"I'm Sammy." Their host cut through her perusal of Ramsey. He offered her a hand to shake, but the moment she took it, he used the hold to pull her close and hug her.

"Man, you do some mean ink, woman," Sammy said as he released her. "You're not too hard on the eyes either. Can't wait to see you in a suit."

He raked her from head to toe and winked at her boldly. "Or out of it. Pool's clothing optional. Don't suit up on my account."

"I'll keep that in mind."

Sammy chuckled. "Ramsey never puts a suit on either." The music producer snapped his fingers. "Someone get my girls here a drink." He looked at Kate and tapped his cheek.

She let out a soft sound of amusement before going toward him and stretching up onto her toes to kiss him. Samuel turned his head at the last second so her lips landed on his.

"Hands off," Syon said as he claimed his wife, pulling her back against him with a solid arm around her waist.

Samuel lifted his hands into the air in mock surrender. His attention honed in on Jewel, or more precisely, something behind her. Sammy lifted an eyebrow, and she turned her head to catch Ramsey moving toward her.

"Really?" Sammy said as Ramsey hooked her hip and kept her in place.

"Nobody brought me a pretty girl?" The music producer offered a few fake sniffles. Two girls sitting nearby took instant advantage, cozying up to him.

"That's better." He looked down one of their dresses, then back up at Jewel. "Nice to meet you. Have some fun. Party is just getting started."

Jewel tried to step away from Ramsey. The people around them melted away with his touch.

"We need to talk," he muttered against her hair.

She'd be a real bitch to say no. But her feelings were injured. She wasn't exactly sure why, only that she was fighting off tears now that he was so close.

"You're making me crazy," she said with a little sigh.

He snorted. "I know the feeling."

For a moment, they stood there, both of their defenses down, uncertain of what to do. His scent awakened all sorts of impulses. Honestly, all she wanted to do was let him surround her until the connection numbed her wits and she forgot all about thinking.

"Ramsey!" There was a squeal from the pool as a girl got out. Water streamed down her body as she came across the deck toward them.

"Oh…that's bad," Taz said nearby.

Ramsey snorted before she heard him draw in a stiff breath. His fingers tightened on her hip for a second. "Be back."

The girl had grabbed a towel and was drying off. She tossed it aside and squealed when she made it to Ramsey. She launched herself into his arms, wrapping her arms around his neck. She reached up and cupped his nape before pressing a kiss against his mouth. A full on-the-mouth mashing of their lips sort of kiss that made Jewel see red.

"Maybe we'd better go change into our suits," Kate said.

"Sure," Jewel answered. "But I'm good. Really. You don't need to wingman me."

Syon trailed kisses down his wife's neck. He lifted his head and sent Jewel a grateful smile. He whispered something in Kate's ear that made her blush. A moment later, he pulled her by their clasped hands through an open side door.

Ramsey was still holding the girl in the bikini. He'd broken off the lip-lock, but she was still pressed against him, her hands on his chest beneath his leather vest as she fingered his nipple bar.

"You know…you should give him a few minutes to straighten things out," Taz said beside her.

"Sure." She turned around and headed into the house. The sight was branded into her memory though, and her temper sizzled.

I'm jumping to conclusions…

Maybe, but that didn't change the fact that she was jealous.

And she wasn't going down without a fight.

The thought just came out of all the emotions churning inside her. Determination sent her looking for a bedroom to change in. There was no shortage of them, but finding an open one proved challenging. When she finally succeeded in getting a doorknob to turn, the sight behind it distracted her from her temper for a moment.

The room was made up as a sex pad. There was a bed with the sheets already turned down. On the bedside table was a basket of condoms, lotions, and small sex toys.

"The party's just getting started, my ass," she said to the empty room.

The suit she'd settled on was more of a sports model. Even with someone else picking up the bill, she hadn't been able to bring herself to buy something superficial. She'd settled on one with boy shorts and little cap sleeves that looked like something a surfer might don.

Considering herself in the mirror, she nodded with approval. She was going out to…well, to be herself. If that wasn't enough to draw Ramsey's attention…she'd embrace her fate.

———

"Vicky, I'm here with someone."

"In your dreams."

Ramsey looked up and found Rage considering him. Vicky wiggled against him, making him feel about two inches tall for the first time in his life because she thought nothing of being so brazen in public. A fact he was responsible for; he'd sure as hell encouraged it enough. Throwing Vicky off him wasn't exactly fair and he owed her an explanation.

"I'm here with someone," Ramsey repeated.

Vicky shrugged. "I don't mind sharing." She rolled the bar through his nipple, her touch practiced and refined. There was a steady confidence in her eyes, no doubt or hesitation. "We've done it before."

They had. The knowledge stung for the first time. He realized he wasn't interested. Not a bit.

Vicky made a soft sound under her breath and pinched his nipple. "I love that sexy grin of yours. Where is she? Let's have a drink together. Get to know each other."

Ramsey jerked and set Vicky back. "You've got it wrong."

Vicky propped one hand on her hip and eyed him knowingly. "Don't I always do you right?"

"Every time I've been here, you have," Rage interjected.

"Get out of my face, Rage," Ramsey growled. "What the fuck business is it of yours?"

Rage shrugged. "You've been working pretty hard to make sure everyone knows you don't give a shit about whoever you're screwing. I'm not the only one who's taken notice."

Ramsey moved closer to Rage. "Still didn't tell me what business it is of yours."

"Not that I expect you have any clue what I'm talking about, but Jewel is worth more than you leaving her the second another woman calls your name," Rage said slowly. "You lump all females into the category of available orifices for your cock."

Ramsey saw red. He launched himself at Rage, catching the man by surprise. Not with the attack, but with how fast it landed on him. Rage wasn't a newbie when it came to brawling. The singer came up with a hiss, jabbing his thumbs into the soft spot behind Ramsey's earlobes.

There was a snort as Ramsey rolled away and came back at the singer. Patio furniture went skidding across the pool deck, umbrellas jerking back and forth like they were caught in a hurricane-force wind. Ramsey didn't care. He went after Rage, the sound of flesh on flesh taking the place of the party conversation.

People started to interfere, but pulled back when they realized it was the two singers. Most of them were there to impress, and that didn't include getting between brawlers.

―⁓―

"What the—" Jewel blinked when she stepped out of the house and back onto the patio. The universe had obviously decided to tilt while she was putting on her swimsuit, because the party was now a cage match. There was a crackle of energy in the air that belonged at a blood sport.

Her mouth hung open as she recognized the two fighters.

"God damn it, Ramsey!" she said.

Rage turned to look at her. Ramsey nailed him on the chin during the moment of distraction. Rage went reeling, but managed to maintain his balance and came back around to jab at Ramsey's midsection.

"Stay right here," Syon said, his missing shirt and half-closed pants telling her more than she needed to know about what he'd been doing. Kate was ten paces behind her husband as she tried to close her corset top.

Syon launched himself into the fight, shoving his way between Ramsey and Rage.

Samuel Moss appeared in the doorway. "What the hell?" The drink in his hand went crashing onto the deck. "Someone pull them the fuck apart!"

Action was swift. Now that the music producer had voiced his command, half the guests jumped forward to do his bidding. Ramsey and Rage didn't have a choice. They were pulled away from each other by sheer numbers.

Well, at least there was a positive use for all the brownnosers.

"It's the middle of concert season, you ass wipes!" Samuel snapped.

"They were fighting over her," Tia said as she

delivered a new drink to Samuel. He looked at the drink and the girl like she was brainless, before he rolled his attention over to Jewel.

"Weren't you just inside?" he asked, proving he was taking in details as well as having a good time.

"Yes."

"It was still over her," Tia insisted as she tried to cozy up to Samuel. He brushed her off.

"I'm dealing with business here," Samuel told her. "Since you don't seem to know to cut the party crap when life gets real enough to threaten profits, why don't you get lost, so the big boys can work."

He stepped away from her and hooked Jewel by the upper arm.

"It was my fight." Ramsey was suddenly there. Something dropped over her shoulders, and she realized it was a towel. Half-wet, the terrycloth stuck to her, and the scent of chlorine pool water tickled her nose.

"But over her?" Samuel demanded. He pointed at his deck. "Why?"

"My point exactly," Rage added as he came closer. "You haven't got a fucking clue how to behave."

"Neither do you," Sammy shot back at Rage. "I've already warned you to keep your pretty face...pretty. Especially during concert season. And if either of you two clowns don't get that part, let me tell you how much I don't like the pair of you risking a broken jaw while the stadiums are sold out. If you wanted the sort of job you could call in sick to, this sure as shit isn't it. We pay every union worker, even if you can't go on and we have to refund the tickets."

Ramsey hooked his hands into his waistband, his jaw

set hard. Rage glared at a spot on Sammy's shoulder. It was as submissive as either of them was likely to get. Sammy made a low sound in the back of his throat.

"You know what?" Sammy said. "You two"—he released Jewel and pointed at Ramsey—"the pair of you, get down the hallway, find a room, and lock the door behind you. Talk...fuck...I don't care, just get the bug out of your ass, Ramsey."

Her checks felt like they caught fire, but Sammy didn't bat an eye.

"And you...come with me." The music producer dragged Rage away.

Half a dozen people heard it. But what bothered Jewel was the way Ramsey's eyes glittered. He was digging in. Making ready to refuse, because that wild part of him just needed to rebel. She reached down and caught his hand before she questioned the protective urge taking hold of her.

"Come on," she said softly.

He stayed exactly where he was. People were watching them, the gleam in their eyes making it clear they were enthralled by the idea of having a juicy tidbit to carry to Sammy. Jewel reversed course and flattened herself against Ramsey.

"Really?" she asked under her breath. "You're going to entertain the brownnosers? I thought you wanted to talk."

He looked past her, noticing the other guests. Two seconds later, he was tugging her down the hallway by their joined hands.

"Three more..." she offered.

He shook his head. "I know where I'm taking you."

Of course he did. Where she'd thought the hallway

ended, there was actually a door. Ramsey pushed through it. There was another section of the house. This one had doors much farther apart.

"Family wing," he said over his shoulder. "I'd sure as hell only let someone I call family talk to me like that."

He selected a door and tried the knob. It turned, and he pushed it in.

"Don't cut your nose off to spite your face," she said as she followed him inside.

Ramsey raised an eyebrow and gave her a dry cough as a reply.

"Seriously. He had a decent reason for chewing you out. Even dream jobs have business sides." She walked past him and into a gorgeous suite. She'd probably even have time to appreciate it if Ramsey wasn't inside it with her. But he was captivating her, as usual.

He shrugged and turned the lock on the door. A hint of satisfaction glittered in his eyes as he crossed his arms over his chest and faced off with her.

Her belly did a little flip.

"I was an asshole this morning."

Whatever she'd thought he might say, an apology hadn't been it. Her breath caught, and she put her back to him as her hold on her composure slipped. It was stupid, really. She'd made her choice and should be able to face the man she'd chosen as her lover. Logical thinking, however, was completely deserting her as usual when faced with Ramsey. All she wanted to do was dissolve into a puddle of receptors.

He let out a grunt, betraying his frustration. "Why didn't you tell me?"

She winced. "I'm sorry." She turned around. "I'm not

trying to guilt-trip you. I wanted to be there…last night. I'm not saying I didn't, and you don't owe me anything."

He was coming toward her, and it was too much. She was on overload and spun around, seeking space to escape. Ramsey didn't let her make it more than a single step. He wrapped his arms around her, pulling her against his body as he nuzzled her hair.

"Why?"

"It wasn't on purpose…just, whenever guys at the shop would find out, they'd start trying to get in my pants like I was some sort of prize."

"You're that, alright," he muttered as he kissed her temple.

"And you make me a little insane," she finished. "I forget how to think, much less talk."

"I do," he whispered against her hair. "I made sure I drove you crazy. I'm an asshole for doing that. For pushing you. For treating you like just another handful of candy I could grab."

She snorted, two tears trickling down her cheeks.

"I made my choice." At least her voice came out smooth. "There's nothing for you to feel guilty about."

He released her and came around her. He cupped her chin and raised her face so their eyes met, reading her emotions like they were in print.

"Except fighting with Rage," she said quickly. "What was that about?"

Ramsey's lips twitched. "He pointed out that I was an idiot for leaving you to go to Vicky."

An image of Ramsey holding the bikini-clad girl came instantly to mind. Her temper flared back up. "You were." She walked past him, taking in the suite for the first time.

"What in the tar is that?" she demanded as she blinked, trying to absorb the reality of what she was seeing.

"One of Sammy's playground toys," Ramsey answered in a tone edged with amusement. She turned on him.

"Don't laugh at me just because I've never seen one of those"—she gestured with her thumb over her shoulder—"in the flesh."

Ramsey laughed outright at her. He rocked back on his heels as he chuckled. Jewel turned around to study the object in question.

It was a swing.

A bondage swing made of straps similar to seat belts, and thick metal bars. The thing was black and suspended from the ceiling. Once again, the room sported a basket of sex supplies like a hotel put out toiletry items.

"You should see your face," Ramsey said from behind her.

Jewel turned back to look at Ramsey. He was watching her, his dark eyes full of appreciation. "Like seeing me blush, is that it?"

"*Like* isn't a strong enough word," he clarified. "I love your unjaded mind, your honest responses."

His expression darkened as he looked past her at the swing. "I think I've got a bellyache." He shook his head and reached out to grasp her hand. Once he had it, he tugged her through the suite, leaving the swing behind.

"I think I've been sick to my stomach for a long time without realizing it," he said. The admission shocked her.

As well as warmed her. Some sensation was spreading

through her, an emotion that caught her off guard as she struggled to put a name on it.

Cherished.

The word didn't fit with his badass persona or his prowling jungle cat reputation.

But it sure suited her needs, soothing the hurt that had been sitting on her chest so heavily that she'd been fighting to breathe.

He opened a patio door. Outside was a private deck. There were padded lounge chairs and a hot tub. He punched the controls, and the water started bubbling. The sun was almost gone, leaving them in semidarkness. Sounds drifted over from the party, but all they did was make her shudder.

"You've got to be sore." He shrugged out of his vest. "Let's soak."

"Hot tubs aren't good for healing tats."

"Sammy employs the best people in the biz to disinfect his house, because he likes to party with his groupies and doesn't want to catch anything."

"Makes sense."

He crooked his finger at her.

She worried her lower lip, more focused on him opening his pants than the mild discomfort left from the night before. His cock was hard, jutting up the moment he freed it. The dragon tattoo was almost healed now, the reptile breathing onto that hard length.

He climbed into the tub, settling back but watching her. She ended up grinning. He lifted an eyebrow. "It was an invitation, Jewel, not a challenge."

"You toss the gauntlet down just by being yourself."

His lips parted, flashing his teeth. Unrepentant. Rebellious. The trait she liked best about him. Because it made her bold enough to unbuckle her own leash and run free.

"You're an enabler, you know that?"

He snorted at her accusation. "According to my parents, I'm leading all my fans to Satan with my music."

He'd meant it as a joke, but the ease with which the words crossed his lips told her it was true.

And that was sad.

Bitterly so.

"That's—" she started.

"The way it is," he finished for her. "I've gotten to the point where I just accept it's the way things are. To be mad about it would be to say they don't have the right to disagree with me. I can't go on demanding the world let me be myself if I'm going to deprive others of the same privilege."

"You have a good heart."

"No, I don't," he insisted with a shrug. "I sold it at a pawn shop back when we were trying to get Toxsin launched."

She bit her lip, quelling the urge to argue with him. Now wasn't the time. There was a guarded look in his eyes that told her he was thinking he'd said too much.

"So what are you going to do now?" he asked her.

"I thought I might…" She fingered the bottom of her swim top. "Take my top off."

His eyes narrowed. "So do it."

There was a touch of arrogance in his tone now, but she realized it was also need. Ramsey style. The man didn't do anything normally.

"Maybe I'm still thinking about it. Enabler."

He nodded. "Tough call. Considering how much I love your tits. Take that top off and I'm going to cup them"—he lifted his hands out of the bubbling water to mimic the action—"and then I'm going to tease those little nipples of yours until they are hard points…before I lean over and lick them…"

Her nipples were puckering already, pushing out the soft fabric of her swim top. His gaze settled on them, satisfaction glittering in his eyes.

"And then, I'm going to suck them…one at a time."

Her breath was coming harder, her heart accelerating. His words were intoxicating, and she wanted more. She pulled off her top, enjoying the feel of the night air on her bare skin. His expression turned hungry.

"Now if you take off those shorts…" He moved to the edge of the tub and rested his hands on the edge like he was making ready to vault over it. "I'm going to have to dig deep for restraint, because I can't start off fucking you. No." His voice became a soft, menacing promise. "I'm going to have to keep my cock out of you for a good long session of foreplay. Tease that little clit of yours, play with it until you scream like you did last night. Your G-spot is so sensitive, you loved having my fingers inside you…"

She was already wet, her pussy aching and empty. It shouldn't have turned her on so much, except there was a glitter of sincerity in his eyes that was more like determination. He was holding the edge of the hot tub, gripping it. Her heart was racing, her clit throbbing.

"I think that water might be a little too hot for me… right now." She pushed her swim shorts down and stepped out of them. "But I should warn you, if you come out, I'm going to wrap my fingers around that cock of yours and—"

There was a splash as he vaulted over the side of the

tub and landed on his feet. Water slithered down his skin as he slowly stalked her.

They collided like thunder, the sound shaking her and rattling her teeth. Her core felt like it was melting, and she was sort of sure steam was rising off her as he claimed her mouth in a kiss, his fingers cupping her nape as he captured her.

There had never been a more willing victim.

———

There was an explosion of laughter from off in the distance where the pool was, and the party was still going strong. Jewel forced her eyes open and found herself staring at the ceiling above the bed that had a spotless mirror attached to it. She got a great view of the man-animal stretched out beside her.

"They might have heard you." Ramsey rolled over onto his side and lay there grinning with victory. "You screamed really loud…and a…lot."

He was laughing. Jewel was on her back, her arms flung above her head. She closed her hand around the corner of a pillow and swung it at him.

He raised an arm to block her attack, laughing harder. She flipped over but stopped, because if she hadn't been sore before, she sure was now. Her body wanted vengeance for what she'd been putting it through. Going after Ramsey seemed a poor choice compared to finding some painkillers.

Ramsey changed moods instantly. "Come on."

The bed rocked as he stood and reached over to scoop her up.

"I can walk, ya know."

He carried her out of the suite to the hot tub. "I like

claiming you." The water was still warm, even though the jets had turned off.

"You have control issues." She settled back against him as the warm water soothed her aching muscles.

"You love the way I come after you," he countered as he cupped water and rubbed it over her shoulders. "That I don't behave. It excites you."

"Maybe." She sighed. "But I don't like all of your caveman tactics. I want to talk about Steven."

"Only if you want to talk me into getting him a partner so he can have set hours off, because you're worried he isn't getting his beauty rest."

She started to push away from him. Ramsey closed his arms around her and held her still, her back to him as she sat between his thighs and reclined on him.

"You don't know my world, Jewel. It's vicious at times. You were run off the road within hours of being linked with me."

She snorted, frustrated by his undisputable logic. He rubbed her arms. "Steven stays."

"You still should have discussed it with me."

She felt him nodding against her head. "I was having self-discipline challenges. Couldn't seem to focus on anything but getting between your thighs."

"You poor thing."

He was chuckling again. "It's been a strain."

She snorted at him.

He became serious. "I shouldn't have gone over to Vicky like that. Rage called it right."

He was still stroking her, cupping the water and keeping her shoulders from getting cold. "I didn't ask you to change," she said.

"You didn't," he whispered against her hair. "That just makes me a double asshole for not realizing you're worth straightening up for."

He held her for a moment longer before there was another outbreak of amusement from the pool area.

"Time to go show my face," he said. "Sammy didn't fly us all out here to have us hiding in his guest wing. He wants to discuss details."

He eased out from behind her and climbed out of the tub. She bit her lower lip as she tried to decide what to do next. He used his thumb to pull her chin down and free her lip.

"He did drop a fair amount of money on this party," she said.

Ramsey tossed her a towel once she'd climbed out of the tub.

"He's sharp." Ramsey used another towel to mop the water off his skin before he moved into the suite and found his pants. "He wants us in the recording studio as soon as the concert tour ends. There's no contract as of yet, but investing in bringing us here is a drop in the bucket. Especially since Morcant is sniffing around."

"That would explain the Jurassic Park feeling I got when we showed up." It also gave her a very unsavory sensation about Quinn Morcant's offer.

Ramsey flashed a huge smile. "Yeah, there are flesh eaters out there, for sure. But only the ones Sammy's sure are on his side."

"So…why didn't you tell Sammy about Tia? It seems to me he would be a little pissed if he found out about the cherry blossoms."

Ramsey finished securing his pants and shrugged into

his vest. Jewel pulled her swimsuit back on so she could go and find her dress. He brushed her hair back from her face.

"I told you, Jewel. I own my fuckups."

"Yeah. You do." It was a compliment, one she truly meant. An acceptance of his apology.

He knew it. For a moment, they stood there, both of them uncertain but chained together by the current of emotion that seemed to bind them.

Another outburst from the pool broke the spell.

"Time to work," he said. "But first, some more clothes for you."

"So says the man who walks around in an open vest."

He clasped her hand and started pulling her down the hallway. "I said I own my fuckups, not that I was going to start playing fair."

He was unrepentant and arrogant, but ever so adorable. He offered her a shrug and a sincere grin.

"Wouldn't recognize you if you did," she said.

Chapter 6

THE TRUCKS HAD CAUGHT UP WITH THEM IN DENVER. What had first seemed like a frantic level of activity now struck her as a well-oiled process. Like a pit crew jumping into action the second the race car drove in. Every man knew his job, and together, they were really awesome.

It was close to six in the evening by the time Jewel crawled out of Ramsey's bed.

Honestly, she could have been passed out in the back of one of the busses for all she'd been aware of her surroundings. Plain and simple, she'd been beat. Worn out. Both physically and mentally. The change in activity level woke her, and shame made her get up. There was a piece of hotel stationery on top of her cell phone.

Sound check rehearsal. R.

Her mouth went dry as she looked at it. She had no idea how to deal with details that confirmed she was in a relationship.

Crap! That had come out of left field.

Relationship?

With a rock star?

Okay, now you're being judgmental.

It was a valid charge. Rock stars needed love too. She groaned. The l-word was really going too far. At least before coffee it was. She put down the note and went searching for the kitchen. Nothing like coffee to toast to the setting sun. The coffeemaker filled the suite with a nice aroma as she found her suitcase and dressed.

Her phone buzzed, and she went back into the bedroom to pick it up.

"Hello?"

"Ms. Ryan, Bryan Thompson here."

"Hi." She was repeating herself. She went back into the kitchen and took a quick sip of the coffee.

"Mr. Morcant was hoping you might take a meeting with him tomorrow, if your schedule is open," Bryan continued.

"Well, I'm in Denver. Colorado." She added the state at the last second. "And under contract at the moment, so travel is out of the question."

"Mr. Morcant is in the States. Your next stop is Milwaukee. Could we put you down for next Tuesday?" Bryan pressed. "It would save you a trip to Scotland to discuss the offer."

Scotland?

She took another sip from her coffee before answering. "Sure." Her response lacked a lot, like professionalism. "I mean, I'll do my best to make it. Could you text me an address?"

"We'll have a car call for you," Bryan assured her smoothly.

The line went dead. She stared at her phone for a long moment before ordering herself to stop worrying about it. Her future was something she needed to get focused on. And quickly. Maybe it was judgmental, but thinking there was anything secure about her relationship with Ramsey was foolish.

And that hurt.

She forced herself to get over it and enjoy the ride. Savor the moment. If she wanted to indulge in pity parties, there would likely be plenty of time later on. Once Ramsey went on with his life and she got on with hers.

So yeah, she was taking a meeting with Quinn Morcant.

—◊—

Hotel suites were starting to look the same.

She was also feeling a little unsure about making herself at home in Ramsey's suite; there was a lot unsettled between them. But going back to her room seemed like a slap in the face, so Jewel wandered down to the lobby, intending to find a restaurant. The Toxsin crew was moving around as she made her way to the hospitality desk and started nosing through brochures for the local highlights.

"You're okay."

Jewel looked up and found Taz considering her. He played bass and did backup vocals for the band. He was also the only member of Toxsin with short hair. It went with his Asian features. There was a slight accent to his English, and she knew he spoke Korean, because he often engaged Kate's bodyguard Yoon in that language.

"You need to come have sushi with me tonight," Taz said.

There seemed something significant about the invitation. Jewel had no clue what it was, but Taz's tone was edged with seriousness, his expression somewhat formal.

"Would love to," she answered with a smile as she put down the brochures.

Taz nodded before he turned around and joined Syon

and Brenton, who had arrived sometime while she'd been looking at the brochures.

Her senses tightened, her body feeling like she was poised on a cliff top.

Ramsey.

She turned slowly, looking for him.

"Took you long enough." He was half-hidden behind a potted silk plant, watching her with his midnight dark eyes. There was a pleased look on his face that told her how much he enjoyed sneaking up on her.

"Stalking me?" she asked.

"I'm definitely looking forward to the pouncing part," he declared, but he suddenly frowned, abandoning his lazy stance and coming out of the foliage.

"Where's Steven?"

"Ah…" She'd completely forgotten about the bodyguard.

Ramsey clearly hadn't. "Do you have your cell phone?"

"Sure." She pulled it out of her bag. Ramsey plucked it from her grasp and swiped the screen. "Are you saying Steven can track that?"

"Yes." Ramsey was punching at the screen and glowering.

"Do you think you might have mentioned that to me…or, gee…asked?"

He looked up at her, all traces of playfulness gone. Instead, she was facing a side of him that was ruthless and all business.

"When it comes to security, I won't ask." His tone was like a gavel pounding, but her temper still stirred. "You're too inexperienced to identify the threats."

"So explain it to me," she said. "Keep me in the loop, and I'm not asking either."

One side of his mouth twitched. "I noticed."

"I mean it," she insisted. His eyes narrowed, but he seemed to think better of continuing the argument and held up her phone.

"This is a piece of crap. The location chip is fried. You need a new one. Now."

He punched in something and dropped the phone in his inside vest pocket. Now that the sun was setting, he was back to being bare-chested except for the leather vest.

"Come on." He clasped her hand and pulled her toward the door. He let out a whistle, and Taz turned to look at him.

"We'll meet you there. Text me."

Taz barely had time to nod before Ramsey was tugging her along behind him. They went through a huge revolving door and into the warm summer night. The flash of cameras was almost normal now. Along with the rude questions, in fact, she was beginning to be entertained by them.

"Jewel…who's a better lover?"

Ramsey turned his head toward the reporter who had hurled out the question. The guy actually shook with excitement. "The fans want to know," he insisted.

"Dude, you need to get out more," Ramsey informed him to the delight of the other reporters.

There were four Harleys parked in front of the hotel. Ramsey swung his leg over one and offered her his hand. The cameras flashed as she climbed on behind him. He handed her a helmet before putting one on himself.

"Great ass!" someone yelled before Ramsey revved

up the engine and pulled away from the curb. Jewel wrapped her arms around him and felt like it must have been a month since she'd touched him.

She was an addict for sure.

It was a weeknight, but the cell phone store was busy. She felt a twinge of temper as Ramsey pulled up in front of her carrier. But a memory surfaced of him telling her about serving in Bomb Disposal.

"I guess you can take the uniform off but you can't take the squid out of the ex-sailor."

He nodded as he joined her on the sidewalk. "We hooked up with Taz and Drake there."

"Sounds like your family had a problem with you going back to being a band boy." She realized once the words were out of her mouth how insensitive they were. "Sorry. That was somewhat…crass."

He shrugged and walked right up to the newest models on display. Which were also the most expensive.

"Ah…you know one of those will be a good upgrade." She pointed to the other side of the store.

"I told you, Jewel. When it comes to security, it's my way." He looked at a salesperson and handed them her old phone.

"And I told you, we're going to have these things called…discussions."

He pulled her close as the salesperson happily went to the back room to get the new phone. "We can't ditch Taz, it'd be a major social gaff, but after that we could go back up to Sammy's and try the swing. I would love to hear which position—"

Jewel twisted her knuckle into his chest, her face on fire. Ramsey chuckled, low and deep, sending excitement through her. He captured her nape and buried his head in her hair as he bit her earlobe.

"Don't you want to have a discussion with me?" he asked.

She groaned in the face of his sarcasm. He chuckled and placed a kiss against her neck.

"You know you're thinking about the swing."

"Right now, I'm thinking about hosing you down." She wiggled until he released her. "With cold water."

He shook his head, making his hair fly, and bit the air between them.

"Animal," she accused him softly.

He moved up beside her, hooking his arm around her back and locking his hand on the curve of her hip. "I love the way you pet me."

He did.

And she enjoyed knowing he did. She'd never thought she'd get such a buzz from going down on a guy, but the truth was, it excited her. Did that mean she was a control freak? If so, they had that in common. Her cheeks remained scarlet as the salesgirl completed the transaction. But the reason behind the blush changed to temper when Ramsey tried to hand his credit card to the girl.

"It's going to be my phone," Jewel argued as she extended her arm so her bank card was closer to the girl.

"Which I'm insisting you buy." He winked at the salesgirl and sent her a grin. "Make sure you pay up the account for the next year. We travel a lot. Monthly statements can be a hassle."

The girl promptly nabbed the card out of Ramsey's hand, clearly seeing her commission increase.

Jewel wanted to argue, but she realized it was deeply

personal, at least on her end, and she wasn't sure she
wanted to share it just yet. She had trust issues, there
was no way around admitting it, and honestly, a big
part of it came down to lack of confidence in herself
and her ability to hold on to the attention of a man like
Ramsey. She stood there biting her lip as Ramsey signed
the sales slip and the girl handed her a little bag. Ramsey
didn't give her a chance to open a conversation either.
He knew she was simmering, but he clasped her hand
and pulled her toward the door.

"We can't be late to Taz's sushi dinner." He unlocked
the helmets and handed her one.

"Lucky you."

He paused before slipping on his helmet. "Chill-lax.
What is the point of me being successful if I can't enjoy
it once in a while?"

She snorted at him. "Way to turn things back on me."

He offered her a grin of victory before he pulled on
the helmet. She followed his example and climbed onto
the back of the bike.

She'd lost this round, fair and square.

Except you got a new cell phone out of it…

That part bothered her the most, because she didn't
want to be kept, and since she'd signed on with Toxsin,
she'd done little work. Sure, it could be argued that what
Ramsey had purchased was her time, bringing her along
to suit his schedule, so he owed her for the business she
was missing out on. Still, she battled with accepting
that idea entirely. There was something inside him that
expected to be used. She'd seen the bitterness in his eyes.
No matter what, she didn't want to be part of causing it.

Now you're trying to save him…

Fine, maybe she was. At least it was a good intention. She got the impression too few people remembered
there was a man inside the rock star.

―∽∽―

Taz certainly did take sushi seriously.

Ramsey drove to a huge restaurant in a Japanese-
inspired building that had a red tile roof with the corners
turned up. There were scores of people waiting outside
for tables, a sure mark of how good the food was.

"Taz will be upstairs in one of the private rooms."
Ramsey clasped her hand and pulled her through the
door. He took a moment to bow at the threshold. The girls
behind the counter all greeted him with warm smiles.

Jewel had to tug back on her hand so she could bow
as well. He grinned when he looked over his shoulder to
investigate why she was resisting his pull.

"Can't go shaming my host," she said. "He said I was
alright. It sounded like a significant compliment."

"It was," Ramsey confirmed. "You can bet Taz never
invited Tia for sushi."

She was half-ready to take offense, but realized she
was too busy enjoying the knowledge that Ramsey's
bandmates saw her as more than a hookup.

Ramsey took her up a set of stairs to a second level.
Below, it had been noisy from the congestion of people
tightly packed around tables to get as many customers in
as possible. Upstairs, there was the soft sound of flowing water from fountains set into the corners. Orchids
decorated the fountains, and there was even one big
enough to have koi swimming in a pool.

The waitresses wore long, flowing gowns of Asian

design. They had empire waistlines, and the girls had their feet slipped into shoes that they took off the moment they came to any of the closed entrances that led to private dining rooms.

Those doors slid opened. Ramsey had his cell phone out and was following the route on the screen.

"Are you tracking Taz?" She pushed forward to see the screen.

"Yeah." Ramsey pointed to a door at the far end of the restaurant.

"And here I thought I was special."

He coughed at her as he dropped his phone into the inside pocket of his vest. He turned around, cupping her nape. She ran into him, because he did it so fast, ending up with her hands resting on his chest.

"You are," he said.

In pure Ramsey style, he'd changed the tempo instantly. She quivered, her body heating as her insides churned.

"Food is suddenly the last thing on my mind," Ramsey muttered against her lips.

"Ditto." It was a confession, one she might actually have thought twice about if she could have thought at all. There was only the way he felt against her. His hard body, the way his skin smelled. It kicked off a pulse deep inside her that made her nipples pucker and her clit throb.

The screen door slid open. A sweet-faced girl stood there, her eyes widening as she took them in. She started to smile but pressed her lips together to control her expression as she looked down for her shoes.

"Get in here before the mama comes out of the

kitchen and thwacks your ear for misbehaving," Taz called out to them.

"My ear, huh?" Jewel asked as she stopped to remove her shoes and cross into the room. Taz used a pair of chopsticks to push a piece of sushi into his mouth. He paused with it in front of his lips.

"It will sting for an hour," Taz confirmed. "My mother is a master of the art."

Jewel sat down on a large pillow. There was a place beneath the table for her feet. It was a clever design, making the table appear to be on the floor, but having the added space for those who weren't comfortable kneeling through an entire meal.

Ramsey settled in beside her, reaching beneath the table to squeeze her thigh.

"Behave." Taz looked like he was focused on the plate of sushi near his end of the table, but he shot Ramsey a look and pointed his chopsticks at his bandmate.

"Jewel is my guest," Taz said before the screen slid open and more food arrived. Taz ran the dinner, switching between Korean and English as the food kept coming. Jewel was grateful she'd worn leggings because her belly soon felt like it was distended. Taz kept pushing more food toward her. At last, she waved her napkin in the air.

"Can I ask you something?" Taz had slowed down and was now contemplating her across the remains of the banquet.

"Sure."

"What sort of setup is Morcant trying to sell you?" Taz's eyes had hardened, his expression becoming pensive. "I mean, he's a businessman. I wouldn't think tattoos would bring in enough profit."

Her nape tingled, but she clamped down on her emotions when they tried to rise. It was a good question, and instead of getting huffy, she needed to recognize a valid attempt at understanding her motives.

"He's suggesting a line of art that would be sold in both graphic format and studios. My freedom to tattoo would actually be tightly limited to keep the price where he wants it."

As in a stranglehold. She'd reread the contract offer several times and still didn't like how tight the language was, but it was still art, her dream field.

"And you're considering it?" Ramsey demanded beside her.

Jewel turned to look at him. "So far as reading the offer. Are you actually suggesting I ignore it? Didn't you guys talk to more than one producer when you were trying to sign with a big label?"

For a moment, she thought he was going to say yes. He wanted to. She could see the need flickering in his eyes.

But Ramsey shook his head. "We did. Morcant is good at what he does."

"Too good," Taz said. "He draws blood in more than one market around the globe."

"Which makes it understandable that you'd consider his offer," Ramsey said. He moved, pushing back from the table and standing. "I've got to walk off some of this."

"Restroom break," Jewel agreed. Ramsey offered her a hand.

She went into the ladies' room to freshen up. Her emotions were still sort of stirred up. On one hand, Ramsey had voiced his understanding of her need to explore the offer with Morcant. On the other hand, she really wondered if she wasn't just kidding herself. After all, Ramsey was a proven artist on a global scale; she'd just gotten lucky when he'd walked into Ted's shop.

Oh Lord, pull up your britches, girl!

Jewel smiled at her own sarcasm. Okay, she really did need to work on her confidence. She took time to play with her hair and apply a fresh coat of lipstick, in an effort to bolster her self-esteem before emerging. The hallway was still full of soothing, low-volume music and the sound of the water flowing through the fountains.

There was also a burst of giggles. Jewel tried to ignore it; after all, it was a fairly safe bet that the private rooms had seen more than their share of flesh eating that had nothing to do with fish.

But she looked down the hall and ended up frozen. Ramsey was lying across the seat pillows of another room as the girl from Sammy's party lay across the table and looked down on him with her cleavage in his face while he gave her a sexy little smile that Jewel recognized. She moved forward, pressing a kiss against his mouth while he reached up and clasped the back of her neck in a hold that Jewel knew as well.

Her confidence fell to the floor like a dropped tray of fried rice, scattering into tiny little bits that were impossible to scoop up.

Jewel was frozen in shock; icy pain went stabbing through her. She must have gasped, because the girl looked up, and so did Ramsey.

Jewel felt her face catch fire. She jerked her gaze away but couldn't seem to recall which screen hid the room she'd been in with Taz. She caught sight of the stairs and decided they would make an excellent escape route.

"Jewel…" Ramsey called after her.

She didn't stop. She ended up at the ground level and kept going, because people looked up and stared at her.

Of course they did. She must have looked like she was ready to burst into tears.

She certainly felt like it. With so many people at the restaurant, there were a couple of taxis waiting. She pulled open the door of one and ducked inside.

And started crying.

———

"Do I have to kick your ass?"

Ramsey whirled around to face Taz.

"Actually, I think that's my line," Vicky said. She was wearing a micromini with a plunging neckline to show off the fact that she wasn't wearing anything under the dress. She preferred being naked, something Ramsey had once enjoyed…fully. She made a low sound under her breath and bent down to grab his boots. She straightened up and shoved them at his chest.

"Get going."

"I'm a dumb ass," he said.

"You are," Vicky said as Taz agreed. "But you need to go tell your girlfriend that."

"I do."

He turned and took the stairs two at a time. A quick scan of the curb area told him Jewel was gone. He dropped his boots and stepped into them before swinging his leg over his Harley.

He would be telling her, and she would listen.

Or he just might end up begging her to.

The taxi pulled up in front of the Marriott. Jewel slid her bank card through the slot and signed the screen before getting out. The driver tactfully ignored her red-rimmed eyes and the sniffling sounds she'd spent most of the ride trying to muffle behind a wad of tissue. She took a deep breath and dumped them in a trash can before walking toward the entry doors.

"Jewel…Jewel…?"

She blocked out the questions as one of the security men opened the door for her. The lobby was blissfully clear of the Toxsin crew and Brenton. It offered her the chance to make it to the elevators and up to her room.

But the idea of getting into an elevator bothered her because at the moment, all she wanted to do was run. She looked over her shoulder, but still rebelled at the idea of going inside. She pushed open the door to the stairs and started climbing.

Twenty floors later, she was pretty sure she'd made a mistake. Her thighs were on fire, and her butt felt like it had turned to stone. But there was a sense of satisfaction in making it under her own power. She had to slide her key card through a slot to gain access to the floor. The door chirped as she opened it, and she ended up facing Ramsey.

"That damned phone," she snarled.

He was leaning against the wall, his arms folded over his chest while he waited for her. He dropped his phone into the inside pocket of his vest as he shot her a look that was full of hard promise.

"We need to talk." Each word was clipped as he straightened up and reached for her hand.

"What do you want me to say?" She jerked on their joined hands.

Ramsey released her and pushed his hands through his hair. "I don't know, but damn it, I want you to demand something from me. Tell me what a dick I am for letting you find me like that. Tell me you're jealous."

Her eyes widened with shock. "So you…can what, exactly? Feel justified? Know you were right all along, and I'm just another person trying to control you? Change you, use you to live out my idea of happiness? When it clearly isn't what you want?"

"Fuck no!" he growled.

"What then?" she demanded, going on the offensive and moving toward him. Her composure was nothing but a taper of smoke. "You're driving me crazy, do you know that? You want me to understand you aren't the guy I see you as, but you're following me when I walk away to deal with my emotions by myself. And now… you're mad because I left you to your…fun! But then, you got ticked when I went to dinner with Rage." Her eyes were full of tears again, infuriating her. "I'm so *stupid* for giving a shit!"

"Yes, it pissed me off to see you with Rage. Tell me it makes you mad to see me kissing other girls."

She felt like she couldn't form another word, because the circumstances of their lives were crushing her. "So you can…what? Feel victorious?"

"So I can feel like you care enough to try and talk some sense into me when I fuck up, and that you won't just give up on me."

His words seemed to surprise him just as much as they did her. For a long moment, they just stared at each other, breathing hard as they both tried to come to grips with how deeply they felt about each other. It scared her on a level she hadn't realized she had, a place that felt like she was just going to shatter if he didn't return her feelings.

"You want to know my inner secrets?" He captured the hand she'd been poking him in the chest with. "Fine. I hate sushi."

She blinked, totally stunned.

"And I eat it by the plateful because to Taz, going out for sushi is a deep bonding experience." He clamped her against his body, bring her flush with him, allowing her to feel his erection. He had his other hand fisted in her hair as he buried his face against her and drew in a deep breath. "The only raw meat I want against my tongue is your pussy. But I will do anything for the people I care about."

He was shaking. His words sent a jolt of arousal through her, but it was the tremor raking him that tore her nearly in half. The elevator arrived, the soft ding making her jerk. It felt like any company would be the same as a crowd pushing against them.

"Take me...somewhere...dark," she said.

He made a low sound of agreement against her hair before he pulled her down the hallway. There was a chirp as he opened the door of his suite, and a click when it closed behind them. She walked past him, into the center of the dark suite. Ramsey reached behind him and locked the door.

The sound made her smile with relief. She wanted

him to be hers, all hers until the sun came up and they
had to deal with reality.

"Yeah." He shrugged out of his vest and tossed it
onto the kitchen table. "No more interference." He
unbuttoned his leather pants and stopped to get out of
his boots before he was able to shuck the pants. "You...
and...me..."

"Sure you don't want to join Vicky's party?" Maybe
it might be a cheap shot. Honestly, she knew it made
it clear her heart was on her sleeve, but she just had to
know for sure.

He moved closer, until he was a dark shadow looming over her. He captured her hand and pressed it against
his heart.

"So sure, it scares me," he rasped.

Uncertainty surrounded her like a cloud of smoke,
but she didn't miss the tremor running through his hand.
She rolled her lips in because she was nervous, not
wanting to mess up something important. She squeezed
his hand before stepping away from him. He watched
her, his gaze making her feel more attractive than any
declaration of flowing prose. He was riveted in place,
his focus aimed at her as she pulled her bag free and let
it slip to the floor. His features tightened as she tugged
her dress up and over her head. The drapes were open,
allowing the city lights to bathe her bare skin.

"I don't deserve you," he whispered, his tone harsh
with self-loathing.

"I want to be here."

He sucked in a breath through his teeth as she spoke,
his eyes closing for a moment as he appeared to be
savoring her words. His eyes glittered when he opened

them. Unshed tears? She was stuck contemplating the inconceivable idea when he moved forward and grasped the waistband of her leggings, drawing them down her body. She stepped out of them, a little sound of relief escaping her lips.

"I get why you like to be nude when you're in your suite," she said.

He'd straightened up and was standing impossibly close to her. All the tiny hairs on her body felt like they were rising up, functioning as receptors and taking her to an extreme level of awareness. Somehow, she'd never realized what her body was for. Just what sort of extremes she could feel.

"It's because you're finally able to be yourself," Jewel finished.

He reached out and slid his hand along the side of her face, sending a flood of sensation through her. It was so intense, she wanted just to close her eyes and nuzzle against his hand, but she first wanted to see what he thought of her observation.

"You get me, Jewel." He pulled her close, or maybe he stepped up; she really wasn't sure, because all that mattered was being folded into his embrace.

"From the moment you saw me, you really saw me." He inhaled the scent of her hair. "It scares the shit out of me."

"It's not any easier for me." She stroked him, letting her hands roam freely over his shoulders, delighting in the way her fingertips seemed to have become ultrasensitive, transmitting every little ridge to her. "Harder, I think."

He lifted his head, their gazes fusing as he cupped her nape. "I'm a dick when I'm rattled."

That made her smile. "Most of us are."

He shook his head. "You've been more than patient with me."

It was an admission, one she didn't have time to contemplate. He was kissing her within moments, and she rose onto her toes to kiss him back. They weren't close enough. She tightened her grip on his shoulders, pulling him harder against her. The kiss changed, becoming demanding, but she kissed him back with just as much insistence.

She wanted to take, drawing her fingernails down his back as he growled against her neck and bit her. The tiny pain ripped through her, tearing the lid off something she'd never before realized she'd had inside herself. A dark craving suited perfectly to the moment. She arched back and clawed him again, lifting one leg so his cock slipped between her thighs and into the wet folds of her sex.

She cried out, the contact jarring. Her pussy quivered, aching.

They were suddenly moving. Ramsey withdrew and turned her around, pressing her against the dinette table. It chilled her, making her suck in a harsh breath, but he was hot against her back, his hands cupping her hips as he spread her feet with a quick swipe of one of his.

He was surging into her before she finished gasping, using the grip on her hips to lift her bottom. He slid in easily because she was so wet.

"Yes!" he grunted; but honestly, Jewel felt like she'd cried it out.

Nothing had ever felt so good. Maybe, when her head was clear, she might question why she was so aroused at being bent over a kitchen table.

But not now.

Now she pushed back against his next thrust, gasping when his balls slapped against her. "More!" she demanded. "Harder!"

"No," he growled against her ear, holding her in place when she would have reached back and clawed him for refusing her. The urge was there, a violent need to take what she wanted from him, any way necessary.

"You're mine, Jewel." He pulled free and thrust into her again. The force of it drove a sound out of her that was low and primal. "I'm going to take you, make you scream."

"Yes!" She was fighting his grip on her hips, but he was lying over her back now, completely imprisoning her with the help of the table.

"And it's not...*not*...going to be over fast," he bit out against her ear before he straightened up and started fucking.

There was no other word for it. But she liked it. He kept her exactly where he wanted her, holding her hips captive as he worked his cock in and out of her with a skill that threatened to drive her mad. He was shaking with the effort of holding back. She felt him fighting his own needs and snarled at him. It earned her a growl and a hard, deep thrust that he paused after, keeping her impaled as he lay back down and whispered against her ear.

"Feel that?" His voice was just a husky rattle.

"Yes," she snapped.

"Good." He was in far too much control for how insane he was driving her. "I want you to be mine. Completely mine."

"I am…" Two little words had never felt like they meant so much. She felt exposed by them, stripped bare and so completely at his mercy. So she bucked, trying to fight her way to freedom, or at least a dark corner where she might lick her wounded pride.

"No way," he said against her ear. "No way are you leaving me to deal with the shreds you make of my life. We're in this…together."

He groaned with the last word, his cock twitching inside her as he lost control. He arched back, pumping her through his release, growling with frustration as his body won the battle over his will.

Jewel smiled. There was a triumph in feeling his seed flooding her. The feeling was so deep, it frightened her, but at the same time, her body jerked, a ripple of enjoyment going straight through her womb. It shocked her as she tried to claw the glass top of the table and hold on to something. Ramsey's hand was suddenly against her belly, pushing through the curls on the top of her sex and into the folds of her pussy. He found her clit and rubbed it, pressing on it with the perfect amount of pressure and friction to send her spiraling into climax. He held her down through it, placing another bite on her neck as she writhed and cried out. It was sharp and hard, the pleasure snapping through her like a whip. It left a sting that burned her insides while she panted and realized just how much she was sweating, because now her cheek was wet against the glass of the table.

"I love the way you come." He gathered her up, cradling her against his chest as he walked through the dark suite and somehow found his way into the bathroom. There was a red light that kept it from being a dark cave. Just the right amount of light to keep them in the dark and not shatter the mood.

"But I screwed up," Ramsey said as he turned on the shower. "I didn't use a condom."

The proof of that was on the top of her thighs. She stepped into the shower without waiting for the water to warm up. Ramsey was right on her tail.

"You have a flee response," he said as he hooked her around the waist and pulled her against him. The water was only slightly warm, and it felt cold against her heated flesh. "You're worth more than you give yourself credit for."

Whatever she'd thought he'd say, that wasn't it. "Excuse me? I'm trying to respect your wishes. I thought that was what you wanted."

"Don't fucking make excuses for me. You're worth a whole hell of a lot more than my kissing another girl the second you're away from my side. Shit…" he mumbled. "I want to be better than that, because you're…just… the kind of girl I gave up thinking would be interested in having me."

He kissed her, like he was trying to avoid any further discussion. She recoiled, needing to tell him what he meant to her, but he followed her, pressing a hard kiss against her lips and not stopping until she kissed him back. Determination didn't seem to be a relevant factor. Where her mind wanted to stick to her guns, her body was overly ready to get on with surrendering.

"I'm being a dick," he said when he lifted his head.

"No, not entirely."

He'd turned to grab the soap. She listened as he tore the paper wrapper off it, the scent of sandalwood teasing her nose.

"You're just disappointed in human nature," she said. He'd frozen, the soap held in the air between them, his fingers tight around the bar.

Jewel plucked it from his grip. "Disappointed in how many people want to ride your coattails"—she smoothed the bar across his chest, one side and then the other—"but more disappointed in how many of them think you don't earn what you have, and you've heard it said so much, you're starting to believe it. Don't."

"I get why you're considering the offer from Morcant," he said. "Still going to tell you the guy is trouble."

"I don't think he'd be successful if he wasn't a predator in the business world. I mean, that's part of it, isn't it? Accepting the job side of being an artist."

Ramsey took the soap from her and cupped her shoulder to turn her around. The water was warm now, but not hot. He washed her back, awakening a new craving for him as he stroked and lathered the soap across her shoulders.

"True," Ramsey agreed. He worked the soap lower, never hesitating when he reached her bottom. She shifted, uncertain, and heard him make a soft sound. "I always thought success would bring me happiness…"

"Hasn't it?"

He stroked the soap around her hip and onto her belly as he moved up behind her so he could wash her belly and move lower to her pubic hair. She shifted again, losing focus. "I can do…"

"I'm doing it." He closed his arms around her for a moment, imprisoning her as she battled mortification. "I made the mess, after all."

She groaned, certain she was going to die on the spot.

"Don't shut me out." His voice was low and needy. "You're right. Success has a disappointing side. I haven't wanted to admit it." He worked the soap through her pubic hair and between her legs. "Makes me feel like a wuss to cry about anything when I have so much."

"Feelings don't differentiate between tax brackets," she said.

He snorted and guided her beneath the water to rinse. She turned around to face him and took the soap from his hand. He didn't want to release it, and she ended up with half-soft soap oozing through her fingers as she increased the amount of pull.

"If you want it to just be us…here…together…it's my turn to wash you. I encouraged you to make the mess."

His lips twitched, and he released the soap bar. "I love your suggestions…"

It was cocky and so very Ramsey. She started to lather him up, noticing the way the soap held his chest hair against his skin. So many little details she was sure he wasn't willing to share with anyone else. Normal details that any other couple might have shared. It was a privilege, and she had to let down her own defenses for him to enjoy it too.

It was give and take on an epic scale, or at least it felt like it was rocking her to the foundations of her world.

His cock was hard again. She stroked it, covering it in lather before he backed up and let the water wash him clean. He shook his head, and his long hair flipped back, flinging water across her as she laughed. He emerged from the spray like the god she'd always thought him to be, moving toward her. Her insides tightened and her nipples drew tight with renewed arousal.

It was a slow stalk he clearly enjoyed. She backed up, taking one step at a time, finally ending up at the rear of the stall. There was a bench seat that he pressed her down onto with a half smile lifting his lips. It was all the warning she got before he sank down and cupped her knees.

"Now, for that course of pussy I was craving…"

Jewel found herself grateful for the stack of folded towels on the seat as Ramsey buried his face between her thighs and she fell back on her elbows. The soft terry cloth kept her from bruising her elbows, but she gasped.

And then moaned.

Ramsey pulled the folds of her sex wide and fastened his lips around her clit. He sucked the little nub without mercy, sending shafts of white-hot pleasure through her. He let it go only when he moved down her slit to the opening of her pussy, rimming it with his tongue before stabbing up into her.

"Mmm…" he growled against her flesh. "I love it…"

"You do…not!" she squeaked, still unable to completely believe him.

He lifted his head and looked up at her. A moment later he was standing in front of her. Whatever thought she'd been about to express died as his cock came into view. She reached out and stroked it, confidence surging through her when he sucked in a harsh breath. That sound fanned the flames of boldness. She clasped his length and pumped her hand down to the base, the water making it easy. There was another sound of male enjoyment, and she leaned forward to take the head inside her mouth.

Ramsey thrust toward her as she worked her hands along the length that didn't fit inside her mouth. She used her tongue on the sensitive underside of the head and enjoyed the way he grunted. His balls tightened as he neared climax, the slit on the top of his cock filling with the first few drops of his cum. She lapped it away and sucked more of him inside her mouth. He had a hand fisted in her hair as he bowed out toward her, every muscle in his body taut. His cock jerked, and he cursed and started filling her mouth with come. It was thick and hot, and she swallowed it as she let him pump though the release, pleased beyond words to know she'd taken him over the edge.

He sank down in front of her on his haunches, and she felt victory warming her. But he opened his eyes, showing her a warning.

"You enjoyed that," he accused softly.

She nodded, reduced to blunt honesty. Although maybe stripped was a better word to describe how she felt, because he had a way of ripping away everything she wanted the rest of the world to think about her, and left her facing herself.

"It's a control thing," he continued.

She had to agree again. One side of his mouth rose as she moved her head up and down.

"So," he said softly, "I'm not the only one with control issues in this relationship. But I do have them. Big time."

He scooped her up and carried her out of the shower. In some part of her brain, she was thinking about the fact that the water was still running. Ramsey didn't care. And neither did she when he placed her on the bed.

"I offered you my cock back there." He was standing next to the bed, watching her.

"You did." She'd risen onto her elbows, trying to decide what he was doing and only managing to feel exposed. It dawned on her that was exactly what he wanted. There was a pleased expression on his face and a gleam of anticipation in his eyes.

"Show me your pussy."

It should have sounded like a line from a lame pornographic movie. Instead, it twisted her insides and curled her toes. The bed had an ornate ironwork headboard. She took a deep breath and lay back, reaching above her head to grasp it. She was on her back, and pulled her legs up until her knees were over her breasts. Submissive, yet defiant as she hid her body from him.

"Tease," he accused her.

"You're going to wait for your treat," she warned him.

"The real question is, can you wait for yours?" he countered.

Her clit didn't want to. It was already throbbing, the knowledge of what he planned making her mouth dry and her pussy wet. She lifted her feet into the air, pointing her toes toward the ceiling. She felt the air against her sex, where fluid was seeping from her aroused body.

"Show it to me, baby," he drawled softly. "Give me submission."

She suddenly understood what people meant by the submissive being in control. At that moment, he waited on her. Seconds felt like hours as her respiration accelerated, her skin became ultrasensitive again, and her clit begged for the touch of his tongue.

More than tongue. He'd eat her out. And make her scream.

She parted her legs and opened them wide, letting her

feet touch either side of the bed in a straddle split. She quivered, feeling exposed and vulnerable.

And still, so very much in control.

"Perfection…"

The bed swayed as he crawled onto it, pausing on all fours as he contemplated her. Satisfaction glittered in his eyes and drew his features tight. It made him look dangerous, and she craved him even more because he was there, demanding her, when he might have had anyone.

He settled over her spread sex, his gaze lowering to it as he wrapped his arms around her thighs and pulled them wider. She jerked, an involuntary motion, and started to snap her legs closed. He made a soft sound and stroked the insides of her thighs, pushing them open again.

He leaned forward, capturing her folds in his mouth. She lost her train of thought as he tongued her clit. It sent a shaft of pleasure through her that didn't seem to have a beginning or an end, because he kept at her. Licking, sucking, stroking her sex but never giving her that last amount of pressure needed to send her into climax. Instead, he'd move away from her clit and rim the opening of her pussy, teasing it until she was ready to beg for an end to the torment.

When he gave her that release, every muscle she had was tight and aching from straining toward his mouth. He had two fingers deep inside her, thrusting up against her G-spot as he sucked her clit and let her explode. The orgasm twisted her, wringing her while she flopped against the bed. The only thing she saw was his head between her thighs as rapture jerked her into a spinning vortex.

She woke up to him lying next to her, brushing

the hair back from her face. Soft, gentle motions that touched off a tremor deep inside her heart. No one had ever made her feel cherished before. She reached up, catching his fingers, letting hers mingle with his. Time just froze and she had no idea how much time passed as they just watched each other. But he was hot against her and she finally shifted.

"Man, I miss my ceiling fan," she said. "And the bay breeze."

He snorted. "Hotels get stale." The bed moved as he climbed off it. He disappeared into the bathroom and turned off the shower. When he came back, he crossed to the large sliding doors and opened them to let in the night air.

"Too noisy?" he asked, his hand still on the handle. The sheer drape that covered the sliding door was blowing in like a bride making her walk down the aisle.

"Perfect." She rolled over and kicked the bedding down so she was on the sheet. She was sitting on the bed, hugging her knees to her chest when he came back to her. Uncertainty had her worrying her lower lip as he sat down beside her. They'd always ended up in bed as a result of passion. Now? The rush was satisfied, leaving them with whatever else they had between them. Something that was largely undefined. She still didn't know very much about him.

It was awkward—painfully so—until he reached out to stroke her arm, just his fingertips moving along her skin. She realized she could feel the calluses from the many hours he spent with his fingers on the strings of his instrument.

"Some women would have done that for my fame… to kiss my ass and get me to open my wallet…"

He locked gazes with her. "You called it right. I strip down in this room because I'm trying to shed that creature. I'm trying to get back in touch with who I am because I'm lonely and I believed fame would solve that problem for me."

"Fame has its advantages," she said. "It is more comfortable to cry in the seat of a Jaguar than on a city bus."

He snorted at her and flopped onto his back. She enjoyed the sound of his amusement, realizing it was a privilege to be around when he had his defenses down. He opened his eyes and looked at her.

"You see me because we're a lot alike." He crooked his finger at her. "Come here. We've never cuddled."

She felt her cheeks heat and ducked her head. He made a soft sound in the back of his throat before curling up and capturing her.

"You blush a lot," he groused as he took her back down with him, somehow managing to drag a sheet and blanket over them.

"You make me blush a lot," she answered as he curled around behind her, his legs tangling with hers.

"I like the sound of that," he whispered against her hair.

"Well…you don't have the right to be so exclusive." Her wounded emotions had decided to surface. "Not when I leave you alone for five measly minutes and find you lying across a bunch of pillows like some sultan preparing to enjoy his harem."

"I still want to be exclusive." He tightened his arm around her when she started to wiggle. "I want you to be all mine, no exceptions. Just…mine."

His voice was muffled by her hair, but she heard

the need in it. She shook, feeling that need herself.
She pressed back against him, even though they were
already locked together. She felt him quiver in response,
a kiss pressing against her temple before she let herself
believe the moment was real. Sleep claimed her shortly
after she stopped worrying about everything, taking her
away while Ramsey held her.

Epic.

Just epic.

The shower was running when she woke up. Jewel
rubbed her eyes and tried to decide if they'd left it running the night before. California-drought guilt helped
her wake up fast and remember Ramsey turning it off.

Not that she escaped drought guilt completely. They'd
played around in that shower for a good long time while
the water was running. Even out of the state, she felt a
pinch of guilt for having squandered natural resources.

Ramsey was warming up his vocal cords in the
shower. Jewel kicked her way free of the tangled bedding and went looking for the other bathroom. Her bag
was lying on the floor, her new phone chirping with a
message. She pressed her thumb against the screen to
unlock it, marveling at the upgraded security.

Not that it seemed to keep Ramsey from tracking her.

"Don't like it?"

She jumped, earning a chuckle from Ramsey. He
was standing in the doorway, toweling himself. He
was insanely attractive in nothing but skin and ink. She
indulged herself in a long consideration of his lean form
and the way the dragon wrapped around his hip line.

"It looks like I can do the additions," she said.

"No hurry," he cut her off. "We've got a show tonight, and tomorrow Sammy wants us to come by and cut a demo of the new song. Since Rage is gone, you can fly with us to Milwaukee. Sammy extended an invitation."

"He did?" Jewel asked skeptically.

Ramsey grinned. "I might have mentioned how happy it would make me."

"I see." She hadn't found any of her clothing yet, but stood up and refused to cringe. His eyes closed to slits, his gaze roaming over her as his features tightened in a manner that was becoming familiar. He liked what he saw, she knew it from the way his lips thinned and his eyes narrowed. It was the purest form of compliment, an honest reaction.

"You like it when I look at you."

Her cheeks reddened as he spoke. She shrugged.

"Don't do that."

There was a reprimand in his voice, but a caring one. He moved toward her, stopping only when he was looming over her.

"Don't think you're not worth my attention—" He touched his fingertip to her lips when she started to answer. "Don't make the mistake of lumping yourself into the hordes of fans who are into hookups."

"Well, they do seem to have a lot of confidence." Which she was feeling a lack of at the moment.

"So do you, Jewel," he said softly. "That's why you were waiting. Taz has been chewing my tail about it for a while now, but it took meeting you for it to sink in. Quality, not quantity."

His words sank in deep and warmed her entire core.

She reached out and grasped his cock, needing to stand up to him, to give as much as she received.

"I'm hoping that doesn't mean you're planning on slowing down on my account…" She stroked his cock, humming as it hardened to marble.

He made a low sound in the back of his throat before he shifted and looked around her shoulder, cupping it and turning her.

"You have ink," he drawled huskily.

"Be sort of odd if I didn't." But the fact that he was just noticing rammed home how explosive their relationship had been. It was their first true "morning after" moment in the bright light of day.

"It's Japanese." He fingered the symbol on her lower back.

"Yeah," she answered, shivering at his touch. "It means music."

He cupped her shoulder and turned her back to face him. "Why?" His voice was edged with emotion, his dark eyes glassy with it. She was shaking him down to his core.

"Because music is the only true universal language. It defines the human element, shows the nature of our spirits."

"Yeah, baby, it does," he choked out. For a moment, she gained a glimpse at the man inside him who was lost. He was looking at her, to her, for solace. She reached for him, settling her hands around his neck as she rose on her toes to kiss him. It was a sweet kiss, a tender exploration of the moment, an exchange of need and hidden fears.

He lifted her off her feet and pressed her against the wall, his cock buried in her to the hilt.

"You love it when I go slow, baby…"

The members of Toxsin knew how to get down to business. They rolled out of the hotel before noon and rode their Harleys up to Sammy's mega mansion. Unlike their stage personas, when they hit the recording studio, they had their hair back and their game faces on.

The music producer was in top form too, taking up a position of command in the control booth. Toxsin was behind glass, headphones covering their ears as they watched the screens for the music. Ramsey worked the strings of his instrument like the pro he was, fascinating Jewel with the raw talent coming out of him.

Tia slid up beside Jewel, her attention on Ramsey. "He is an animal. One hell of a good fuck. Better enjoy the time you have his attention."

Tia had chosen her moment well, waiting until Kate had moved off to the other side of the room to talk with Sammy.

"Is that why you took him to Spike?" Jewel asked.

Tia rolled her eyes. "He had it coming. You'll see. He's hot for your snatch now, but the moment he decides he wants a different flavor, he'll drop you." Tia's features turned mean. She squinted at Jewel like she was a cockroach, one she wanted to squash. "Unlike me, you won't have any way to get back into his world. You'll be rolled out to the curb like garbage." She made a gesture with her manicured fingers.

"I'll take my chances," Jewel offered as nonchalantly as she could.

Tia wasn't impressed. "Don't you wonder why he never told Sammy about Spike? It's simple, darling.

I'm part of his world. You don't have any connections,
just a pussy he wants to screw. He's not the first man to
get an itch for a good girl. For what it's worth, you'll
have a hell of a memory to take with you. Maybe that
will keep you warm when you end up married to some
cubicle troll."

Jewel's eyes narrowed.

"Hey now…" Sammy proved he wasn't as focused
on his conversation with Kate as he appeared. "No cat-
fighting in the studio. Take that shit outside."

Jewel offered him a smile. "Tia was just explaining a
few things to me."

"That so?" Sammy asked, his lips curling into a
smug grin. "Ramsey's a lucky dog. That's all I'm going
to say."

"Not that lucky." Tia was moving across the control
room, looking like some sort of fashion model. She
smoothed her hands over Sammy's chest and up around
his neck as she pressed her perfect little body against
his. "You're the only man I have eyes for in this room."

Sammy's hands cupped her hips for a moment, his
fingers spreading out over the curve of her butt before
Drake started marking the count with his drumsticks
again. The second he did, Sammy pushed Tia aside,
missing the glare she sent him.

Jewel almost felt sorry for her. She was only a toy.
Tia caught her watching and sent her a smug look, but it
was less than convincing.

Clearly she was right where she wanted to be. Better
to pity the people who felt the sting of her claws. Tia
made her way back, flashing Jewel a warning look.

"You're smart," she said after a long moment of

listening to the music. "Just don't be stupid enough to pull the 'bun in the oven' maneuver. A man like Ramsey will never be leashed. He enjoyed your cherry, just don't think you know shit about keeping him satisfied."

Jewel swallowed the lump that suddenly formed in her throat. There was a wealth of experience in Tia's eyes. It struck her as ugly, but at the same time, damned hard to ignore. "Unlike you, I wouldn't want to see him tethered."

Tia made a little humming noise before scoffing at her. "Glad you understand that. He's not going to think about things like birth control pills. That's your problem."

Victory flickered in her eyes before she sauntered off. The hairs on the back of Jewel's neck stood up as she looked up and found Ramsey watching her. The music playing was a recording. He frowned at her. She shook her head and sent him a smile.

But her belly was roiling, the urge to run to the bathroom and throw up nearly too much to ignore. She forced herself to quell it—there was no way Tia was going to scare her.

They'd been careless.

It was a blunt, harsh fact that horrified her.

And there was nothing she could do about it. Sure, she knew about the morning-after pill but rejected that idea instantly. She couldn't stop life, and if it was growing inside her, well, she'd just have to deal with it.

Even if Ramsey walked away.

<center>~~~</center>

"She upset you."

Ramsey didn't waste any time. The moment he could

break away, he tugged her down the hallway to the suite they'd used during the party. The swing was still there, and once again, she was distracted completely by Ramsey as he closed the door.

"Tell me what the bitch said."

"It doesn't matter—"

"The hell it doesn't," he said, cutting her off.

Jewel reached out and flattened her hand against his lips to silence him. "It doesn't. Being in a relationship with you means I have to deal with crap being said. And so do you. Wasn't the last headline about me being Syon's lover?"

He licked her hand. She jumped back, but not before a crazy twist of need went through her, raising goose bumps all the way down to her toes.

"I know you aren't messing around with Syon."

"So…what then?" she demanded. "Is this the real reason you have Steven trailing me?"

"Fuck no," he snapped. "You're redirecting, Jewel, and picking at me to avoid sharing your feelings with me. Answer the question."

He was right, and she didn't like it, largely because she didn't want to face her own reckless behavior.

"I can go ask Tia," he threatened. "She'll tell me in a heartbeat."

"Don't be a prick." Jewel drew in a deep breath. "She'll lie to you just as easily as tell you anyway."

He shrugged. "Maybe, depends on the topic."

Her insides twisted, her belly doing a little flip. Tia would happily blow the top off a subject so touchy. But her temper sizzled too. "I get your point on Steven. Don't go thinking I'll take your controlling me like that on matters that aren't about safety. If I'm not ready to tell you something, you don't threaten to go check up on me. Not when it's personal." She was drawing a line. Maybe it was risky, but she decided she wasn't going to be a doormat.

Ramsey cursed. "Jesus, Jewel...you're tearing me to sheds. Just tell me. I can't stand knowing you're upset. I want to help, be a part of...stuff. You're shutting me out."

He meant it. Her temper fizzled out, leaving her nursing guilt for being too chicken to share her concern with him. "It's stupid, and for the record, I'm trying not to whine. I do know how to pull up my big-girl panties."

"Not stupid if it upset you," he countered. "Tia is messing with you because of me, which was my screwup. So that means I'm going to stay right here until you tell me."

"You own your fuckups?"

He nodded once, firm and hard, with determination glittering in his eyes. "Spill it, Jewel, we're in this together."

It was his last word that broke her down. *Together*. It was an idea really, a shimmering concept that she was still too scared to accept as reality. She really should have had more pride, but the reality was, she was pretty sure she'd crumble like a dried-out sand castle if he cut her out of his life. So that meant trusting him. Jewel swallowed the lump lodged in her throat. "She was being a bitch—"

"She's good at that," he interrupted.

Jewel propped her hand on her hip. "Well, you're the one who dated her."

"Hooked up with. And in my defense, it was a little more like I didn't shove her off when she sat in my lap. I didn't chase her. Tia is a groupie," he explained. "You're the first woman I've dated since I was in high school."

"But she has connections," Jewel finished, feeling a little hollow and out of her league. Sure, she should have been able to hold on to her confidence, but she'd be lying to herself if she didn't admit to being just a little envious of Tia's ability to stay in Ramsey's world.

"Don't," he said firmly.

She'd been lost in her thoughts. "Huh?"

He reached out and flattened his hand on her chest. Just above her heart. "Don't think Tia has anything compared to this…connection between us."

She knew instantly what he was talking about. The current was there, his touch awakening her body. It was immediate and so strong, her breath caught.

Breathless. Yeah. That's what he did to her.

"I fucked Tia. She made the offer, and I took her up on it. I sure as hell never spent any time trying to impress her or find a way to keep her near me. I put off having you work on my ink because I don't want you to have a way to leave."

The admission shocked her, hitting her directly in the heart. It was the sweetest thing she'd ever heard. Ramsey pushed a hand through his hair in exasperation.

"What…did she threaten you with?" he asked roughly. "Please."

She was going to have to step up and meet him. Take a chance on letting him see her at her weakest.

"She…" Jewel got stuck, because her emotions were swirling around, making thought difficult. "She said it to be a warning, and I can ignore it, except…I realized the core point was something I should have addressed. That's what I'm dwelling on."

He reached out and cupped her shoulders, his face warning her he was just about out of patience with her hedging.

"I'm not on birth control," she pushed out. "And I lost my head the other night and…"

"Tia somehow knew you weren't on the pill?" he asked, his tone gone dead serious.

"No," she answered quickly, realizing his mind had instantly jumped to security. She saw the man he must have been in the Navy, his focus clear and unwavering. That sort of thing came only from knowing your life and those of your comrades hung in the balance. But she realized what Tia had known, and it made her stop.

Ramsey lifted her chin when she looked down while she contemplated.

"Tell me exactly what she said." His tone was deadly serious.

"Um…she knew I was a virgin. I didn't think a lot about it at the moment."

But she should have. "It's really weird the way she knows what's going on in your bed."

He grunted. "That's because I'm a meal ticket to her."

That made sense. Jewel nodded, but Ramsey kept her chin cupped in his hand. "So tell me how she threatened you."

"You're not dropping it, are you?" It was a pointless

question that earned her a half grin from him that was full of promise.

Well, no guts, no glory…

"She told me you'd dump me…"

He snorted. The little sound filled her with happiness. It was just there, in her chest like a huge bubble of joy. He read the realization right off her face, one side of his mouth lifting into a grin, but he held up one finger between them.

"And she said…what?"

"That I shouldn't try to hold you with a bun in the oven." Reality was killing the mood, puncturing that bubble of joy as she was forced to face hard facts. Standing still became impossible. She walked by him as she flung her hands into the air. "And I realized I should have done something about making sure…"

He caught her from behind, wrapping his arms around her and resting his chin on top of her head. "We."

He kissed her temple and smoothed his hands down her arms. "We should have done something, Jewel, not you. We are in a relationship. It's both our responsibilities to discuss birth control. And stop making everything so easy for me. I don't deserve that."

She turned around, cupping his cheek. "Yes, you do."

He captured her hand and kissed her palm. It was a soft press of his lips, but what hit her hardest was the way his hand shook. "No, I don't. But I'm going to start trying to be worthy of it."

She smiled, couldn't help it. Joy filled her, and a sense of tenderness she was positive she'd never felt before.

"Oh…man…" he groaned. "I really am a dick."

"Huh?" she asked, confused.

"I should have given you reasons to smile like that

before now," he said huskily.

The sound of his voice dropping hinted at growing passion. She recognized it and reacted, her nipples tingling as they drew tight. His gaze lowered to her chest, his eyes narrowing as his lips thinned.

God, she loved seeing that look on his face. It was a shot of pure confidence, making her bold.

"So…how does that"—she gestured with her thumb at the swing—"work?"

He made a low sound in the back of his throat. "You strip first."

"Hmm…" Jewel hummed as she lifted her bag off. She moved a little way back, enjoying the way Ramsey watched her. If that was vain, fine. Guilty as charged.

But it was also a total buzz.

His eyes glittered with anticipation as she smoothed her hands down her body and over her hips in search of the hem of her tunic top.

"Down to your skin," he clarified.

She found the hem of her tunic and pulled it up, not because she was submitting to him. Oh, no. Nothing was further from the truth. She was being brazen. The desire to wave the red flag in front of the bull raged through her. The night air hit her bare skin.

"It's so fucking sexy to know you don't have a bra on." He moved toward her, dropping his leather vest behind him so his chest was just as bare.

"I love knowing there is nothing but a layer of fabric between me and these." He slid a hand around her waist and leaned over to capture one of her nipples between his lips. She ended up arching back and over his arm as he tongued her nipple and sucked on it.

He surprised her by releasing her. "The rest."

There was the ring of authority in his tone. A touch arrogant, but it teased something inside her that made a curl of heat lick her insides. The intensity in his eyes had her pushing her leggings down.

She waited for him to strip, her gaze lowering to where his leather pants were tied. He chuckled, catching the laces with his fingers. Her mouth went dry, anticipation building inside her as he tugged the laces free and the leather opened. His cock was already swollen, the length pushing out the moment the leather no longer contained it.

"Nice." She reached for it, for what she craved. The skin was smooth and hot, but beneath that satin covering, the organ was as hard as stone. That curl of heat set fire to something, making her feel like she was dancing in the middle of a firestorm. Being naked didn't make her feel exposed any longer. It felt perfect, just perfect.

"Glad you like it," he whispered against her ear. "Because it's all you're ever getting."

He threaded his fingers through her hair, binding her with the strands and tipping her head back so their gazes locked. She felt the connection as much as saw it. His black eyes glittered with hard purpose.

"You're mine." It was a declaration and also a request. His features were drawn tight as he waited for her response.

Jewel stroked his cock, reaching down to the base and pulling her hand up to the head. "Then I guess you'd better let me do the additions to your ink, so I know you trust me."

He closed his eyes but opened them a moment later.

His lips curved slightly. "Later," he rasped out. "Right now, I want to put you in that swing."

His words had barely crossed his lips when he pressed a kiss against her mouth. A firm kiss that spiked the level of arousal boiling her blood, and anticipation was a living, breathing thing inside her. He scooped her up and carried her across the suite, his cock hard against her bare bottom.

The swing moved as he angled her into it. The straps were more comfortable than she'd thought they'd be, while the position in which they supported her body was far more intimidating than she'd expected. She was mostly on her back, reclining against the black straps, while the bars above her supported her weight.

"Hmm… I like the view." Ramsey cupped her knees and slid his hands to the tops of her thighs.

Jewel gasped, arching into the touch, her clit throbbing. Ramsey chuckled, the sound more a promise than anything else. He drew his hands back up her thighs, but with his fingertips set against her flesh like talons. His fingernails were clipped short, keeping her from getting scratched, which left her with nothing but the pure exhilaration of his touch.

"Claw me," she whispered. "Be the jungle cat I thought you were the first time I set eyes on you."

She was still exposed, still hanging in midair like bait, but she was also bold. Demand pulsed through her, and there wasn't going to be any tempering it with rational thought. When Ramsey made it to her knees again, she lifted her eyelids enough to see him.

His expression stole her breath.

It was a combination of need and conquest that defied

her entire comprehension of sex. He wasn't just contemplating appeasing his lust, he was set on claiming her on a much deeper level. He slipped his hands beneath her knees and lifted her legs into the air, all the way up so that her nose was hitting her thighs for a moment. With a slow motion, he spread them and let them down on the opposite sides of the straps that secured the swing to the bar above her head.

She gasped.

His lips lifted into a pleased grin. A damned cocky one too. She was spread open for him, the evening air touching the already wet folds of her sex. There was a second set of straps by her shoulders that she suddenly realized came equipped with bondage cuffs.

That made her shiver.

"Don't worry, baby…" he cooed softly as he teased the curls on the top of her sex. Each little hair was suddenly ultrasensitive. "I want to control you with my own hands."

It was a promise he didn't waste any time getting started on. "Great thing about swings is…the adjustability factor." He moved away from her, toward the wall. Ramsey pulled something off the small table that had all the sex aids on it. When he returned to her, he pointed a small remote at the ceiling, and the swing was suddenly lifting her. He stopped it when his head was directly between her spread thighs. She tried to close her legs out of instinct.

"Not a chance, Jewel." He teased her curls again before using his fingers to spread her folds away from her clit. "You know how much I like to eat you out."

His breath hit her clit, making her shudder, before he

leaned in and lapped her.

She cried out, her voice hitting the ceiling where the spotless mirrors waited to reflect everything right back at her. She ended up watching in fascination as Ramsey licked her slit, from the opening of her pussy to her throbbing clit. She felt it and saw it, the combination beyond anything she'd ever felt.

"Mmm…" he murmured against her clit, the vibrations adding to the stimulation. Her nipples had puckered, the mirror above her showing off their hardened peaks. He teased the opening to her body, rimming it with his tongue before licking his way to her clit and capturing the little nub between his lips.

She was straining toward him, lifting her hips as the need to climax nearly drove her insane.

"Not a chance," he warned her, looking up her body as he rubbed her belly with one open hand. "It's not going to be that simple tonight."

She shivered at the harsh edge to his words. She'd gripped the straps of the swing on either side of her shoulders, and suddenly realized she was holding on to the bondage cuffs. Ramsey noticed too. But he returned to the table, contemplating it for a long moment before he came back.

"Um…what's that?" She knew it was a dildo, but couldn't seem to keep the question from popping out.

"I'm almost jealous of it." He held up the glass dildo so she could see it. "But not enough to keep me from enjoying every last second of having you on the edge"—he looked up and locked gazes with her—"while I'm still clearheaded enough to not blow my load because my cock is lodged inside you."

She blushed. It was rather ridiculous, considering

they were having sex, but his blunt talk made her feel about as naive as a teenager.

He flashed his teeth at her before there was a hum, and the swing lowered. A moment later, she lost track of everything. At least as far as her thoughts went. There simply wasn't room in her brain for anything except what she was feeling. Ramsey teased her, stroking her belly and threading his fingers through her pubic hair. The first touch of glass against her folds was shocking. She jerked, and he soothed her back with a soft motion of his hand against her belly.

"It's sexy…" He sounded far away, and yet almost inside her head. She settled back into the hold of the swing as he slid the tip of the dildo across the edges of her labia. Sensation shot up into her belly, her clit feeling like it was about to pop.

"It's so damned sexy watching you…"

"Yeah…sure…" Her lips had gone dry. She swallowed and tried again, but he trailed the dildo across her folds again; this time, the smooth glass slipped easily between them, because of how wet she was.

"I am sure." Each word was hard and blunt. She lifted her eyelids to find Ramsey shooting her a hard look. "Surer than anything, I need to please you, Jewel. Need to ensure you never want another man. I don't just want you to be mine, I want you to believe you belong with me."

"I want it too." She tried to curl up, seeking a tighter connection with him, needing him deep inside her. The swing made it too hard. Ramsey pushed her back too easily. "I want you!" she demanded.

His features tightened. "But you could want me more…"

His gaze lowered to her spread sex. The determination glittering in his eyes made her belly knot. He was going to drive her past the edge of reason. It was both exhilarating and unnerving. But she lost all grip on thought as he teased her body, using the toy expertly, gliding it across her clit, through her slit, until she was sure she was going to climax just from a single touch. Only then did he insert it into her. The very walls of her pussy felt like they were trying to grip it. When he penetrated her to her core, she cried out, the sound deep and primitive, because he'd touched some spot inside her that seemed to have been made as a secret collection of nerve endings that were just waiting for him to discover.

"That's the spot." He withdrew the dildo and thrust it back until she jerked when he connected with the same spot. "Your G-spot. You like it….right…there…"

The term for the fabled sex promised land got through to her. Jewel opened her eyes, feeling like her eyelids were almost too heavy for the lifting, and caught the look of triumph on Ramsey's face. He pressed the dildo back into her, teasing her clit with his thumb as he rotated the toy against her G-spot.

She jerked, crying out as it felt like she was going to snap in two. She'd never needed to fuck so badly, never craved having the motion of a cock inside her so much. It was overwhelming, and she flung herself into it willingly.

"Fuck me." Her voice was loud, bouncing around the suite, and she didn't give a rat's ass. "Fuck me… *Now!*"

Ramsey looked up her body, triumph shimmering in his dark eyes. "Yes…ma'am."

The toy dropped to the floor with a clatter. There was

a slight hum as he lowered the swing again, right to the perfect height for him to impale her.

"Get me out of this thing," Jewel insisted, craving his weight on her.

"No way." He ripped open a condom and sheathed himself before he grasped her hips and seated himself to the hilt with one hard thrust. "You're mine right now. All mine."

He grasped the straps of the swing and pulled her toward him as he fucked. She loved every second of it. Their bodies met with a wet slap, and the room was filled with the sounds of their groans. There wasn't thought; there was only needy purpose. It seemed to root in the very walls of her cells. A part of her nature she'd never realized was there, just waiting for the right man to touch.

Ramsey let it loose. Set it free. Set her free. She strained toward him, fought against being controlled so completely, and finally cried out in rapture as he delivered on his promise. Was she conquered? Possibly. All Jewel knew was that she was twisting in the grip of something that could only be called rapture. It surpassed pleasure or climax. It was zenith. It wrung her and stole her breath and dropped her into the hold of the swing as Ramsey collapsed on top of her, his head falling to rest on her chest.

———

Ramsey cupped handfuls of the bubbling water in the spa and smoothed it over her shoulders. The moment was perfect, and yet her mind insisted on returning to the business of thinking, a major killjoy for sure.

"You need to let me do the additions," she said at

last, realizing she was being a coward by holding off the conversation.

He tensed behind her, cupping her shoulders. She turned around, straddling him, and the bubbling water teased her nipples. "I need to know if you'll ask me to stay."

"Christ," he cursed as he buried his head against her neck. "I'm a fucking coward."

He lifted his head back and looked into her eyes. "Stay with me. Please, Jewel."

His tone was needy, just as needy as she felt. She cupped his chin. "I will."

Something felt like it was lodged in her chest, and she realized it was a bubble of happiness. Oh, it didn't make any sense, there wasn't a bit of logic to be found anywhere, but it was there.

And she was not going to question it. Instead, she lifted up and sheathed his cock, taking refuge in the physical pleasure their flesh created. It was time to live in the moment.

And savor every second of it.

Because tomorrow wasn't promised.

"Epic."

Jewel had been chewing her lip as Ramsey inspected his ink. The additions had been challenging, but she realized she wanted to excel, because it was Ramsey. He turned in front of the mirror a few more times before looking at her. For a moment, she felt a connection between them that was unexpected.

Uncertainty.

She smiled back and realized it was an awkward

smile, which made her choke. Ramsey gave her a
harassed look. Jewel lifted her hands into the air. "I've
finally found something you've never done before.
Something you're a virgin at."

He snorted and turned to face her. "Something tells
me you're not referring to the ink."

"Our relationship." It felt like she'd pounded a gavel.
The silence in the room was heavy. "I hope you aren't
going to turn into a nice guy or anything."

He grunted but came across the room to settle in front
of her. He sank down on his knees and hugged her to
him, his head against her chest.

"I should," he said at last, his voice muffled.

"Should...what?"

He loosened his grip on her and looked up from
where he'd settled on his haunches in front of the chair
she was sitting in. "Become a great guy..."

He was thinking. She could see his thoughts buzzing
as he contemplated her.

"Come on." He was in action before he'd finished
talking. Ramsey jumped to his feet and yanked a T-shirt
off a hanger. The staff took their jobs seriously, even
hanging up T-shirts.

Ramsey shrugged into it, never giving even a stiff
breath over his new tat.

"You're an animal," Jewel said. "That has to at
least sting."

He had the shirt in place and was grinning at her
with an expression that she was pretty sure said "seriously?" "Okay. Okay..." She lifted her hands in mock
surrender. "Sorry I questioned your badassness."

"You should be." He pulled her bag off the chair it

was sitting on. "I feel the need to prove myself."

She snorted out a giggle. "Can't wait."

He had the outer door to the suite open for her. Once they were in the hallway, he captured her hand and pulled her toward the elevators. Steven opened his door as they passed, but Ramsey waved him off. "I'll take this watch." The bodyguard grinned as he reached up and loosened his tie.

"You need to tell him he can ditch the suit," Ramsey said when they hit the elevator.

"I did," she countered. "I think he's trying to keep up with Yoon."

Ramsey grinned. "Yeah. Yoon will die in that suit. His grandmother bought it for him when Taz got him the job."

"Well, I wouldn't want to mess with Yoon's grandmother. So I can't really blame Steven for not wanting to either."

A Harley was waiting outside the door, but Jewel hung back, tightening her grip on Ramsey's hand. "Your ink is fresh."

Ramsey tugged her toward the bike. "Told you before, sweetheart, I like to play rough." He swung his leg over the bike and jerked his head at her in invitation. "Scratch me a little, kitty cat. I promise only to bite when you're in the mood for it."

Her insides curled, anticipation prickling along her skin. She moved forward and joined him. The moment she wrapped her arms and legs around him, he took off into the Milwaukee evening, handling the bike expertly as the scent of his skin filled her senses.

Wherever she'd thought he was taking her, a public high school parking lot wasn't it. The dated building of the gym was painted with the school's mascot. It was a falcon of some sort, or maybe a hawk, the cartoon nature of it making it hard to interpret. Ramsey angled the bike and drove right through the closed gate and up to the entrance of the football stadium. The lights were on, the members of the football team down on the field in their sweats as the sound of the coach's whistle floated up to them.

"Come on. I want to introduce you to my past." Ramsey was off the bike and offered her a hand.

"You went here?" she asked, feeling slightly giddy, like she was being invited inside his secret sanctum for a peek at his personal secrets.

He nodded. "Spent plenty of sunsets on that field."

He came up behind her, wrapping his arms around her in what she'd come to recognize as the position he took when he was in the mood to let his personal guard down. It was a privilege, one she didn't take for granted. Below them, the football team continued to drill, the sun beginning to sink on the horizon.

"I like being here with you a lot more," he whispered against her ear.

"You must have had plenty of girlfriends."

He snorted. "I was a god among geeks, more nerd than the science fiction junkies. I put practice in Syon's parents' garage above dates."

"Come on, you were on the football team," she offered hopefully.

He shook his head, his chin rubbing against her shoulder. "Track. I ran sprints. The faster I moved, the sooner practice was over and I could get back to music. My parents insisted on sports."

Her gaze moved to the running track that went around the football field. There were a couple of youths taking turns timing one another.

"I wanted to run away and did my best."

She angled her hands up and rubbed his forearms. Wanted to reach back and soothe the teenager he'd been. Somehow help lift some of the pain away.

"Not that any kid at that age really understands what he wants anyway," he finished off in an effort to be nonchalant.

"You did," she answered softly. "You just needed time to catch up with yourself and make it possible for you to seek your own path. Parents do the best they can. Even if it seems like they aren't understanding."

He grunted and went silent.

"Does that sound mean you hate your parents?" Maybe she was digging deeper than he was willing to go, but the question just felt natural.

Ramsey shrugged behind her. "Nope, they hate me."

"No parent hates their child."

He was quiet for a long moment, and his embrace tightened. "Fine, they deeply disapprove of my life choices."

"You mean your music," she clarified. "I would imagine they were proud of your Navy service."

He nodded.

"I'm guessing you learned a lot of your vocals in a choir."

He laughed softly. "I can sing a hallelujah pretty good." He shifted, stroking her arms and inhaling against her hair. "Syon's parents let us listen to heavy metal. My parents had a meltdown when they discovered what they considered a lapse in parental monitoring."

"Like you wouldn't have found the music without that."

"Exactly," he agreed. "I can't recall when I heard it first, but I knew it was the music in my soul."

"I hear that," she said. "When you're on stage, or any-time really. But I realize I see your military training too. The first time I saw you perform, I thought you looked like you were storming that stage. Your training showed."

"I hated going, but you're right, that experience, being on the ground in a hot zone, it tightened things up inside me, gave my music an edge I'd only been faking before that."

They were quiet for a long moment, hearing only the sound of the coach's whistle. She felt the tension in him, the pain left from childhood that really needed to be dealt with. "Well, your parents just need to get past their objections. They don't have to share your taste in music. You will always be their son. Are they still in the area? Because if they are, you better have called them and tried to meet for lunch. Leave it up to them to reject you, but you gotta try. Right is right."

"And wrong is always wrong?" He laughed, but it was hollow and stung her. She ached for him, for the dark pit he was still dealing with where all the hurt of his youth was piled up.

"I'm serious. Our past shapes us, so don't let it make you bitter. You've used that part of your life to fuel who you are. You've got to appreciate that much, and the choir. You did learn how to play…right? And read music? Respect the need for practice? Without that foundation, what would you be?"

He moved so he could look at her. "You know, from anyone else, I'd call that a line intended to worm your way into my heart."

Jewel slowly smiled. "Oh…so you admit you didn't sell your heart at a pawn shop?"

His lips rose into a grin. "Maybe I went back and paid up, since I thought I might need it now."

She blushed and looked away. He reached out and lifted her chin with two fingers, bringing her gaze back to his. What she saw there stole her breath.

And hit her square in the solar plexus.

Ramsey leaned forward and kissed her. A sweet kiss, one reminiscent of high school sweethearts and full of all the uncertainty they both felt. But most important, his fingers trembled, and she shivered as she realized how truly important the kiss was.

It was a pledge of affection.

"Okay, we'll try it your way," Ramsey said while offering her a hand. When she was standing beside him, she caught the uncertainty in his eyes. "But you might regret it. Actually, I'm pretty sure you *are* going to regret it."

"Umm…regret what exactly?" She needed clarification, because the promise in his tone sent a ripple of apprehension down her spine. One thing she'd learned to trust Ramsey on was that the guy delivered in grand, over-the-top style.

His lips curved up. "Telling me to make up with my family, because there is no way I'm going in alone. You're my wingman. So gird your loins, I'm taking you to meet my parents. And just so you know, the last time I saw my mom, she was shaking a Bible at me."

Jewel felt her belly do a little flop, but she forced her lips into a bright smile. "No guts, no glory."

Ramsey was tense, his body tight as he rode the Harley through a residential neighborhood and around a corner to a house several decades old. He pulled up in front of it but didn't kill the motor immediately. The house was coated in fading paint. But the lawn was nearly flaw-less, hinting at attention. There were seasonal plants in the flower beds, and even a bird feeder hanging from one corner of the porch. A pair of finches flew into a large tree as they realized she and Ramsey were stay-ing. The birds voiced their displeasure at having their dinner interrupted.

"My mom feeds those. They peck on the kitchen window when the feeder is empty," he said.

"Sort of impressive, considering their brains must be the size of a gumdrop."

He grunted and killed the motor. Jewel climbed off the bike and waited for Ramsey. His expression was tight, his jaw set against the rejection he clearly expected. She decided he needed to be put out of his misery.

"Come on. Right is right, and wrong is wrong, and you are not the only person who struggles with impressing his parents. At least you aren't wearing a suit, like Yoon."

Ramsey snorted at her. "My mom would love it."

"But it would be a lie, and you're better than that."

He shook his head and grasped her hand before turn-ing and walking up the path that led to the front door. He pressed the button for the doorbell, and they heard it chiming inside the house. Seconds crawled by like hours as they waited, Ramsey's grip tightening on her hand.

There was a scuff and then a muffled word on the other side of the door before they heard the dead bolt turning.

"This is a surprise." Ramsey might have thought he didn't have anything in common with his parents, but he was definitely a chip off the old block. The man standing in the doorway was the image of his son, with thirty years of age on him.

"Hi, Dad," Ramsey said. "Is it a problem that I didn't call first?"

His dad grunted. "You know it isn't. I might disapprove of your life choices, but I never disowned you. Was hoping you'd come to your senses."

"My dad, Calvin Brimer," Ramsey introduced them. "Joan Ryan."

"Who is it, Cal?" a woman called from the kitchen.

"Matthew."

There was a clatter from the kitchen and a hurried step on the tile floor before a woman appeared. She was wearing an apron and looked over the rim of her glasses at them. Her lips pressed into a hard line, but there was a glitter of happiness in her eyes. "Well, don't just stand there in the door. About time my son came by to see his mother, instead of leaving me standing in a hotel lobby."

"We were going to fight that night, so I walked away before it happened."

His mother's face darkened, but she bit her lip and nodded a single time. "I was being a bit judgmental that night."

It seemed like some sort of peace offering, because the tension between them eased.

Calvin backed out of the way, pulling the door open

wide. Ramsey hesitated, but crossed the threshold with a death grip on their joined hands.

"I was just getting to making supper," his mother said. "Nothing fancy, but there's room at the table."

Ramsey suddenly drew in a deep breath. "Are you making scalloped potatoes?"

His mother cracked a smile, one full of motherly pride.

"She is," his father said as he closed the door. "And she still hasn't adjusted the recipe to serve only two. Looks like I won't have any leftovers."

"I'll make another batch tomorrow. It's not like I have any grandchildren to take up my time, despite all my prayers." His mother swept Jewel from head to toe. "And there is no ring on her finger."

The barbed comments started flying. Jewel accepted a glass of iced tea and tried to lend a hand. Mrs. Brimer deflected her attempts with impressive skill. Her husband had popped open a couple of beers as he stood just outside the open kitchen door, where a huge barbecue was sitting. Mrs. Brimer was quickly marinating a couple more steaks to add to the ones waiting to go on the grill.

"Those warehouse stores do have good deals on meat," she said. "Calvin loves steak, even though I tell him we don't need so much, now that both our children have abandoned us. It's not like Matthew even has a home, but that doesn't keep him from avoiding ours."

Ramsey spoke slowly over the top of his beer. "Jewel...*Joan* made sure I knew today was a good day to start on new habits."

His mother turned to consider Jewel. "Jewel, is it? You don't respect the name your mother gave you either?"

"Actually, my grandmother started calling me her

precious jewel when I was about three. My mom said I decided it was her special name for me. She died a little while after that, and I wanted to keep the name to remember her by."

Ramsey's mom smiled. It was only a half smile, but her lips were curved nonetheless. It transformed her face. "Well, I suppose that's a fine reason. And your mother agreed." She nodded, like she was trying to convince herself it was acceptable to bend on the issue. "Yes, that's fine, I suppose."

There was a sizzle as Ramsey's dad laid the steaks on the grill. Ramsey had taken to leaning against a support beam to the shade canopy that covered part of the patio. There was an ominous crack before he straightened up. He reached out and pushed on it experimentally. "I'll get someone out here to replace this." He was taking charge, as he so often did, but his father's eyes narrowed with injured pride.

"So now our house isn't good enough for you?" Calvin Brimer growled.

"Can't I step up and lend a hand when I see a need for it?" Ramsey countered. "Be a good son?"

"What you can do—"

"Hey, would you two fight over something important already?" Jewel interrupted. Calvin looked like she'd pulled up her top and flashed him, while Ramsey cocked his head to the side and tried to decide what she was up to.

"And what might that be?" Calvin Brimer demanded as he brandished a long, stainless steel spatula at her.

"How long to grill the steaks," Jewel answered

without skipping a beat. "Isn't that the age-old battle of men who are in front of the grill?"

Ramsey hid his grin behind his beer bottle, but Jewel was pretty sure his father saw it when he turned to glare at him. There was a long moment as Calvin contemplated his son and the meat sizzled. Jewel held her breath, and she realized Mrs. Brimer had gone still in the kitchen. Calvin suddenly sniffed and pointed at the grill with the spatula. "Not going to be any debate. I've grilled about ten thousand more steaks in my time than either of you two youngbloods. Daddy's doing the turning tonight."

———

Ramsey stripped the second they made it back to the suite. He left a trail of clothing on the way to the mini fridge, but all he did was stand with the door open as he contemplated the contents.

"You don't want that," Jewel said softly.

The suite was dark, just a little light coming through the sliding glass door. The city lights cast his features in silver and shadow when he turned to look at her.

"You're sick of covering up your feelings," she continued as she pulled her tunic dress up and over her head. The door of the mini fridge closed with a soft sound as he turned completely toward her. She gained a full glimpse of his nude body, the perfection of his form and his erection.

Hard.

Basic.

He needed to be free, and that meant fulfilling his appetites. All of them, without excuses or explanations.

She pushed her leggings down and stepped out of

them. Reached up to tug off the two ties she had holding her hair. The ends were just long enough to brush her bare shoulders.

"You want—"

"You," he rasped out, cutting her off with a kiss that was just as hard as his cock. Jewel kissed him back, taking as much as she received before she pulled her head back and locked gazes in the dark.

"You want me…to invite you to be yourself…with me."

"Yes." He sucked in his breath and buried his face in her hair, inhaling the scent of her skin as his cock twitched between them. "Yessss…" He grunted as he pressed a kiss against the sensitive skin of her neck and then another one and another.

Jewel threaded her hands through his hair and raked her fingernails across his scalp. He reared back, the muscles along his jaw tight and corded.

"Claw me," he demanded.

She pulled her talons down his back, and he let out a low sound of primal enjoyment. She felt him shudder, her body melting in response. Skin to skin, she couldn't stay still, had to rub against him as the need to be closer nearly drove her insane.

"Fuck me." She punctuated her demand with a thrust of her hips against him. "Right now…right here."

He flashed his teeth at her, the grin primitive, savage, and so damned exciting, she was sure she was going to climax on the first thrust. Ramsey followed her to the floor, spreading her thighs with his body.

"Hard," she instructed in a breathless whisper that came from some place deep inside her where her cravings lived. "Do it…*hard!*"

She was fixated on him, time moving slower than normal as he came closer, closer, until she felt the warmth of his body on her skin. His cock touched her, sending a jolt of excitement through her. It tore away everything except the need to be joined with him. She curled up, intent on taking hold of him.

"Mine…" he growled as he captured her wrists and pinned her to the floor with her hands stretched out over her head. "Tonight…you're mine…all…mine."

She strained toward him, desperate. He didn't deny her. There was an arching of his body over hers, and then the hard thrust of his hips as he impaled her.

"Oh…*yes*…" she cried out. There was no controlling the level of her voice as he stayed embedded in her and slowly bit her neck.

It was a soft bite, merely hinting at discomfort. But it was the last component needed to send her spiraling into climax. He held her down through it as she strained to get closer to him. The pleasure burned through her, dropping her abruptly when it was finished with her. She was breathless, her chest heaving as she tried to pull in enough oxygen to keep up with her racing heart.

"And now…for round two," he whispered against her ear. She shivered, feeling too overloaded to engage in another climb up the ladder of arousal.

"I don't think…I can…"

"Then let me lead the way, baby." He leaned back, taking his weight off her clit, and settled on his haunches. He grasped her hips and pulled her toward him as he thrust into her spread body. His cock tunneled into her, teasing her G-spot with just enough pressure to rekindle her need.

He took her up slowly, pinning her beneath him only when she was once again mindless with the need for release. It was more than sex; it was intimacy on a level that scared her as much as fulfilled her. It showed her in blunt clarity how alone she'd always been in life. There, in the dark, after they'd both spent, Ramsey pulled her close, close enough she was sure he was touching her soul.

Chapter 7

SOMEONE BANGED ON THE DOOR OF THE SUITE JUST after noon. Jewel managed to open her eyes as the bed moved and Ramsey lifted his head.

"Chow!" Syon called from the other side of the door.

Ramsey had a hand on one of her breasts as she lay on her back in the middle of the bed. His cock was hard against her thigh, but she groaned as she realized how sore she was; one little attempt to move sent an ache through her. She lay still as she tried to decide how to gather up enough resolve to leave the bed.

Ramsey's lips curled back into a smug grin.

"Ha-ha," she groused as she sat up and rolled over the side of the bed. "Bet you won't be so satisfied with yourself when you realize you aren't getting any for a bit."

He smacked his lips and flipped over so he was lying on his back, braced on his elbows and giving her a million-dollar view of his buff body. His cock was standing rigid, but it was the look of victory in his eyes that made her reverse course.

"Two can play that game," she warned a second before she dove back onto the bed and grasped his length to lick it from base to tip.

"I love letting you kick my ass in this game."

They had to order a second round of breakfast

by the time they made it over to Syon and Kate's suite. Drake and Taz were hanging out as well, the scent of pancakes and hash browns filling the air. Ramsey dropped a packet of painkillers in front of her, making her cheeks heat. Taz reached over and whacked his ear.

Ramsey jumped and turned on his bandmate. Taz greeted him with a raised eyebrow. "Don't mess up."

"He's not," Jewel assured Taz. "Even went to see his parents last night."

There was shock all around the suite. Ramsey shrugged and dove into a mountain of scrambled eggs he'd dumped Tabasco sauce over.

Taz suddenly smiled. "See? I'm right to tell you not to mess it up. Jewel is a keeper."

"Which means everyone can turn their attention on you," Ramsey retaliated with a smack of his lips.

Taz's expression became guarded as the other members of Toxsin took the opportunity to laugh at his expense. He shook his head. "I'm not the one with the commitment issues. Joi is."

Jewel was itching to ask who Joi was, but a warning look from Ramsey made her reach for a piece of toast instead. There was a knock on the door before Brenton appeared.

"How are we feeling today?" he asked brightly. "Ready to rock? We've got a packed stadium to play."

The buzz in the room started to build. Jewel enjoyed being part of it. The members of Toxsin began to put on their game faces as they scattered to their suites to shower and begin the trip to the stadium. Ramsey kissed her good-bye before running down the hall to dive into an elevator with Taz. The hotel lost its homey feeling with their departure, becoming more of a lonely building. A necessity of success.

Her phone buzzed, showing Bryan Thompson's number. "Hello?"

"Good evening, Ms. Ryan, Bryan Thompson here. Mr. Morcant is hoping you have time to meet with him tonight."

There was a tingle on the nape of her neck—the timing of the call was just too perfectly matched with Ramsey's departure. Jewel shook it off, realizing that she really didn't have the right to be picky. A mega offer was a mega offer.

"I do," she answered clearly.

"Excellent," Bryan replied. "A car will call for you, say around six?"

"Great."

She ended the call and ordered herself to look forward to the meeting. Being in a relationship with Ramsey didn't change her dreams of having her own career. In fact, she needed to be her own person more, because the last thing Ramsey needed was a woman trying to ride his coattails. It would be too simple to get lost in the whirlwind of his bigger-than-life persona. Caught in that gravitational pull she'd noticed about him the first time they'd met.

Yeah. She was going to her meeting with Quinn Morcant, and she was going to give his offer serious consideration. Because there was no way she was only going to be Ramsey's toy.

No matter how much she enjoyed being played with. The reason was simple. She needed to be his match.

When Jewel made it down to the lobby at six, she had the contract offer in hand. It was decorated with high-lighter now, questions written into the margins. Steven followed her silently until he spied the uniformed driver waiting in the lobby, holding a card with her name on it.

The bodyguard stepped into her path. She was so used to him trailing her, his action surprised her. When she locked gazes with him, she realized she'd misjudged him completely. Steven often came off as a happy-go-lucky guy. It had been a mistake to think Ramsey would have hired anyone who wasn't deadly skilled. She was looking straight at that reality now. And Steven was making it clear she wasn't going any-where until he approved.

"Sorry," Jewel started. "I'm a little new to having someone along with me. I have a business appointment this evening with Quinn Morcant to discuss the proposal he has made."

As far as explanations went, it was polished and pro-fessional sounding. But she still felt off balance and wet behind the ears.

Well, straighten up, girl. Opportunities are calling.

Steven considered her for a long moment. "We need to work on communication, Ms. Ryan."

"Yes. My fault," she admitted.

He turned around to look at the driver. "Ms. Ryan has her own car at her disposal. I'll see that she arrives."

The driver wasn't amused. For a long moment, there was a stare down that had the hotel security moving closer. Morcant's driver finally reached into his jacket pocket and withdrew a business card. Steven plucked it from his fingers before lifting up his cell phone and tapping something into the screen.

He held his tongue until she was settled in the back of a dark-windowed sedan that appeared in front of the hotel fast enough to make her realize she had been selling Steven short. The guy was a polished professional.

"I hope you understand why it isn't a solid idea to get into a car with a stranger?" Steven asked softly.

Too softly, because she heard the judgment in his tone loud and clear. "I'm a little new to the lifestyle."

Steven pulled something from his jacket pocket. It looked like a hair ornament. He held it up. "Press the center, and it sends a signal to my earpiece." He demonstrated. "And I won't ask any questions before I extract you. To be clear, there won't be any conversation until I have you in a secure location. You'll move under your own power or mine."

"So 'oops, I didn't mean that' isn't something you want to hear?"

He shook his head with a menacing look. Jewel held out her hand. "Got it." She slid it into her hair and made sure it was secure. "No oopsies."

Steven returned to what she'd come to consider his normal expression. Guess that meant her apology was accepted. But she was still left feeling a little hollow, like she had no clue what she was doing.

Well, she was going to have to learn.

Fast.

Because she was going to be her own woman. She loved Ramsey for the no-excuses artist he was. Didn't fucking care she was admitting she loved him either, because it only fueled her determination to make sure she was someone he'd be proud to have near him.

His counterpart.

The car pulled into traffic as she opened the contract and focused on the meeting ahead.

～～～

"Jewel is good for you," Taz said from a makeup chair.

"Can't believe she got you to go see your parents," Syon added from where he was fingering the strings of his guitar.

"Believe it." Ramsey made his way across the performers' backstage room to pick up his own guitar. "That woman holds awesome powers of persuasion. It was good. My mom even fell into line. Sort of. She didn't bring the Bible out, anyway."

Syon looked shocked for a moment before he slowly smiled. "The fans are going to be devastated."

"Yup," Ramsey confirmed.

His decision felt right.

So damned right it scared him, but in a good way. It had been too long since he'd had something in his life that he was afraid to lose.

But Jewel had been worth the wait.

～～～

The car delivered her to another posh, upscale hotel not too far from where Toxsin was staying. A huge revolving door was centered in front of it. Steven took her through it, insisting on walking ahead of her. Inside the lobby, there were polished marble floors and desk personnel in bottle-green suits.

A woman in a smart brown suit was waiting for her. "Good evening, Ms. Ryan, I'm one of Mr. Morcant's assistants."

It was an obvious tactic, replacing the burly driver with a less intimidating female. Jewel didn't buy it for a second. There was a sharpness in the woman's eyes that said she was every bit as capable as the driver, even if she was wearing a skirt.

Well, mostly because of the skirt and the fact that the woman looked a little unaccustomed to it.

She was suspicious, but decided it was a healthy approach to take into a meeting with one of *Forbes*'s most eligible bachelors. Quinn Morcant wouldn't be giving anything away, so neither would she.

"This way please."

The assistant didn't blink an eye as Steven followed them. She took Jewel to a private elevator that required a key card. She swept it through the card slot, and the elevator door opened.

She led the way forward, inserting a key into the control board of the elevator before the doors would close. There was a soft hum and vibration as the car engaged and pulled them upward. The doors opened into a very nice entryway. The assistant swept the key card a final time to open a pair of double doors.

"I'll show your escort to our waiting lounge," the assistant stated firmly.

Steven sent her a look before he followed the woman through another door. Jewel was left standing in the entryway, facing a pair of doors that just might lead to her future. She tightened her grip on her resolve and reached for the door. There wasn't much use in knocking. A man with a personal assistant certainly wouldn't be in the dark on just where his appointment was.

She hesitated two steps inside the door. There was music playing in the background, and a table set up for dinner.

"Excellent." Quinn Morcant didn't waste the opportunity to let her know he noticed her shock. He was watching the doorway from a position near the floor-to-ceiling windows that made up two sides of the room.

"My plan to impress you is working." He had on a three-piece business suit that was expertly tailored to his body; there was also a slight Scottish lilt to his voice, making the "you" sound more like a "ye." Damned if that didn't tickle her just a little.

She pushed herself forward, repeating her self-imposed dictate to face him head-on. "I didn't realize it would be a dinner meeting."

Quinn had closed the distance between them, allowing her to see how blue his eyes were. Oh, hell, he was Scottish through and through, in that way every girl fantasized about after reading a Highlander romance novel.

"Can hardly keep you during the supper hour without feeding you." He held out a hand. Jewel took it, thinking he meant to shake. Instead, he lifted it to his lips and pressed a kiss against the backside of her fingers.

Man, it was suddenly clear how the man had made it onto the *Forbes* list. Eligible didn't even begin to describe him. There was a vibe to him that sent a shiver down her spine.

"I see you've gone through my offer," Quinn continued as though she wasn't standing there frozen.

"Yes." Her brain fired up as she lifted the contract

between them. Quinn plucked it neatly out of her hands and dropped it on a nearby table.

"After supper," he declared softly, but not so softly that she didn't hear the ring of authority in his tone. The guy was used to commanding everything around him, and she got the distinct impression he enjoyed it.

There was no way she was going to let him steamroll her. "Sounds delightful," Jewel said, her confidence coming to her rescue. Quinn was charming and over the top, but she realized he didn't steal her breath.

Only Ramsey could do that.

"Excellent." Quinn actually held a chair out for her. "I like to get to know people before jumping into bed with them."

He was testing her. Using the word "bed" instead of business. Jewel sat down. The moment she did, a waiter appeared with a bottle of wine. Quinn settled down across from her, but she wouldn't say he sat down. He swung his leg over the chair and settled onto it. There was something less than civilized about the motion.

"I tend to take that approach in business myself," she added. The waiter had opened the wine and poured out a sample for Quinn. He smelled it before tasting it.

"Perfect." His speech slipped into a burr again. The waiter filled both their glasses before moving away on silent feet. Quinn lifted his glass. "To new ventures, Ms. Ryan."

—⁓—

Ramsey rubbed a hand over his face, happy to be free of his stage makeup. He was still pulsing from the show, his blood up. Brenton appeared, but it was the set of the man's body that drew a second glance from more than just Ramsey. Syon, Taz, and Drake all turned to look at the road manager. There was something serious on his mind.

Dead serious.

"Sammy called," Brenton began.

"And?" Syon prompted him when he fell silent.

"Someone tipped him off," Brenton responded. "Claims Jewel went to a dinner meeting with Quinn Morcant."

Ramsey eyed Brenton. "He's trying to contract her art work." It was the right thing to say, but he didn't like it. It meant Jewel was out with another man. A thick wave of jealousy crashed into him.

"Sammy's source claims she's there selling your new piece of music." Brenton dropped the real reason he was so tense.

"Bullshit," Ramsey said.

"I don't think so," Taz agreed.

"Neither do I." Syon added his two cents' worth.

"Jewel doesn't roll that way," Drake stated firmly.

"Well, Sammy thinks so. It's a good source. She had opportunity."

"So…she's guilty?" Ramsey countered. "Was that source Tia, by chance?"

Brenton's eyes narrowed. "Don't know."

"Well, find out," Ramsey shot back. "Because Tia started in on Jewel the second she could, and Tia isn't one to quit while she thinks she's ahead. Someone is feeding her information. She knew Jewel was a virgin."

"That's not good," Taz said. "It's someone with top-floor access."

"I'll get on that," Brenton added.

Quinn Morcant was smooth and as much of an appreciator of the ladies as Ramsey had been himself. He suddenly realized exactly what sort of asshole he'd been. "I'll go find her," he said.

"Wait for me," Syon insisted, but Ramsey was already on his way out the door of the performers' area. The press was camped out, flashes going off as he emerged. For the first time, he felt crowded. There was something hollow about it all, and he realized what he was feeling was fear.

Fear that all he was going to have was his rock-star life.

It wasn't enough.

Shit.

His parents were right.

Jewel's head was spinning when she made it back down into the car. Steven was watching her, but Jewel had her hands full trying to keep her thoughts together. Quinn was cutthroat. A business shark that made normal sharks look cute and cuddly. She'd taken to sipping the wine in an effort to maintain her wits. The trip back to the hotel wasn't long enough for her, and she was still struggling to sort her thoughts into order as she headed into the lobby.

"Why did you go see Quinn by yourself?"

Jewel jumped, looking up to find Ramsey bearing down on her.

"I was discussing the contract offer he sent me." The paparazzi were surging to life, the scent of a fight rousing them. Jewel walked through the lobby toward the elevators, because Ramsey was tense, clearly spoiling for a fight.

She made it into a car, but Ramsey followed her. He pointed Steven toward another car before the doors slid shut.

"What are you doing jumping on me like that?" she asked the second the doors shut. "Couldn't you wait? Or maybe…trust me?"

"It looked bad," he continued, as though she hadn't spoken. "Really bad that you went alone to see someone you know is in direct competition with my producer."

"So that's why you're barking at me in front of half the crew, like I was stepping out on you?" She bit back her temper and dug deep for some patience. "It was a business meeting, about my career."

Ramsey scowled at her as the doors opened on the top floor. "A meeting that smells like it included wine."

That stopped her in the middle of the hallway. She turned around, unbearably conscious of the fact that they weren't alone. She struggled to make her tone even. "The last business meeting I went to with you included naked people in the pool and a topless woman in a shoe-string bikini bottom kissing you. I'm not planning on coat-tailing my way through life, which is exactly why I went to the meeting. To discuss my art."

She was losing it. In some corner of her mind, she realized he was jealous and lashing out at her. Jewel turned on her heel and headed down the hallway, away from the suite she shared with him. She ended up in a conference room, reaching for the sliding glass door and pulling it open for air.

She needed air!

It was just a misunderstanding.

Like hell. It was an epic failure on his part not to

trust her. Her phone buzzed, and she reached for it. Her mother's number flashed on the screen. She opened the line, desperate for a distraction. She didn't want to face the fight she was having or its destructive implications. Suddenly, all of the confidence she'd had in her relationship with him went dead like a jet engine that just stopped in midair.

Just falling, and all the time, she was aware of her impending death when she hit the ground.

Ramsey was suddenly there, pulling the phone out of her hand. "Whoever it is, they can fucking wait."

He punched the power button on the phone, killing it completely, and dropped it into a chair.

"That was my mom."

He froze, her statement impacting and making it through the haze of jealousy holding him in its grip.

"And we are not talking about this now." She held a hand up between them. "I am way too pissed off and you're…" Words failed her.

"I'm jealous," he confirmed. "Aren't you happy?"

"What?" she asked in a hollow whisper. "How could I be happy to see that you don't trust me?"

"Morcant isn't just anyone," Ramsey continued. "The guy could charm the habit off a nun."

"Oh…so I'm expected to understand when I come out of a restroom and find you lying across a bunch of pillows and kissing someone, but how dare I have a dinner meeting with a man who is equally as attractive as Vicky?"

"Someone said you gave him our new music piece."

She felt like he'd punched her in the chest. Her heart just stopped between beats. "How can you even say that to me?"

The other members of the band were in the doorway. "I would have walked out of the meeting if he'd even asked!"

"I had to bring it up, because someone told Sammy about your meeting with Quinn."

His face was red, but she interrupted him before he got out his next argument.

"That is such lame logic. You should be smart enough to realize Tia is just trying to clear me out of her way," she said. "We need some space to cool off."

"Agreed." Syon was suddenly there, along with the other members of Toxsin. Ramsey snorted, but realized he wasn't going to win. In some corner of her mind, Jewel discovered herself admiring the way the members of the band came together to help one another. Taz and Syon were muscling Ramsey out of the room, while Drake offered her a key card and gently guided her down a different hallway.

"I'm fine," she informed him, and swallowed when she realized how sharp her tone was. "Really. Thanks for the key card. I'll be fine."

Kate was hovering as well, considering her with a critical look before nodding. "Give me a ring if you don't want to drink alone."

"Yeah." Jewel slid the key card through the slot and pushed in the door. Inside the room, there was blissful privacy, but it rang with a silence that was nearly deafening.

She sank down onto the bed, reeling from the way life had turned a full one-eighty on her in less than the space of a day. She was back to being on her own, and the reality of it was overwhelming.

And too painful to face. She lay back as she lost her battle against her tears. They slid down the sides of her face as she felt the flames consuming the wreckage of her relationship with Ramsey.

He didn't trust her.

Didn't see her as anything but an ornament decorating his life.

Maybe they could come back from the trust issue. It could be excused by the newness of their relationship.

But she had to be her own person.

Knew it and felt it burning in her gut so badly, there was no way she was going to abandon her art. She'd know she was a sellout, and someday Ramsey would see it too.

Tia would end up calling things right.

He'd leave her because she wasn't his partner. Loving someone meant taking them the way they were. Not trying to change them. But true relationships needed to be balanced. She couldn't be his poor, rescued, starving artist forever.

Which sucked on an epic scale, because she loved him.

"Getting drunk isn't the answer," Taz said.

Ramsey wiped his mouth on the back of his hand, an empty bottle already sitting on the table beside him. "Last time you saw Joi, it worked for you."

"The difference is, Joi refused to leave that restaurant with me," Taz countered as Ramsey tipped the beer bottle back and drained it. "Jewel is here, and smart enough to know when to walk away and let both your tempers cool off."

"So…I'm chillin'." Ramsey chucked the bottle in the direction of the trash can. "Get lost. I'm a big boy."

"You're a big something," Taz said without moving off the sofa. "But I'm staying. Team code. When one of us gets drunk, he gets a wingman."

Ramsey flopped back onto the floor, staring up at the ceiling as the alcohol numbed his brain. He shouldn't have guzzled it. That was his last clear thought before it stole his wits, leaving him prey to the regrets his temper had shielded him from, and too intoxicated to physically do anything about it. Like get his ass down the hall and beg Jewel to forgive him.

"I'm an asshole," Ramsey informed the ceiling.

"No argument."

"I need to tell Jewel," he said as his words slurred.

"When you sober up," Taz replied.

Ramsey rolled onto his side. "It was only a couple of beers." But the room was spinning.

"And two shots of rye," Taz enlightened him. "Only place you're going is to the throne room."

"I never puke."

But an hour later, he wished he had. The room spun, and his belly knotted from the poison he'd ingested. The thing that tormented him the most was the fact that he was helpless to remedy his actions while his system was dealing with the alcohol.

"Tomorrow, I'm going on the wagon," he informed Taz.

"Told you, Jewel is good for you."

"Yeah," he agreed. "Got…got to straighten up." Ramsey turned onto his side and tried to fix his gaze on Taz. "Kick my ass…if I mess up?"

Taz slowly smiled. "You got it."

"Thanks."

Jewel deserved better from him, and he was going to make sure she got it.

—⁓—

The phone in her room rang at two in the morning. Jewel woke with a start, fumbling for the receiver in the dark.

"Hello?"

"Ms. Ryan?" someone far less groggy asked on the other end of the line.

"Yes." She rubbed her eyes and squinted at the bedside clock. Yup, it was two in the morning.

"This is the front desk. Could you come down to the lobby please?"

"Huh?" she asked.

"I am sorry, but there seems to be some concern over your well-being, and I would like to maintain the privacy of the top floor." The manager sounded stressed beyond his limits. "There is someone here claiming to be your mother, and she is insisting on seeing you, or she intends to call the police to investigate the matter."

"My mom?" Jewel asked as her brain started to function. "I'll be right down."

Jewel was suddenly wide-awake, the severed phone call clear in her mind. She was a rotten daughter for not making sure her mom wasn't worried about her. She flipped on the light in the bathroom and wiped her face with a washcloth before dragging a brush through her hair a few times.

She felt the tension the moment she got out of the elevator in the lobby. There were four members of hotel security standing near the front desk, clearly trying to keep someone there. There was a very familiar sounding "harrumph" before her mother pushed through them.

"Mom, what are you doing here?" Jewel asked, even though she already knew the answer.

Her mother stopped two paces in front of her and propped her hands on her hips as she scanned her from head to toe with a knowing eye. "Being your mother."

The security force was still standing in place, the manager wringing his hands. "We're good," Jewel said.

The manager didn't look appeased.

"Don't placate him," her mother said. "He's just worried his rock star guests will have a problem with me showing up to keep them from abusing my daughter."

"I'm not being abused," Jewel insisted.

"Well then, you can explain why someone cut off a call, and you didn't answer when I called back." Her mom was in full mother-hen form. "You know my feelings on oppressive relationships."

"Yeah…" Jewel reached out and hugged her mom. "I'm fine, and I'm so sorry I didn't call you back. I fell asleep."

Her mother pegged her with a knowing look. "Fell asleep crying."

Jewel didn't bother to lie. Her puffy eyes betrayed her anyway. Her mother suddenly abandoned her defensive mode in favor of being the compassionate shoulder Jewel desperately needed. "Come here and tell me what happened."

Jewel indulged in a long hug, but pushed away when tears flooded her eyes. "I can't. Not just now. I need to sort out my feelings."

Her mother made a low sound under her breath.

"Well then, are you coming home with me? No better place to think things through."

It was a good idea.

And yet, it filled her eyes with fresh tears. Jewel blinked them away as she tried to get a grip on her emotions. Her mother made a low sound under her breath.

"Come on," her mother said in a firm yet understanding tone.

Jewel let her mom take over. She knew she was being a coward, but the wounds on her heart were just too fresh for her to do anything but stumble through life. She didn't want to see the suspicion on the band's faces. Not on the men she'd come to think of as friends.

But what she really wanted to escape from was Ramsey. She was being a chickenshit. Sure. She knew it, freely admitted it. The reason she followed her mother out of the hotel was that she just couldn't lose what was left of herself. If she saw Ramsey, she'd fold, like she always did. He'd overwhelm her, and she'd talk herself into making it work. Every relationship called for compromises.

It was that idea of compromise that had her sliding into the front passenger seat of her mom's car and pulling on her seat belt.

Ramsey deserved better.

So did she.

Sure, it might work for a while. While the sex was hot enough to overpower everything else. But the day would come when passion wasn't enough, and they had to face each other as partners. That was when it would all crumble, because she hadn't been strong enough to become her own person. Ramsey deserved that in a partner, and she wasn't going to be the one to disappoint him.

Even if it meant walking away.

———✦———

He stank.

Ramsey groaned and squinted at the morning light, and he was forced to notice just how much he reeked. Taz was punching the keys of his laptop as he scowled at an online game. His headphones might have led some people to think he wasn't aware of what was going on around him, but Ramsey knew his bandmate better.

And there was no way he was going to get so lucky as to escape having a witness to his stupidity.

Ramsey climbed to his feet and went toward the bathroom. He flipped on the water and stripped out of his pants. The dragon tattoo sent a prick of pain through him, as well as remorse.

He really needed to stop being a dick.

As in, immediately.

The water was still cold, but he walked beneath the showerhead and let it shock him. His brain was clearing, allowing him to think.

And he had a lot to think about.

Or in this case, plan.

By the time he finished dealing with his stubble-covered chin, he was grinning. Jewel was about to discover just what happened when she got what she wished for.

Because he was going to be the man she thought he was.

—⁓—

"Open it," Ramsey hissed through his teeth.

Brenton eyed him dubiously.

"Are we rolling out of here in an hour?" Ramsey supported his demand with fact. His fist was still resting on the door to Jewel's room. He hammered the wood again, but there was still no answer.

"We are," Brenton confirmed as he produced a master key card and slid it into the door. Ramsey took over, pushing the door in.

"Jewel?"

It took exactly sixty seconds to confirm she wasn't in the room. His stomach dropped. The bed was messed up, but there wasn't a single other sign of Jewel having been there.

"Steven!"

The bodyguard yanked his door open, wearing nothing but a pair of pants. He was looking at his phone. "She's in the conference room. East corner."

Ramsey felt a flash of relief, followed by an intense twist of dread. His head might be splitting with a hangover, but his brain was working just fine. The memory of tossing her phone onto a chair was crystal clear and chilled his blood.

"Shit!" he cursed as he found the phone. Steven was on his heels, buttoning a shirt.

"Oh, crap," the bodyguard agreed. He was in motion immediately, dialing the security center of the hotel.

Ramsey swept the screen of the phone and used his own fingerprint to unlock the screen. Jewel was going to have something to say about him putting himself as second security protocol on her phone, but he didn't care, so long as she said it to him. Profanity, anger, just something to prove he hadn't screwed up so badly she was giving up on him.

The ten calls from her mother were blinking, along with several text messages.

"Her mother was here."

Ramsey and Steven spoke at the same time.

"Oh, man, you hung up on her mother last night," Taz said from the doorway.

"And she left the phone in here when she needed to get away from me," Ramsey finished.

"The manager says her mom showed up around two, threatened to call the local cops if her daughter wasn't allowed to leave," Steven filled them in.

"Why the fuck didn't that manager call up here?" Ramsey demanded. It was a ridiculous demand; he recognized it the moment the words were out of his mouth.

Brenton put on his game face, the one he used when he was trying to remind them all of the merits of professionalism.

"I'll meet you in Detroit," Ramsey said as he started out of the room.

"Now wait just a moment." Brenton stepped into his path.

"Clear out of my way, Brenton," Ramsey warned him. "I am going after her, and when I get back, someone better have some answers from Sammy."

"Got your answers right here. It was bullshit," Sammy said from the doorway. The music producer folded his sunglasses and slipped them into the pocket on the breast of his shirt. "Although, in my defense, if you'd filled me in on Tia, I wouldn't have let her twist my balls last night while I had a couple of drinks in me. Caught the little bitch cackling about her victory this morning. Don't leave my ass flapping in the breeze like that."

Ramsey grunted. "She was your groupie."

"Yeah, yeah, I've got to tighten up the guest list," Sammy agreed.

"The vultures made good use of the opportunity your girl Jewel offered them this morning when she left with her mom."

Ramsey pulled out his phone and checked it. The headlines were vicious.

Romance Over for Tattoo Princess Jewel!

Leaving in Mom's Car, Jewel Is History!

Toxsin Fans Rejoice, Ramsey Is a Free Man!

"I'll catch up with you in Detroit," Ramsey repeated. Something prickled along his nape, and he realized it was fear. Stone-cold dread that he might have just fucked up worse than he ever had before.

"The plane will be waiting for you," Sammy said.

Ramsey flashed him a look.

"Don't be so surprised," Sammy said. "I might enjoy having a good party, but that doesn't mean I don't know a keeper when I see one." He turned and grabbed something from the assistant hovering behind him. "Give her this, and tell her I'm open to negotiation." He handed over a thick folder. "I sure as shit can't stand by and let Quinn scoop her up without a fight. That bastard would never let me live it down."

Ramsey tucked the contract under his arm and headed out.

It was action time.

―――ᴍᴍᴍ―――

"Mom?"

Jewel was still rubbing her wet hair with a towel when she caught a glimpse of her mom hurrying from the front room to the kitchen.

"Is something wrong?" Jewel dropped the towel when she realized her mom had grabbed a rolling pin from the kitchen and come back across the hallway, holding it like a club on her way toward the front door, with an expression that said she was going to war.

"Nothing at all." Her mom was clearly distracted by what was happening in the front yard. She was looking through the spy hole in the door.

"I can't remember the combination for the gun safe," her father said as he came back into the living room.

"What is going on?" Jewel asked again, but both her parents turned bright smiles toward her.

"Nothing to worry about."

"Everything is fine."

Which sent Jewel's heart racing. She marched across the room and grabbed the curtain pulled across the window. She'd moved it only a few inches when the flashes started. Jewel recoiled instantly, releasing the fabric. It swished back into place, earning a muffled cry of dismay from the paparazzi camped outside.

Oh…shit…

Of course the hyenas were there to feast on the carcass of her crashed and burned relationship with Ramsey.

"I remember," her father announced before he headed back into the bedroom and the gun safe.

"Oh God," Jewel moaned, "I shouldn't have come here."

"Nonsense." Her father was back with his service pistol from the seventies. "This is your home. No better place for you." He held the gun up and checked it before pushing the loaded clip into it. "It's those squatters who need to clear out. Don't you worry none, Daddy's got this."

Her father started toward the door with a determined look on his face. Jewel slid between him and the door. "Dad, you can't just go out there and start waving a gun around."

"Watch me," he declared firmly. "I didn't break my back earning the money for this plot of land to see anyone trespassing on it or threatening my daughter in the house where I raised her."

There was a rise of noise from outside. Jewel looked at the curtain, suspecting it had shifted. It hadn't. The window was still covered, but there was a definite commotion taking place outside.

"Better dial the emergency services, Patti," her father warned. "Sounds like things are heating up."

"Dad." Jewel flattened herself against the door. Her father had the gun tucked into his belt as he leveled a firm look at her.

Someone pounded on the door before her father got the chance to argue with her.

"They're bold," her mother said.

"Good," her father replied. "I prefer a straight fight any day."

He gripped her shoulder and pushed her away from the door. She could have dug in, but respect for her father made her give way. She mentally cringed as she watched her father turn the dead bolt, fairly certain her nest egg from signing over rights to the dragon was about to become jail-bond money.

Her dad pulled open the door, and the paparazzi surged to life. But her tongue was frozen to the roof of her mouth as the open door revealed Ramsey. He stood there on her parents' front porch, looking like a Ferrari parked outside of a fast-food restaurant. The reporters behind him filled the air with flashes from their cameras, making him look like he was sparkling. Pain knifed through her, but so did a protective urge. The paparazzi were pushing forward, acting like a hungry pack of vultures.

"Are you here for Jewel?"

"Did you run away, Jewel?"

"Why were you crying last night, Jewel?"

"Did Ramsey cheat on you?"

"Ah…come in." Jewel reached for him and pulled him through the open door. There was a cry of outrage from the crowd on the lawn and a grunt from her father as Jewel closed the door, sealing Ramsey inside with them.

"This is Ramsey," Jewel began lamely.

Her mother lifted the rolling pin and hit her palm in an unmistakable warning. "Mm-hmm."

"We need to talk," Ramsey started, his eyes glittering. He pulled himself up and looked at her father. "May I come in?"

Her dad grunted. "Seems my daughter thinks so. Don't think I won't throw you to that pack out there if you make her cry."

"Dad," Jewel groaned, writhing against a wave of embarrassment.

"Yes, sir." Ramsey hooked her by her bicep. There was a warning sound from her mother that made him turn and look back at her. Her mom slapped her palm with the rolling pin with clear intention.

Ramsey released her arm and offered her his hand instead. Jewel hesitated, scared to death that touching him would be her undoing. Just seeing him was almost too much to bear.

"I'll stand right here and discuss this with you, Jewel," he said firmly.

"There is nothing to discuss." She moved away from the door. He reached out and caught her wrist.

"There sure as sh…is." He bit back the word of profanity. "You were the one who realized we needed time to cool off."

"Actually"—she pulled her wrist out of his grip, not caring too much for the fact that he let her go—"you needed time to—"

"See what a dick I was being." He looked at her mother and shrugged.

"Acceptable in this case," her mom replied before she turned and headed toward the kitchen. "Just call out if you need me, Jewel."

Her father made a sound in the back of his throat before he followed her mother through a doorway and into the kitchen.

"I was being a dick, and then I got drunk, which was stupid," Ramsey stated. He was full of all the confidence she'd felt radiating from him the first time she'd set eyes upon him.

She loved it.

Loved him.

But tears filled her eyes without a care for the way she tried to control them. Ramsey cursed and wrapped her in his embrace, gathering her close when she tried to squirm away.

"You have to forgive me," he muttered against her temple. "I love you. I want to be everything you've always thought I could be, but I can't do it without you to anchor me."

She gasped and pushed against his chest. He finally released her with a snort of frustration.

"It's not about forgiving." She suddenly felt drained. She knew she had to let him go, and it was going to suck everything wonderful out of her.

"The hell it isn't," Ramsey argued. "Sammy came by this morning to apologize in person. I should have ratted Tia out to him. Should have made sure she couldn't take another shot at you. Even Sammy told me I was a dick for leaving him open to her attack."

Jewel snorted. "He should clear out that pack he has brownnosing him."

"He plans to."

"Good." That was what really mattered. "But that's not the real problem."

Ramsey went still as he read her emotions off her face. He'd been tense before, but something shifted between them as he went rigid.

"Then what is it about, Jewel?" His tone had gone deadly. "Why did you leave me?"

She had to tell him, had to be straight. He deserved that.

"Because I have to be my own person too." She was shaking, and wrapped her arms around herself. "You have to see… I can't be less devoted to my own career than you are to yours. It would be a mismatch. You'd realize it…in time…and I'd know I was a sellout."

Understanding dawned on him. It was a horrible sight to see, because it confirmed everything she'd known to be true, even if some part of her heart had been holding out hope. It was all over now.

"Yeah, I get it," he said softly.

"Anyway…I'm glad you understand." She was holding on to her composure by a thread. Ramsey reached out and stopped her when she tried to walk past him, the connection making her stiffen.

"I know what it's like to have a passion burning in your gut." He delivered his next words in a menacing tone. "So don't ever call me dense about the need you have to be successful."

She stepped back, trying to decide what he was driving at. "But you don't want me signing with Morcant."

"I don't want you near that guy, because I'm fucking jealous of him," Ramsey informed her. "I may like girls, but I'm not blind. The guy is smoking hot, and did I mention that I love you?" He opened up his hands in a "get real" gesture. "Knowing you are anywhere near him makes me jealous. Which is just another way of saying I love you, because I have never cared about another girl taking off. There were always plenty more to take her place. Not you."

His admission made her smile, just a tiny curving of her lips. Oh, it wasn't really the right thing to feel, but she couldn't help it. He'd been jealous. It was one of the best compliments he'd ever given her.

"You smiled," he said softly. "I win the point."

She rolled her eyes as the memory of Portland flashed

through her mind. "This is about more than one encounter. This is about…" Words suddenly failed her, because she didn't want to let go of the fragile hope springing back up.

"I get it." His tone had deepened. "You're worried I can't deal with you being more than mine."

She nodded, once, and it felt like the motion tore her heart in two. She was laid bare, everything exposed.

"Honey, I sure as hell want to have you stuck to my side, but that's only because I value every bit of you. The drive to be successful is part of that, and I never said I couldn't deal with it." He was furious, but drew in a deep breath and let it out slowly. "I still don't want you anywhere near Morcant…at least not without me there to remind you how much more you mean to me."

"Ha," Jewel said. "You mean so you can glare at him."

"That's what guys do." Ramsey shrugged. "Some girls too. I saw the way you warned Tia off with a glance."

Jewel defended herself. "She had it coming. She thought you were just some possession."

"But I'm more?" he demanded, forcing her back to the topic at hand.

"Yes, much more," she admitted.

He captured her, taking the opportunity to fold her into his embrace. It was her undoing; the connection between their flesh as jolting as the first time. She gripped the fabric of his T-shirt and drew in the scent of his skin, trembling as it raced through her senses.

"I love *you*…" he whispered in her hair. "All parts of you."

"I'm going to sign that contract. It would be stupid

of me not to." She lifted her head and locked gazes with him. "So I am going to see Quinn again."

He didn't like her comment, but he nodded. "At least read the offer Sammy brought over this morning."

Her eyebrows rose in surprise. Ramsey's lips lifted into that arrogant grin she adored so much. "He even left the private jet at our disposal. Want to become a member of the mile-high club?"

"Ramsey…" She squirmed as her cheeks caught fire. "My parents are listening."

There was a smothered giggle from the kitchen before her father called out, "If you're not going to take advantage of that offer, girl, how about letting me take your mother on a date in that jet?"

Ramsey wiggled his eyebrows at her. "I like your dad." He pressed a hard kiss against her lips before he released her. "And I need to talk to him about you."

"What?"

He kissed her again, cupping her chin. "I want to marry you, so I am going to go ask your dad."

"Ah…he's got his gun on him at the moment."

Ramsey winked at her. "I noticed. Why do you think I was going to ask him to be the shotgun bearer?"

"That's not funny," Jewel said.

But her father started busting up in the kitchen, deflating her argument completely. Ramsey smirked before turning around and walking across her parents' home like he belonged there.

And she realized…he did.

Life was suddenly so perfect. Impossibly perfect for how many hours she'd agonized over the reasons why it couldn't be perfect.

Love didn't make sense.

But it did feel absolutely epic.

———

"I just want a band."

No one listened to her. Ramsey was still looking at a tray of loose diamonds, while her mother drooled over a tray of engagement ring settings. Her father sipped a rum and Coke, and tried not to look too nervous when her mother slipped one of the rings onto her own hand and smiled longingly.

"Ramsey…I really just want a band." Jewel tried to sound enticing. "So I can work with it on."

"Not a chance," Ramsey replied as he picked up a huge diamond with a set of jeweler's tweezers. "I want Morcant to see a rock on your finger the size of Texas."

"And men claim women are the ones who insist on a diamond engagement ring."

Ramsey wiggled the diamond gently so it caught the light. There was a bump as one of the reporters trying to get a shot of them inside the jewelry shop hit the window because he was being jostled by the rest of the pack of paparazzi.

Still, the little polished rock was dazzling. She felt herself melting, but honestly, it was because Ramsey was there. He carried the diamond over to her hand, letting her see it over her ring finger.

Her composure shredded, the reality of the moment filling her eyes with tears and her heart with love.

"That's the one," Ramsey said, but he wasn't looking at the diamond. He was looking into her eyes, his dark eyes glittering with love. "The only one for me."

"Yeah," she agreed. "And I plan to make sure you never forget it."

His eyes narrowed. "School me, baby."

That was exactly what she planned to do.

———~~~———

Jewel groaned. Her cheeks heated, and Ramsey wore his smug victory grin. She looked over toward the cockpit door.

"It's not thick enough. They heard you…screaming," Ramsey cooed next to her ear as he settled back onto his back on the private jet's sofa. The thing slid out to make a bed. The fabric was slightly stiff against her bare skin, but most of her body was lying on top of Ramsey, so it didn't really matter.

Nothing really mattered when they were in each other's arms. Her new engagement ring had twisted on her finger. She tried to turn it, but her right hand was pinned against Ramsey's side. He reached up and centered the ring.

"Still think it's too big?" he asked as he squeezed her hand.

She smiled, nuzzling against his chest. "It's growing on me."

"Wish your dad had let me buy that one your mother picked out."

"Well, you know that had about as much chance of happening as you letting Quinn Morcant pay for mine."

Ramsey snorted. Jewel laughed at him. "Just put my dad to work. He hates being retired." She sighed. "Guess I'm asking for nepotism. See? You start getting me things, and I lose all sense of boundaries."

He smoothed the hair back from her face. "Lay your demands on me, baby. I'll satisfy you."

She made a soft little sound and let her eyes close. "You certainly did."

"And I plan to do it again and again," he insisted. "Getting your dad a job will just be part of making sure you can't escape me."

She lifted her hand and slapped him mockingly on the chest. He covered her hand with his, holding it still.

The plane engines droned on, the aircraft vibrating just enough to rock them both to sleep. Ramsey kept his eyes open longer, fighting to stay awake so he could savor the feeling of her in his arms.

He was the luckiest damned fool alive.

Taz sat in his hotel suite, staring at his phone. A Facebook page was open, a notification of a friend request having been approved, keeping his full attention.

Joi Sun Kim had accepted his request.

After two years.

Why?

The question fascinated him as much as it frustrated him. What did she want? He grunted and closed the application. Damned if he had any clue. All he knew was he wanted her. Wanted her so badly, three years of rejection hadn't dulled the urge. She still filled his dreams. Success in the music world had somehow translated into disgrace in her family's eyes. They had forbidden her to see him, talk to him, marry him.

He should move on.

But he couldn't.

Taz opened Facebook again and punched in her name so her page came up. Maybe she'd approved his friend request so he'd see that she'd settled down with some other guy. It would hurt like shit, but maybe it would be better to see the evidence of her with a husband. Maybe that would end his obsession with her.

Instead, all he saw was her face, and it cut him to the bone. Her sparkling eyes, her whimsical smile, and the way her spirit came across in the form of cute animal pictures and encouraging sayings on her Facebook wall.

He still loved her.

There was no doubt about it.

*Keep reading for an excerpt from the first
book in Dawn Ryder's Rock Band series*

Rock Me Two Times

"KATIE...SWEETIE..."

Kate Napier raised her head, shifting her focus from
the strips of leather she had pushed under the industrial
sewing machine she was using. Her partner only called
her sweetie when he was nervous about something.

One look at Percy Lynwood confirmed it. All six
foot four of him hovered in the doorway between the
machine shop and the cutting room of their design
studio. He was pulling on the measuring tape draped
around his neck, looking at her with pleading eyes. She
looked past him to find that their staff members had sus-
piciously disappeared into the prep room at the back of
the building.

"This is part of the Stanton order, Percy," she
warned him. "He wants it for Sturgis in two weeks."

Percy wrung his hands, looking like a gigantic
teddy bear with his naturally curly hair framing his
forehead. He shifted from side to side before taking a
stiff breath and stepping onto the concrete floor of the
machine shop.

"I know, *sweetie...*"

Kate flattened her hands on the edge of the sewing
machine table and narrowed her eyes. Percy grimaced
and lifted his hands to keep her from arguing further.

"I'll put Paula on it," he said in a rush. "Giles just called with an emergency."

She took the opportunity to stand up and stretch her lower back, arching all the way until her neck popped.

"Leather is my department. No offense to Paula, but she doesn't fit ass like I do," Kate said.

"Definitely not," Percy agreed. "But this is an emergency on an epic scale," he finished with a flurry of his hands.

Kate lowered her chin and locked gazes with Percy. His tone was downright miserable. "Okay, so what is stressing you out so bad?"

"It's the Toxsin account."

Kate lifted her hand and pointed to the wall behind Percy. Her personal operating rules were on a corkboard. Number one: no cuts to the front of the line.

"I know about your rules, Kate, but this is urgent!" Percy was back to wringing his hands. "Toxsin is going on stage in four hours, and there is some sort of problem with the lead singer's leather pants."

"As in Syon Braden?" Kate asked.

Percy nodded. "The Marquis." He supplied the stage name of the man currently topping preeminent entertainer lists around the globe with a breathless sigh.

She moved around the large industrial sewing machine and jabbed her finger again at the corkboard on the wall that had her name on it. "Rule number two: I don't do rock stars. Besides, are you really telling me that you don't want to get your hands on the Marquis?"

Percy cracked a saucy grin through his worried expression. "You know I do, and I think even Steve will forgive me for it as long as I share every last succulent detail. That Syon is an animal." Percy made a soft sound that was a cross between a moan and a growl.

"Glad we got that squared away." Kate turned and headed for the leather pants destined for the biker paradise known as Sturgis. The end-of-summer rally held in Sturgis, South Dakota, drew bikers from all over the world. Making leatherwear for attendees was her bread and butter. "Have a blast with the Marquis."

"But, Kate," Percy whimpered again. "Showtime is seven, and they are playing the Staples Center downtown."

"Ahhh…" Kate turned to look at the large clock on the wall next to her corkboard. Every staff member had a corkboard. Schedules were posted there, along with any rule anyone felt they couldn't live with being violated. The boards kept the peace pretty well, but the clock read three sharp.

"With afternoon traffic, which will be even worse than usual with Toxsin playing, I'll never make it down there in time. They've been sold out for months," Percy explained.

"So why did Giles call us? It's his account, his premiere account. Why isn't he flying out to defend his turf?" Percy's costume college buddy had jumped through flaming hoops to score the account with Toxsin.

Percy spread his hands in a pleading gesture. "Because he's in New York, and it's an emergency. They need something fixed immediately. He wouldn't trust just anyone to deal with them. That's why he called us."

"Giles called you, not us." Kate propped her hand on her hip. "I'm still a little sketchy on why you need me for this, Percy. I don't drive any faster than you do."

"They're sending a helicopter from the Staples Center. That's how desperate they are." Percy looked miserable again. "You know I can't stand heights."

Kate's stomach knotted. Percy could get woozy on the third story of their building if he got too close to a window. He'd turn green just looking at a helicopter.

Shit.

"Wear a blindfold and think about what you'll get for your courage," she said.

Percy gave a sigh, which was pitiful until she coupled it with his overall size. He had the body of a linebacker and the heart of a 1950s suburban housewife. A mouse sighting would send him screaming. When it came to his marriage with his husband, Steve, Percy was the wife all the way.

"I tried the blindfold in Alaska, but I still threw up all over Steve before we finished the helicopter tour of the glacier. And it was his birthday present too. I tried so hard." He shook his head sadly.

The knot in her stomach was tightening with the help of guilt. She did love Percy, but rock stars drove her insane. She chewed on her lower lip as her partner looked at her pleadingly. *Yup, hungry, starving baby bear.*

"Take a bucket," she suggested.

"I'll arrive as weak as an infant and light-headed. Definitely not professional." He pointed at the three phrases posted above everyone's corkboards. They were the operating foundation of their business, Timeless Custom Creations:

Always push the creative boundaries.

Always wow the customer.

Always be professional.

"Shit," she cussed as the word *professional* cut through her personal phobias. "Just…craptastic!"

Percy sent her a relieved look. She was folding, and he knew it. "I always fucking cave in when it's our image on the line," she said. "Giles is so going to owe me."

Percy tried to soothe her. "You'll be just fine, sweetie."

"Don't 'sweetie' me." She pointed at him. "You'd better tell them I'm a lesbian, because if even one of those arrogant asshats pinches my butt, I'm going warrior princess on them."

Percy rolled his eyes. "Hardly. You're so strictly dick, I get jealous when you sit next to Steve at lunch."

"I'm not a home wrecker," she defended herself.

"But you are a little uptight lately…maybe it will be good for you." Percy was back to being saucy. "Find out if they know how to use those succulent bodies for more than dancing. You know, just 'cause you got great buns doesn't mean you know how to fuck worth—"

He ducked when Kate chucked a chair cushion at him. It collided with the wall, making a soft, unsatisfying sound before sliding to the floor.

Percy was laughing when he peeked between his hands at her. "Is that a definite no? Because the Marquis does have a whole lot of yumminess going on. I bet he could make you forget all about Todd—"

"Rule number five, no kissing on the first date," Kate reminded him.

"Technically, it's not a date," Percy pointed out with a smirk. "You should exploit that loophole darling, or let it exploit you!"

Kate groaned and stomped off to take a shower. Working with leather was a sweaty business. The water restored her confidence in her appearance, but she was still chewing on her discontentment when she heard the helicopter landing in the back parking lot.

Rock stars. Jeez. Just what she didn't need. Todd and his two-timing had been more than enough.

But at least she could dress how she liked. She pulled on a pair of leather pants and tightened the laces that ran up their sides from ankle to hip. They fit her like a second skin, and she admired the way the blood-orange leather cupped her ass.

No one fit leather like she did. She couldn't help it. She loved the stuff—the scent, the feel, and most especially, the look. She added a thin silk tank top that fluttered over her buns like a teasing veil, ending right at the curve of her butt, and shrugged into a leather corset top with brass closures. Once it was tight, her cleavage was halfway to her chin.

Perfect. At least she had one good thing to say about rock stars: they had good taste in clothing.

"You've got a full set kit." Percy pointed at the black cases being loaded into the helicopter. "So no matter what the issue is, you should be fine."

Kate wasn't sure what she'd expected, but the sleek black aircraft in her parking lot wasn't it. The thing was plenty big enough for the eight heavy-duty traveling cases that made up their "on set" kit. The pilot hadn't even needed to disembark, because he had two burly assistants to help him load everything. They were outfitted in tuxes, and *not* the off-the-rack variety. She knew a custom job when she saw one. They kept those suit jackets on even as they lifted and stowed her gear, which meant only one thing: they were bodyguards too. Had to have something to hide their chest harnesses.

"I am so jealous," Percy whined. "These guys are premium…"

Kate rolled her eyes. "There will be at least a hundred starstruck fangirls willing to grease their poles just for the chance to get near the band."

"I know, Katie girl, but I have to admit that I wouldn't mind playing games with any of them." He made a sound of enjoyment and smacked his lips.

"You're married," she reminded him.

"But not dead." Percy batted his eyelashes at her. "You look like a blood orange. Sweeten up a little and stop letting Todd make you into such a bitch. It's his loss."

Kate offered him a genuine smile. She felt a little tug on her heart, because she did love Percy, quivering insides and all. He had an unparalleled eye for color and could draft a pattern like a fairy godmother.

"Todd who?" she purred.

"There's my girl." He reached out and patted her hair. Newly washed, it was rising up into a cloud of tiny copper curls. She had it clipped back, but there was no way it was going to lay flat. "I think they're ready for you."

Kate looked up to see one of the private security men moving toward her.

"Be careful with the warrior-princess thing. I hear the Marquis likes his women wild," Percy added with a suggestive grin.

Kate stuck out her tongue at him before striding toward the sleek aircraft. One of the security men opened the sliding door behind the copilot seat and offered her a hand as she stepped up into the cabin. The seats were plush and covered in black leather. The security guy waited while she pulled the seat straps over her shoulders and secured the chest harness. He pointed to a set of earphones hanging from the ceiling. The rotor was beginning to spin, filling the cabin with noise.

She pulled the earphones off the hook and fussed with them until she adjusted them small enough to sit on her head. They were the sort that covered each ear completely, and a microphone stuck out in front of her face.

"Once I take off, I'll turn on your feed, Ms. Napier. Push the button on the side of your headset before you talk." The pilot's voice had an electronic quality to it through the headphones, and there was a click the moment he finished talking. The helicopter shuddered as the rotor reached full speed. They began to lift off the ground, Kate's belly doing a tiny flop at the sudden weightlessness.

She leaned forward to look out the window. There was something thrilling about being able to lift up and over the afternoon traffic. They flew over the freeway, confirming her suspicion that there was no way she would have made it by car. It was bumper-to-bumper rush hour in the Los Angeles basin. No one was going anywhere fast.

Unless they were in a helicopter. She smiled, enjoying the moment of being someone important. Because it sure wouldn't last. There was a pile of leather waiting for her back at the shop and a line of impatient bikers to deal with.

In the distance, the towers of downtown Los Angeles rose up. The air was surprisingly clear, and the sun sparkled off the glass-sided skyscrapers. The pilot was talking to some air-control personnel as he made a wide circle around the Staples Center. It sure was a different picture from the air. She'd been to the huge arena plenty of times, but she'd never seen the top of it.

There were three helicopter-landing circles, complete with blinking lights set into the concrete. There was also a ramp that had two black SUVs parked on it, facing away from a glass entry into the arena. A burly body-guard was standing near the driver's door, watching the helicopter hover over one of the landing circles.

What a different world.

"They are waiting for you, Ms. Napier. We'll get your gear unloaded and down to you."

Someone opened the side door before the pilot stopped talking. The rotor was still winding down, and air rushed inside. The suit jacket on the guy at the door flipped up, giving her a peek at a shoulder holster and the butt of a pistol.

Yeah, different world completely.

She pressed the release buttons on the latch holding her harness and managed her way to the open door. The wind and noise were dying down, allowing her to hear something else: the unmistakable sound of people cheering from the street. It was like a roar coming over the top of the building.

It sent a tingle along her spine.

"Don't mind them. They just think you're part of the band arriving."

The bodyguard offered her a hand, but she grabbed the handle on the ceiling of the aircraft. He cupped her elbow the moment her feet hit the pavement and guided her toward the glass entry port from the roof. Now that she'd landed, she could see painted walkways leading toward two huge double doors.

"You don't need to hold on to me." She lifted her arm, earning a stern look from the bodyguard.

"Let's go over the rules." He kept hold of her elbow as someone inside opened the door for them. "No touching the performers."

"That's going to make fixing a costume issue challenging," she remarked.

He lifted a finger into the air. "Unless they give you permission."

Once inside, she had more space and stepped away from the guy. He was burly enough to maintain his hold on her if he wanted to, but he only sent her a annoyed look before holding out his hand.

"I'll need your cell phone before you go any farther. No backstage pictures," the bodyguard continued.

"Oh…" That made sense. She started to dig it out of her purse.

"The whole purse," he insisted.

She froze and studied the look on the guy's face. He wasn't kidding. She handed it over. "That's a one-of-a-kind bag; don't let it get punctured."

He gave it to a man standing behind him and gestured her toward a security-screening machine, just like one she'd find in an airport.

Rule number two wasn't changing.

About the Author

Dawn Ryder is the erotic romance pen name of a best-selling author of historical romances. She has been publishing her stories for over eight years to a growing and appreciative audience. She is commercially published in mass market and trade paper, and digi-first published with trade paper releases. She is hugely committed to her career as an author, as well as to other authors and to her readership. She resides in Southern California.

Backstage Pass

Sinners on Tour
By Olivia Cunning

———— ·∿· ————

For him, life is all music and no play…

When Brian Sinclair, lead songwriter and guitarist of the hottest metal band on the scene, loses his creative spark, it will take nights of downright sinful passion to release his pent-up genius…

She's the one to call the tune…

When sexy psychologist Myrna Evans goes on tour with the Sinners, every boy in the band tries to woo her into his bed. But Brian is the only one she wants to get her hands on…

Then the two lovers' wildly shocking behavior sparks the whole band to new heights of glory… and sin…

———— ·∿· ————

"Olivia Cunning's erotic romance debut is phenomenal."
—*Love Romance Passion*

"These guys are so sensual, sexual, and yummy. [T]his series… will give readers another wild ride, and I can't wait!"
—*Night Owl Reviews*, 5 Stars, Reviewer Top Pick

For more Olivia Cunning, visit:

www.sourcebooks.com

Filthy Rich

by Dawn Ryder

She's fighting for control…

Celeste Connor swore that she'd never be a victim again. After the hell of her abusive ex, the last thing she needs is to be under another man's thumb. But when she catches the eye of fiercely dominant Nartan Lupan at her best friend's wedding, Celeste finds herself drawn into a glittering world of wealth and power that has her body aching and her mind reeling.

He's fighting to make her his…

Nartan is a filthy rich businessman who works hard, plays harder, and doesn't take no for an answer—and he wants Celeste with a hunger he's never felt before. He'll do whatever it takes to have her. But Nartan didn't expect that he'd still want more…

"A sexy, romantic read that will have you rooting for that filthy rich guy that any gal could not resist. A tantalizing read with steamy sex." —*Fresh Fiction*

"Deeply romantic, scintillating, and absolutely delicious." —Sylvia Day praise for Dawn Ryder

For more Dawn Ryder, visit:

www.sourcebooks.com

Full Contact

Redemption
by Sarah Castille

New York Times and *USA Today* Bestselling Author

—◆—

When you can't resist the one person who could destroy you...

Sia O'Donnell can't help but push the limits. She secretly attends every underground MMA fight featuring the Predator, the undisputed champion. When he stalks his prey in the ring, she is mesmerized. He is dominant and dangerous and every instinct tells her to run.

Every beautiful thing Ray "The Predator" touches, he knows he'll eventually destroy. Soft, sweet, and innocent, Sia is the light to Ray's darkness—and completely irresistible. From the moment he lays eyes on her, he knows he's going to have to put his dark past behind him to win her body and soul.

—◆—

"A highly enjoyable romance with deep characters and sexual chemistry that will have readers quickly turning the pages." —*Fresh Fiction*

For more Sarah Castille, visit:

www.sourcebooks.com

Must Love Cowboys

Cowboy Heaven
by Cheryl Brooks

So many cowboys...

Shy computer specialist, dog lover, and amateur chef Tina Hayes has a thing for firefighters, but when she travels to the Circle Bar K ranch on family business, the ranch's cowboys have no trouble persuading her to stay on as their cook. Especially not when she learns that brooding Wyatt McCabe—a man who makes her heart gallop like no one else can—is also a former firefighter.

How does she know he's the one?

Wyatt's sizzling embraces leave Tina breathless. But being surrounded by a passel of smokin' hot ranch hands can be complicated. With so many cowboys courting Tina all at once, Wyatt must prove to Tina that she belongs with him.

Praise for *Cowboy Heaven*:

"The best of both worlds—a steamy, wild fling and a second chance at real love...total female fantasy fulfillment and full of to-die-for cowboys." —*Fresh Fiction* Fresh Pick

"Awesome read...not just hot and sexy, it's intelligent, witty, and well-written." —*Long and Short Reviews*

For more Cheryl Brooks, visit:

www.sourcebooks.com

Rough Rider

Hot Cowboy Nights Series

by Victoria Vane

———

Old flames burn the hottest...

Janice Combes has adored Dirk Knowlton from the rodeo sidelines for years. She knows she'll never be able to compete with the dazzling all-American rodeo queen who's set her sights on Dirk. Playful banter is all Janice and Dirk will ever have...

Until the stormy night when he shows up at her door, injured and alone. Dirk's dripping wet, needs a place to stay, and Janice remembers why she could never settle for any other cowboy...

———

Praise for Victoria Vane:

For more Victoria Vane, visit:

www.sourcebooks.com